HONEY DROP DEAD

Titles by Laura Childs

Tea Shop Mysteries

DEATH BY DARJEELING
GUNPOWDER GREEN
SHADES OF EARL GREY
THE ENGLISH BREAKFAST MURDER
THE JASMINE MOON MURDER
CHAMOMILE MOURNING
BLOOD ORANGE BREWING
DRAGONWELL DEAD
THE SILVER NEEDLE MURDER
OOLONG DEAD
THE TEABERRY STRANGLER
SCONES & BONES
AGONY OF THE LEAVES

SWEET TEA REVENGE
STEEPED IN EVIL
MING TEA MURDER
DEVONSHIRE SCREAM
PEKOE MOST POISON
PLUM TEA CRAZY
BROKEN BONE CHINA
LAVENDER BLUE MURDER
HAUNTED HIBISCUS
TWISTED TEA CHRISTMAS
A DARK AND STORMY TEA
LEMON CURD KILLER
HONEY DROP DEAD

Scrapbooking Mysteries

KEEPSAKE CRIMES
PHOTO FINISHED
BOUND FOR MURDER
MOTIF FOR MURDER
FRILL KILL
DEATH SWATCH
TRAGIC MAGIC
FIBER & BRIMSTONE

SKELETON LETTERS
POSTCARDS FROM THE DEAD
GILT TRIP
GOSSAMER GHOST
PARCHMENT AND OLD LACE
CREPE FACTOR
GLITTER BOMB
MUMBO GUMBO MURDER

Cackleberry Club Mysteries

EGGS IN PURGATORY
EGGS BENEDICT ARNOLD
BEDEVILED EGGS
STAKE & EGGS
EGGS IN A CASKET

SCORCHED EGGS
EGG DROP DEAD
EGGS ON ICE
EGG SHOOTERS

Anthologies

DEATH BY DESIGN
TEA FOR THREE

Afton Tangler Thrillers
writing as Gerry Schmitt

LITTLE GIRL GONE
SHADOW GIRL

HONEY DROP DEAD

Tea Shop Mystery #26

LAURA CHILDS

BERKLEY PRIME CRIME
New York

BERKLEY PRIME CRIME
Published by Berkley
An imprint of Penguin Random House LLC
penguinrandomhouse.com

Library of Congress Cataloging-in-Publication Data

Names: Childs, Laura, author.
Title: Honey drop dead / Laura Childs.
Description: New York: Berkley Prime Crime, [2023] |
Series: Tea Shop Mystery; #26
Identifiers: LCCN 2022052032 (print) | LCCN 2022052033 (ebook) |
ISBN 9780593200957 (hardcover) | ISBN 9780593200964 (ebook)
Classification: LCC PS3603.H56 H66 2023 (print) |
LCC PS3603.H56 (ebook) | DDC 813/.6—dc23
LC record available at https://lccn.loc.gov/2022052032
LC ebook record available at https://lccn.loc.gov/2022052033

Printed in the United States of America
1st Printing

This is a work of fiction. Names, characters, places, and incidents either are the product of
the author's imagination or are used fictitiously, and any resemblance to actual persons,
living or dead, business establishments, events, or locales is entirely coincidental.

PUBLISHER'S NOTE: The recipes contained in this book are to be followed exactly
as written. The publisher is not responsible for your specific health or allergy
needs that may require medical supervision. The publisher is not responsible
for any adverse reactions to the recipes contained in this book.

HONEY DROP DEAD

1

It was politics as usual. Or unusual in this particular case. Because tea maven Theodosia Browning had never hosted a tea party before where a superambitious, overcaffeinated politician had suddenly leaped from his chair to deliver a boastful, impromptu speech.

Of course, it was election time in Charleston, South Carolina, and politicians were thick as flies in a hog barn. Which is why Osgood Claxton III was rambling to an acutely bored audience about his prodigious accomplishments and why they should surely award him a seat in the state legislature. It was also why Theodosia hovered nervously at her tea table while her team readied scones and tea sandwiches.

"He's trying to hijack Holly's event," Theodosia murmured to Drayton Conneley, her tea sommelier and trusted friend. They were gazing out at the dozen or so tables that had been set up in Charleston's gorgeous new Petigru Park, getting ready to plop fresh-baked glory bee honey scones on all their guests' plates.

"This has the makings of a train wreck," Drayton agreed. He touched a finger to his yellow bow tie as if to punctuate his sentence.

Theodosia turned sharp blue eyes onto Holly Burns, the owner of the Imago Gallery, who was seated nearby. As Claxton droned on, Holly's face turned blotchy and her jaw went rigid. Clearly, she wasn't one bit happy.

Oh dear. This was, after all, Holly's outdoor tea party in honor of the relaunch of her Imago Gallery. Dozens of art lovers, patrons, and artists lounged at the elegantly appointed tables while, all around them, large colorful paintings were displayed on wooden easels. A brilliant yellow sun shone down and a cool breeze wafted in from Charleston Harbor to stir the park's newly planted native grasses. Hives from a community bee-keeping project were stacked like bee condos a safe distance away.

"I'm going to go over there and try to disarm that walking, talking dictionary," Theodosia said to Drayton. A self-made tea entrepreneur who'd made it on her own terms, Theodosia was confident, nimble at handling tricky situations, and unimpressed by boastful politicians. Her ice-chip blue eyes matched her taste-ful sapphire earrings while masses of Titian red hair swirled around her lovely oval face. Theodosia also possessed a gracious manner that was poised yet purposeful.

"Watch your step with that fellow," Drayton warned. "He's powerfully . . ."

"Connected. Yes, I know he is," Theodosia said as she grabbed a pink floral teapot filled with Darjeeling tea, fixed her mouth in a bright smile, and headed directly for the red-faced, over-bearing politician.

Osgood Claxton III saw her coming and seemed to lose focus for a moment. He blinked, trying desperately to sputter out a few more words. But that tiny hesitation was all Theodosia needed.

"Mr. Claxton," Theodosia said with a warm lilt to her voice. "Bless your heart for expounding on your many qualifications. Now that we're all familiar with such prodigious talents, you must surely take your seat so my staff and I can begin serving our delicious luncheon of honey scones and tea sandwiches."

Theodosia grabbed a quick breath, faced the forty or so guests, and continued, not allowing the startled Claxton a moment to jump back in. "As you all know, Holly Burns has recently upped the ante at her marvelous Imago Gallery." She smiled as Claxton reluctantly slumped in his seat. "Along with a new partner, and a higher profile in Charleston's thriving art scene, Holly now represents an amazing group of talented and well-known South Carolina artists."

There was a spatter of applause and Holly half rose in her chair to wave and acknowledge her guests. She had long dark hair, was skinny as a wet cat, wore armfuls of clanking silver bracelets, and jittered with anxiety. With dozens of potential art buyers and a few wealthy collectors among her guests, today would prove to be a make-or-break day for her.

Theodosia continued. "And lucky for us, we have on display here"—she gestured at the paintings resting on their easels—"a number of intriguing and colorful paintings—works by Holly's new artists that are here for your appreciation and careful perusal." There was more applause and then Theodosia added, "So please sit back and enjoy this special Honeybee Tea as we fill your teacups with our house blend of Honey Child tea and serve our first course of fresh-baked glory bee scones. Following that, we'll present a tempting array of tea sandwiches that will include honey ham on rye, shrimp with tarragon on crostini, and chicken salad on brioche."

As Drayton poured tea, Theodosia and her young chef, Haley Parker, slipped from table to table, serving scones, dropping off bowls of Devonshire cream, and encouraging guests to drizzle some of their specially sourced raw honey onto their scones.

When the guests were all sipping and munching (even Osgood Claxton III seemed to be making short work of his scone), Theodosia wiped her hands on her apron and gazed about contentedly. This is what she did, after all—and she did it rather well. Yes, Monday through Friday you could find her at the Indigo Tea Shop, a devastatingly adorable tea shop on Church Street. But she also reveled in catering special event teas. And this Sunday's tea, her themed Honeybee Tea, seemed to be going off without a hitch. The weather was gorgeous, Petigru Park was clearly the perfect venue, and there were already small red stickers on several of the paintings—which meant they'd been earmarked as either on hold or sold—a feather in Theodosia's cap as well as Holly's.

As a former marketing executive, Theodosia loved nothing better than to spin out new ideas. These included event teas, tea trolley tours, even catering gigs. She'd draw up a business plan, work out all the nits and nats, then bring the whole shootin' match to fruition. Right now she was making plans for a line of organic, tea-infused chocolates that would be sold at the Indigo Tea Shop. Two of the brand names she was considering were Church Street Chocolates and Cacao Tea.

"This is going well, yes?" Drayton said to her. He'd just made the rounds pouring tea and looked elegant in his cream-colored jacket and matching linen slacks. Sixty-something and always projecting the manner and bearing of a true Southern gent, Drayton was a tea sommelier and a skilled orator and served on several boards of directors.

"I just got a quick read from Holly and she's over the moon," Theodosia said. "She believes she's already made several sales to a few serious collectors and that the Imago Gallery is finally on the right track to success."

"Holly was smart to hook up with that silent partner. Jeremy something . . ."

"Slade. Jeremy Slade."

Drayton nodded. "Right. The one who gave her the infusion of cash."

"She lucked out," Theodosia said. Then she gazed across the tables and said, "Oh bother."

"What?" Drayton said.

"Bill Glass just showed up." Glass was the publisher of *Shooting Star*, a local tabloid that specialized in gossip, unfounded rumors, and glossy photos of the nouveau riche acting badly. Today, Glass was wandering among the tables, taking photos, and doing a skillful bit of glad-handing. His razor sunglasses were pushed up on his forehead and he wore a khaki photographer's vest, sloppy brown pants, and red high-top tennis shoes.

"He's not exactly the vision you want to see at a tea party, but he's harmless," Drayton said. "Besides, most people are thrilled to see their picture in his little rag of a magazine."

"Maybe," Theodosia said.

Haley nudged her and said, "Time to put out the sandwich trays?" Haley was twenty-six, petite, and blond with stick-straight hair. But underneath her sweet appearance, she was a little martinet. And it was woe to the baker or fishmonger who tried to deliver day-old goods to Haley's kitchen.

"Let's do it," said Drayton. "While everything's so perfectly fresh."

"Right down to my edible flowers," Haley smiled.

*   *   *

Theodosia had just placed a three-tiered tray stacked with tea sandwiches on one of the tables when a woman glanced past her, pointed, and said, "Will you look at that. One of the bee-keepers just showed up." She sounded amused.

Theodosia looked over at the colony of twelve white hives where a man (she thought it was a man) in protective gear was aiming a smoker at one of the hives.

"Going to harvest some honey," another guest said, excitement coloring her voice.

"Good thing he's wearing that bee getup, the protective jacket, pants, veil, and whatnot," a man said. "Dealing with beehives is quite an art."

Now more guests had turned in their chairs to watch.

"This really is quite charming," the man's companion said. "It must be part of the event."

"Has to be," another person at the table chimed in.

Theodosia knew this hadn't been planned. It was completely serendipitous that one of the beekeepers had shown up at this exact moment. All the same, she was pleased because it made for an exciting diversion. Especially since the event had been promoted as a Honeybee Tea and the invitations had even made mention of the park's community beekeeping project.

Unfortunately, two tables over, Claxton had jumped to his feet again. He was suddenly spearheading a round of applause for the beekeeper, whipping up the crowd's enthusiasm.

"Not him again," Drayton muttered as he came up behind Theodosia.

"The man's incorrigible," she said. "Looks as if he's trying to take credit for what's really a city-funded project."

They watched Claxton vigorously thrust both arms in the air in a *V for Victory* sign as the guests cheered.

"He thinks the applause is for him," Theodosia said.

Everyone watched as Claxton puffed up his chest, practically busting the buttons on his vest. Then he turned with a flourish and faced the beekeeper.

"Great job," Claxton called out to him. "Phenomenal project, these bees."

He took a few steps in the direction of the hives as the beekeeper moved forward to greet him.

"You see what your city officials can do when they put their mind to it?" Claxton said loudly. "Native grasses planted in this park, all these wonderful hives. Come on over here, Mr. Beekeeper, I want to shake your hand."

The beekeeper advanced on Claxton, his helmet obscuring his face, his smoker held at waist level. It looked a lot like a stainless steel watering can, Theodosia decided. Only with a shorter spout.

As Claxton reached a hand out, the beekeeper snapped his smoker up to eye level and a faint motorized hum suddenly sounded. Then the beekeeper aimed the smoker directly at Claxton's face and sent a milky white vapor spewing out at him.

"Wha . . . ?" came Claxton's startled, garbled response as he was suddenly engulfed in a thick white cloud. Terrified, Claxton began to stumble about aimlessly, his face turning red as he started to choke. It was a dry, raspy AR-AR-AR, as if he was unable to pull in a single sip of oxygen. Then, eyes rolling back in his head, knees beginning to buckle, Claxton batted his arms frantically, as if to ward off the continuing billows of smoke.

Or was it smoke? Theodosia wondered a split second later.

Because everyone in Claxton's vicinity was suddenly coughing and choking like crazy and rubbing their eyes.

No, it has to be some kind of toxic bomb.

The cloud drifted across the tea tables, threatening to engulf everyone. Dark shapes darted back and forth as they fought to escape. Visibility was almost down to zero.

Undaunted, Theodosia covered her mouth with her apron and ran smack-dab into the fray.

"Everybody! We have to get away from this right now!" she cried. Then she raised a hand in a wild gesture. "This way!"

Coughing and crying, shouting and screaming, many of the guests were openly weeping from the toxic fumes and stumbling toward Theodosia as she tried to lead them away from the smoke.

Haley suddenly appeared next to Theodosia, eyes bleary and red, tears streaming down her face. Her cell phone was clutched in her hand.

"Did you call 911?" Theodosia choked out as she led her flock to safety.

"Talking to them now," Haley cried. "They want to know what . . ."

"Toxic fumes, tell them some kind of toxic smoke bomb." In the melee, with people all around her, Theodosia lost sight of Haley for a few moments. Then she found her again. "Are they coming?" she asked.

"They're coming." Haley had to shout to be heard above the cries and screams.

"Tell them to send ambulances, EMTs, everything they've got." Theodosia looked around. "We probably have a couple dozen injured people here."

"The dispatcher wants to know who released the . . ."

"I think it was just the one guy," Theodosia shouted back. "A phony beekeeper who . . ."

BOOM!

That noise—an explosion, really—rattled Theodosia's teeth and rocked her back on her heels. But her brain instantaneously sorted out exactly what she'd heard.

A gunshot? Oh my Lord, I think it was. I know it was.

Wiping her eyes, squinting into the filmy cloud that was slowly starting to dissipate, she saw the phony beekeeper standing there. He had a gun clutched in his right hand with Claxton's body sprawled at his feet.

The beekeeper's protective suit still obscured his identity, and he held the smoker in his other hand. But it was his attitude that chilled Theodosia to the bone. He seemed to gaze at Claxton's body in a gloating, self-satisfied manner. Taking pride in his kill as well as the terrible panic he'd brought about.

The phony beekeeper cocked his head, as if making some sort of critical decision. Then he spun on his heels and began to sprint awkwardly across the park. He obviously had one single burning thought in mind—get away from this place fast!

At the same time, a nugget of white-hot rage exploded inside Theodosia's brain. She took in Claxton's prone body—the man had to be dead—as well as the tearful guests that milled about, still looking panicked. And she was gripped by one all-consuming thought—run the killer down!

Not having access to a weapon, not even thinking all that clearly, Theodosia grabbed the first thing she saw—a tall glass vase filled with bright yellow jonquils. Tucking the vase under one arm, Theodosia took off running.

"Stop!" Theodosia cried as she pounded across the vast expanse of green parkland in hot pursuit of the phony beekeeper. She leaped across a bed of daylilies and dodged a small copse of

dogwood. She saw that, up ahead, the phony beekeeper was running badly. He was hindered by his bulky suit and the clanking smoker that banged against his legs. So, little by little, as Theodosia chased after him, she was beginning to close the gap.

He killed a man, was the terrible thought that spiraled through Theodosia's brain and propelled her forward. *And spewed out some kind of toxic smoke that made people sick. Made my guests sick.*

She lowered her head, hunched her shoulders forward, and forced herself to lengthen her strides, to kick it into high gear. She was a longtime jogger with an abundance of stamina. So maybe she could catch him?

Maybe, but then what?

Her answer came in the form of a black-and-white dog, a kind of collie-Labrador mix, that suddenly sprinted out of a nearby wooded area. Legs churning, haunches bunched like a jackrabbit, the dog began chasing after the running man. The dog probably saw it as a game, but Theodosia was grateful for the help.

Catching up fast, almost running on the man's heels now, the dog let out a series of high-pitched barks. When the man didn't stop to play, the dog gathered itself into a coiled bunch and lunged forward, his teeth catching the legs of the man's flapping suit.

That's it, get him! Theodosia's heart was suddenly filled with hope.

But no. The dog's interference had slowed the man down some, but it didn't stop him completely. Angered by the canine intrusion, the man spun around and lifted his pistol. Half running, half backpedaling now, the man aimed his weapon directly at the dog

He's going to kill the dog! Theodosia loved dogs more than anything.

"Don't!" she shouted.

Startled to hear someone shout at him, the phony beekeeper's hand jerked sideways. He looked around hastily and saw Theodosia running full tilt in his direction.

Then the beekeeper readjusted his aim and pointed the gun at her!

Theodosia ducked her head and threw herself down on the grass just as he pulled the trigger. There was another loud BANG and a high-pitched ZING as something—presumably the bullet—flew past her head.

That's when Theodosia made a split-second decision. Scrambling to her feet, she assumed a power stance, and cocked her right arm. Then she let fly, hurling the glass vase directly at the phony beekeeper with as much force as she could muster. The vase sailed through the air, flipping over and over, spewing water and flowers as it went. Theodosia watched, hypnotized, following the arc of the vase, feeling as if this whole thing were happening in slow motion. Then the scenario seemed to jump ahead into hyperspace and speed up, like super cranked film footage, as the vase smashed hard against the side of the man's helmet. Instantly, shards of glass, water, and flowers exploded everywhere.

Caught completely off guard, momentarily stunned by the direct hit to his head, the assailant was knocked off balance. He stumbled to his left, caught a foot on the turf, tripped, and started to go down. One of his knees hit the ground and his arms flew out to try to steady himself. As his arms flailed wildly, seeking to regain his balance, he also fumbled his gun.

Yes!

"Stop!" Theodosia shouted as the dog, undaunted, circled back around, barking loudly. Then, as the man searched frantically for his gun, the dog dashed back in and nipped his pants leg for a second time.

Hindered by his mask, unable to locate his gun, the phony beekeeper spat out a single harsh word. Then his leg flew up and he kicked the offending dog right in the head, sending the poor mutt spinning.

"The police are on their way!" Theodosia shouted as she reached down and snatched up a piece of broken glass. It was the bottom of the vase and it made a dandy weapon.

The phony beekeeper ignored her and lumbered up a small hill where a stand of palmettos waved in the breeze. Once he'd reached high ground, he spun around to face her.

Theodosia stopped in her tracks.

Now what?

Was she tough enough to rush in and attack this jackhole? Try to wrestle him to the ground until law enforcement could arrive? Probably not. She could hear the faint drone of sirens off in the distance—answering Haley's 911 call, thank heavens—but they wouldn't reach her, wouldn't *find* her, anytime soon.

Theodosia held up the hunk of glass and made a cutting gesture.

As if to retaliate, the phony beekeeper hoisted his smoker and pointed it at Theodosia. But when he flipped a lever with his finger, he was clean out of smoke.

Disappointed and frustrated, the phony beekeeper tossed the smoker on the ground, where it clattered and rolled away. Then he lifted an arm and pointed directly at her. It was a silent, ominous gesture. A clear message that said he wouldn't soon forget this confrontation. Then the phony beekeeper turned and bounded across the grass into a copse of trees. Seconds later, he'd disappeared from sight. There was a loud revving sound and then . . . silence. A few birds, the wind through the trees.

Theodosia stood there, out of breath, scared, and frustrated.

She was also shocked at herself for having sprinted after the man without benefit of a weapon or a serious plan.

She'd been motivated by . . . what? Just good old retaliation, she guessed. Hard-boiled anger had sunk its talons into her and almost gotten the better of her.

Not good. Not smart, Theodosia told herself.

As adrenaline continued to fizz through her body, Theodosia turned and slowly retraced her steps. On a path that was strewn with shattered glass and broken yellow jonquils.

2

Theodosia had never seen so many ambulances in her life. They came screaming in from the surrounding hospitals, one after the other, sirens blasting, red and blue light bars pulsing like crazy. Right behind them was a horde of black-and-white police cars as well as two fire-and-rescue squads from the Charleston Fire Department.

And all around her guests continued to cough, hack, sob, and wipe frantically at eyes that were bright red and stinging mightily. Some of the guests were sprawled on the grass, others slumped in chairs.

Respirators were quickly handed out; many guests were getting their eyes washed out by EMTs who'd arrived early on the scene.

One EMT hurried over to where Claxton's body lay on the ground some forty feet away and bent down to check for life signs. When he found none, he covered the body with a black plastic tarp. But as more help arrived, no one looked at the body. Not a single person walked over there. It was like a smoldering puddle of nuclear waste that nobody wanted to acknowledge.

Theodosia grabbed a police sergeant she recognized and pulled him aside.

"Sergeant Walker," she said. "There's a gun."

Walker beetled his bushy brows and stared at her. He had a hangdog face and looked weary, as if he'd already put in a good long day. But his eyes were still sharp and keen.

"The man—the one dressed as a phony beekeeper—after he spewed smoke all over, he shot Claxton." Still trying to catch her breath, Theodosia pointed at the body.

"What about this gun?"

"The killer dropped it," Theodosia said. "I chased after him until he . . . well, if you want, I can show you exactly where the gun was tossed."

Walker bit his lip. "Show me."

By the time Theodosia returned with Sergeant Walker carrying the dropped weapon as well as the abandoned smoker, the local EPA had arrived. Two men in white hazmat suits wandered through the area with some kind of mechanical sniffer. Trying to figure out what kind of fumes had been released, she guessed.

Then Theodosia looked around for Drayton and Haley.

Haley was gathering up wicker picnic baskets, as if she was trying to tidy up, but where was Drayton?

"Drayton?" Theodosia called out. "Drayton?" She looked around, not quite frantic but certainly concerned.

"Over here," came a croaky voice.

Theodosia spun around and found Drayton sitting at one of the far tables. He was hunched over and coughing viciously.

Oh no, he needs help.

She ran over and grabbed the sleeve of an EMT, a young Black woman with a blue bag full of gear, and pulled her over to Drayton.

The EMT made an immediate assessment. "How's the breathing?" she asked him. "Need some help?"

Drayton shook his head even as he let loose a vicious series of coughs. "No," he managed to choke out. Then, thick-voiced, added a reluctant, "Well, maybe."

The EMT, whose nametag read M. LILAC, pulled out a portable respirator and attached a hose.

"Try to relax and breathe a few of these Os," she said.

Drayton nodded as the EMT placed a clear plastic mask over his nose and mouth and slipped a plastic band around the back of his head. Drayton breathed slowly and evenly as Theodosia and the EMT watched him expectantly. Within minutes, a fair amount of color returned to his face.

"Better," Drayton said to the EMT. "Better than he is." He gestured at the tarp that covered the body of Osgood Claxton some thirty feet away.

The EMT followed his gaze, then grimaced at the sight of the body. "Stay on the Os for a few more minutes until you feel steady," she urged. Then she patted him on the shoulder and went off to help the next person.

Theodosia kept an eagle eye on Drayton. He was a healthy sixty-something but wasn't exactly a spring chicken anymore. "How are you feeling?" she asked. "I mean really?"

Drayton nodded. "I'm better. Better than most, I think. I was far enough away from the . . . what was it? Some kind of toxic smoke or gas?"

"Not sure," Theodosia said. "Something like that."

"Where did you run off to?"

"You don't want to know," Theodosia said.

Drayton frowned, then his brows rose in alarm. "Oh no, tell me you didn't."

"I'm afraid I did."

"You ran after the beekeeper?"

"Someone had to."

"Did you catch him?"

"Not even close," Theodosia said.

"Well, at least you're still in one piece," Drayton said.

Theodosia gazed around Petigru Park and saw that most of the guests were back on their feet again or were being helped to their feet by quick-acting EMTs and police. Thank goodness for these wonderful first responders. They'd come rushing in to help, not knowing how dangerous or toxic the chemicals might be.

But the party wasn't over yet.

A large black Suburban blatted its horn as it nosed its way up and over a curb, rumbled across a paved walking path, and drove into the park. It rolled across fifty yards of green grass, threading its way past the ambulances and police cruisers, heading toward the edge of the picnic area where Theodosia and Drayton were seated.

"This looks serious," Theodosia said.

Drayton pushed his mask aside. "Who is it? Homeland Security?"

Then one of the back doors burst open and a large, burly man clambered out. Theodosia recognized his familiar bulk immediately. It was Detective Burt Tidwell, head of the CPD's Robbery and Homicide Division.

Tidwell was a large man, bearish and brash. He not only commanded respect but demanded the utmost from his officers.

Tidwell was a former FBI officer who'd tired working for the Feds and yearned to get his hands dirty again. Here in Charleston he had every opportunity.

As Tidwell threaded his way toward them, he began to cough. Low, harsh rasps. Then he dipped a hand into the pocket of his saggy, oversized jacket and pulled out a hankie. Unfurled it and held it to his mouth.

Raising a hand, as if offering some kind of benediction, a half dozen uniformed officers immediately clustered around him.

"Talk to me," Tidwell said.

"Two dozen people with minor eye injuries," one officer said.

"The rest with breathing issues," another officer said.

"Everyone being tended to?" Tidwell asked.

There were nods and yeses from all the officers.

"Any idea what caused the problem?" Tidwell asked as he glanced around. "Officer Gandler? You were one of the first on scene?"

"We think it was some type of insecticide," Officer Gandler said. He pointed to the two men in hazmat suits. "That's their guesstimate, anyway, before they run lab tests. Probably something toxic, but only when it's super concentrated. Then if someone breathes in a whole bunch of the gas or ingests a fatal dose . . ."

"Did anyone?" Tidwell asked.

"No," Gandler said. "We got lucky."

"And we also have a GSW?" Tidwell was referring to a gunshot wound.

"Osgood Claxton," Gandler said.

Tidwell looked startled. "The politician?"

"Exactly, sir."

Tidwell nodded, then turned slowly to look at the black

tarp covering the body that lay well away from the crowd. The body that was waiting for the Crime Scene investigators to come and photograph and run tests on it.

Then Tidwell's roving eyes took in the picnic tables, mess of teapots and half-ruined sandwiches, and ruined artwork.

"There was an event taking place here," he said.

"A tea party," Officer Gandler said. "To celebrate an art gallery."

Tidwell's eyes continued to move across the scene. Until they fell upon Theodosia. "Uh-huh," he said with a knowing look.

But before Theodosia could connect with Tidwell and pepper him with a million questions, Holly's boyfriend, Philip Boldt, came rushing in.

"Holly! Holly!" Philip yelled, his voice edging into hysteria. He spun around, looking everywhere, frantic to find her.

"Philip, over here!" Holly called back. She rushed over to meet him and practically fell into his arms crying. They hugged, kissed, and wiped tears from each other's eyes. Then, when they were finally composed, they walked over to where Theodosia was standing, where Drayton was still sprawled in a chair.

Theodosia reached a hand out and gently touched Philip's arm. "Are you okay?" she asked. Philip was a thin, nervous type who looked like he was coming apart at the seams.

Philip gave a vigorous shake of his head. "No, I'm not okay. Not anywhere *near* okay." His mouth curved downward, his chin quivered. "I was at my restaurant and I got a frantic call from Holly. What happened here anyway?"

So Theodosia proceeded to tell him, giving Philip the short, CliffsNotes version with Holly jumping in and Drayton tossing in his two cents worth as best he could. She did, however, leave out the part where she chased the phony beekeeper and then had to hit the dirt when he fired at her. Some things were best left unsaid, she decided.

Philip listened to the retelling of the phony beekeeper's assault with toxic smoke and the beekeeper's shooting of Osgood Claxton. He seemed to grasp the gist of it all. But just as he began to nod with understanding, splotchy tears rolled down his face and he said, "Are all the paintings ruined?"

Holly grimaced. "They're not in great shape."

"Your artists are going to be furious," Philip said.

"If I explain it to them carefully, I think they'll understand," Holly said.

"That's why you carry insurance," Theodosia said.

But Philip suddenly slipped from Holly's grasp, ran over to one of the ripped canvases, looked at it, and started weeping again. "This one was a Herman Becker," he said.

"I know," Holly said. Then to Theodosia and Drayton, she said, "Philip is very sensitive."

Drayton nodded. "I'll say."

Five minutes later, Holly's silent partner, Jeremy Slade, arrived at the scene. He was the cofounder of Arcadia Software, an up-and-coming tech company. He wore a navy blue sport coat, a pink polo shirt, and blue jeans. His feet were shod in Gucci loafers.

"What. The. Hell," Slade said to Holly through gritted teeth.

"It's not as bad as it looks," Holly said, in an attempt to mollify him. As her silent partner, Slade had brought a much-needed infusion of cash to the gallery, so naturally Holly was on eggshells.

But Jeremy Slade remained tense and standoffish, even when the circumstances were explained to him.

"This is outrageous," Slade fumed. "How could something like this be allowed to happen?" He looked directly at Theodosia and glared at her, as if she were at fault.

"It wasn't exactly planned," Theodosia shot back.

"What the Sam Hill happened?" Slade demanded.

"It was a direct assault on a single person that spun out of control," Theodosia said.

Slade continued to stare at her. "On the politician? Osgood Claxton?"

"That's right."

"He never should have been here in the first place," Slade said. "Why was he here, anyway?"

As Holly cowered from Jeremy Slade's wrath, Theodosia said, "I believe he came as someone's guest. Their plus-one."

"That should have never happened," Slade snapped.

"Not my doing," Theodosia said. "I didn't send out the invitations."

"Well, neither did I!" Slade spat out. "What a disaster. This is going to be an absolute public relations nightmare."

"Miss Browning." A voice at Theodosia's elbow, low and deliberate. She'd been trying to salvage as many teapots and teacups as possible, stacking them in the plastic bins they'd brought along.

She whirled around to find Detective Tidwell staring at her. He was his usual rumpled self, but his beady eyes were sharp and clear. There was an intelligence behind those eyes that, at times, could be quite frightening.

"What?" Theodosia asked. She was tired. Couldn't wait to put this all behind her so she could go home.

"That fellow you were speaking to a few moments ago, the one who was so rude and agitated."

"Jeremy Slade," Theodosia said.

Tidwell shifted his bulk slightly to face her. "You know him?"

"Not really." Then she reconsidered. "Well, maybe in passing. He's the silent partner, the money behind the newly expanded Imago Gallery."

"Not so silent today," Tidwell said. "He seemed rather obnoxious. You say his name is Slade? Was he here for the event?" He gestured at the overturned tables and chairs. "Your ruined tea party?"

"Not that I can recall," Theodosia said.

"So he just now showed up." Tidwell turned to watch Jeremy Slade as he walked angrily about the grounds. Slade kicked at one battered painting, then leaned over, grabbed another damaged canvas, glanced at it casually, shook his head, and tossed it aside.

Theodosia, never one to miss a critical nonverbal cue, also watched Jeremy Slade. And began to wonder why he'd shown up when he did. *How* he knew to show up.

"Do you think . . . ?" she began.

But Tidwell just shook his head and walked away.

So that was the messy aftermath of Theodosia's tea party. Ambulances and police cruisers, followed by a shiny Crime Scene van, then a coroner's van with two somber-looking attendants. The Crime Scene techs roped off the area, took photos and measurements, and looked for footprints, hairs, fibers, and whatever it was Crime Scene people found interesting. Anything that might help them piece together the puzzle of why Claxton had been murdered. And who could have murdered him.

Then there was the detritus from her tea party. The rumpled tablecloths, precious teapots that had been cracked or broken, flower bouquets accented with fuzzy faux bees that were strewn everywhere, and the discarded scones, honeyed ham sandwiches, and miniature jars of DuBose Bees Honey. It was all smashed on tables and scattered across the lawn, along with ripped paintings that had been knocked clean off their easels.

Theodosia's heart ached when she saw so many dirtied and damaged canvases. And that the handle had broken off one of her good Sadler teapots.

And she wondered—who was responsible? Not just for this mess, but for the bizarre and brutal murder of Osgood Claxton III. For the devastating blow to Holly's gallery. For injuries to so many guests.

Better yet, who was going to track down that phony beekeeper and drag his sorry ass to justice?

3

KNOCK, KNOCK, KNOCK.

Someone was knocking at Theodosia's back door. A friendly but insistent knock.

And as she hurried through her dining room into her kitchen, her dog, Earl Grey, right on her heels, Theodosia had a fairly good idea of who might be paying her a visit this evening.

"Riley," she said, pulling open the door and favoring him with a bright smile.

"Hey, sweetheart." Pete Riley bent forward, gathered her in his arms, and gave her a kiss.

She kissed him back, snuggling in close, enjoying his warmth and comfort, then said, "You heard?"

"I reviewed the incident report an hour ago. Are you okay? I mean, you were *right there*."

"Saw the whole thing unfold before my very eyes."

"Terrible," Riley said. "A gun was recovered, you know."

"Yes, I know. I mean, I heard."

"And a few people are still in the ER because of the toxic gas or smoke."

"Do you know what it was? Specifically, I mean?" Theodosia asked.

"Not yet," Riley said. "Both Crime Scene and the ME have to run a bunch of toxicology tests. Oh, and a couple of the victims ended up with nasty blisters on their hands and arms. They had to be taken to the ER."

"Gracious!"

"Tell me about it."

"Is there anything new? Has anyone been able to identify the killer?" Theodosia asked.

Riley shook his head. "Not so far. But we'll get him, I have faith."

When he was at work, Pete Riley was a serious, by-the-book, up-and-coming detective. Off the clock he had a charming, boyish demeanor about him. And, from Theodosia's perspective anyway, Riley was easy on the eyes. He was tall with high cheekbones, an aristocratic nose, and blue eyes a shade lighter than hers. She'd fallen into the habit of simply calling him Riley. And he called her Theo. It was as simple and sweet as that because it suited them both.

RWWR. This from Earl Grey.

"Ah, another party heard from," Riley said as he leaned down and grabbed Earl Grey's head in his hands. "How are you doin', fella? Keeping guard over the old homestead?" He rubbed Earl Grey's ears, his muzzle, then patted his broad shoulders. Earl Grey, a mixture of dalmation and Labrador (a Dalbrador), reveled in the attention.

Because it was after six and Theodosia hadn't eaten yet (and Riley was *always* in the mood for a snack), she said, "Are you hungry?"

Riley's eyes lit up. "Are you kidding? I'm famished."

Theodosia pulled open her refrigerator and did a quick check of the goods. She had wedges of baby Swiss and Brie cheese, some cold cuts and potato salad. Add some crackers and fresh veggie slices and she had the perfect antidote to an evening snack attack.

She fixed a meat and cheese board, added dollops of mustard and mayo, then carried it into her living room, where Riley had already flaked out in a chintz-covered chair, his long legs stretched out in front of him.

"This is the life," he said, reaching out to grab a cracker, slice of roast beef, and a hunk of Swiss cheese all in one fell swoop.

Theodosia knew this was the life, but not because of the food. It was her house, her little cottage, that made her heart beat faster. She'd worked long and hard to afford this cozy little Queen Anne–style cottage with its angled roofline, stucco exterior, and crossbeams. Drayton always said if she allowed moss to grow on her roof the place would look like a hobbit house. Of course, the interior of her home was just as intriguing, with pegged wood floors, a brick fireplace, leaded windows, and chintz-covered furniture.

"You didn't just show up for the cheese and crackers, did you?" Theodosia said finally. She knew Riley was here on account of Claxton, the dead politician. Because of the tea party disaster.

Riley shook his head. "Nope."

"So what's up?"

Riley chewed his bite of cheese, swallowed, and said, "Tidwell and the powers that be at City Hall believe Claxton's murder is a disaster in the making. With a complete meltdown to follow."

"A meltdown?" Theodosia was amused.

"On the magnitude of Chernobyl."

Theodosia leaned forward, her curiosity starting to ping. "Tell me."

Riley drew a breath and seemed to gather his thoughts. Then he said, "Hear me out for a few minutes, will you?"

Theodosia nodded. Riley was working up to something; she just wasn't sure what it was.

"Claxton was connected," Riley said. "And by that I mean big-time connected. The man's been a professional politician all his natural born days and has had his sticky fingers in literally hundreds of political issues."

"Such as?"

"Permits, inspections, licensing, you name it. Claxton's held so many city and county offices and served on so many committees, boards of directors, special action groups, and political action committees that it would take twenty single-spaced pages simply to make up his bio."

"And that's a bad thing?" Theodosia asked.

"It is when you've developed a reputation for playing down and dirty. For being someone who accepts bribes and kickbacks and demands favors. Claxton was also a fixer in many cases and the rumor around police headquarters is that Claxton engineered countless political shakedowns."

"You're telling me he was a bad guy?"

"With a heart as black as coal," Riley said.

"But Claxton was running for a seat in the state legislature."

"Moving on up to the big time," Riley said. "Gonna rub elbows with the pros. So far it's been a hotly contested race."

"But not anymore," Theodosia said. "Now that Claxton's dead." She blinked. "Wait a minute, is that why he was murdered? For political gain? Could the killer have been a political opponent?"

Riley shrugged. "It's possible, but the investigation's just getting under way. We won't know anything for sure until we dig deeper. And remember, a whole lot of people wanted Claxton dead. The man wasn't just feared, he was hated. He had mortal enemies in every aspect of his political and personal life."

"So what's the bottom line here?" Theodosia asked.

Riley shook his head. "There is no bottom line. For you, anyway. I just gave you a half dozen reasons why you *shouldn't* come anywhere near this case. Why you shouldn't get involved."

"That's funny," Theodosia said. "Because I thought I was already involved."

"Only peripherally, but not really."

"Actually, really," she said.

"Sweetheart, what we have here is Southern politics at its absolute bottomed-out, mud-slinging, murderous worst. I mean, everyone's in an uproar over Claxton. The mayor, city council, legislators, business community, every political party operative . . ."

"But this is a straight-ahead murder investigation, is it not?"

"Not when a politician of his ilk is involved. And not when so many people have a keen interest in seeing how this investigation shakes out."

"What do you mean? What people?"

"Some people want his murder to be solved, others would rather have the whole case deep-sixed. And we're talking longtime politicians, campaign contributors, political hacks, people who demand and expect political favors, people who've been threatened, others who've been ruined or semi-ruined."

"Claxton's influence extended that far?"

Riley reached out and took Theodosia's hand. "You see now why I'm asking you not to get involved? To not activate that famous curiosity gene of yours?"

"Sure," Theodosia said. "Of course." But in her mind she

was thinking, *There are any number of reasons why I should be involved.*

"Then there's the Lucket factor," Riley said.

"The lucky factor?"

"Lucket, as in Lamar Lucket. He's the political big shot who was running against Claxton."

"Okay, I have heard of him." Theodosia thought for a moment. "He owns that chichi boutique hotel over on Spring Street. Is he a suspect?"

"Not at this point. But, trust me, Lucket is another someone you don't want to mess with."

Theodosia smiled. "You're telling me his daddy's rich and his momma's good-looking?"

"Daddy is probably a billionaire and, back in the day, momma was Miss Georgia."

Theodosia leaned forward, interested. "Wow."

"There you go," Riley said. "That's exactly what I've been talking about."

"Hmm?"

"You've got that telltale look in your eyes. That overly curious, meddlesome gleam."

"No, I don't," Theodosia said, wondering if she could somehow will her interested expression away.

Riley sighed heavily. "Yes, you do."

"Well." Theodosia leaned back in her chair. "Inquiring minds *do* want to know."

4

Tea kettles whistled and steeping teapots released aromatic puffs of Assam and Darjeeling into the air. Theodosia sat at a table sipping her morning cup of tea as Drayton, looking formal and altogether serious in his Harris Tweed jacket and Drake's bow tie, bustled about behind the front counter. It was early Monday and a long, busy week spun out ahead of them. Daily tea service, luncheons, two event teas to host, dozens of special orders, and catering requests.

And then there was the issue of Claxton's murder.

Drayton hadn't said much about Claxton, about all of yesterday's goings-on, but Theodosia knew it was hanging over his head like a little gray cloud. Still, Drayton remained perpetually busy, selecting today's offerings from his floor-to-ceiling wall of tea tins, fussing over his various strainers, and lining up bone china teapots like a sweet little armada.

"Well?" Theodosia finally said.

Drayton glanced over at her. "If each day is a gift, can I please return yesterday?"

Theodosia managed a faint smile. "I agree. It was just plain awful."

"I keep turning the whole mess over and over in my head— the beekeeper, the toxic smoke, the shooting . . ."

"And?"

"Words escape me."

Theodosia gave a wry smile. "Just as Claxton's killer escaped me."

Drayton picked up a pink famille rose teapot, came around the counter, and stepped over to her table to pour a refill. "I've been meaning to talk to you about that." The serious look on his face seemed to complement his disposition.

Theodosia lifted a single eyebrow. "Yes?"

"Why on earth would you risk life and limb by trying to chase down a crazed killer?"

Theodosia fidgeted with her teacup for a few moments, then said, "You ask a good question. Maybe because I was furious beyond belief? And felt violated that someone crashed our lovely event, assaulted one of our guests, and caused so much misery?"

Drayton sighed. "I can't fault you for being upset. But running after a stone-cold killer the way you did . . ."

"Please don't tell Riley about that."

"He doesn't know?" Drayton was incredulous.

"Not yet, anyway. And I prefer to keep it that way, if you don't mind."

Drayton sat down across from her. "Okay. Mum's the word. Just don't do anything that foolhardy again. I almost went into cardiac arrest when I saw you running through that cloud of toxic smoke."

"I tried not to inhale."

Drayton shook his head. "Where have I heard that before?"

*   *   *

Tables were set, candles were lit, and Theodosia had just hung out her sign, a little painted, curlicued affair that said TEA AND LIGHT LUNCHES, when the front door cracked open behind her.

"That was fast," Theodosia murmured to herself. She didn't think their first customer of the day would arrive quite so quickly. And on a Monday morning at that. Then she stopped, spun around, and did a double take as Riley stepped through the front door.

"Hey," Riley said, a smile lighting his face.

"I didn't expect to see you again so soon," she said.

Some of Riley's smile faltered. "Truth be known, I'm here to talk to Haley. If she's around, that is."

Theodosia felt a sudden flutter in her stomach. "Talk to Haley? Why? What for?"

"The thing is, some new information has come to light."

"What do you mean? Explain, please."

"It concerns yesterday. Haley has a boyfriend, yes?"

"Ben," Theodosia said. Haley had been dating a guy, a young man, by the name of Ben Sweeney. He was a grad student, studying public administration at the College of Charleston.

"That's the guy," Riley said. "You know him?"

"Not really." Theodosia stopped to think for a moment. "Well, I've *met* Ben in passing a couple of times. You know, when he stops by on his bike to pick up Haley."

"He rides a motorcycle."

"That's right. Why are you asking?"

"Because a motorcycle was seen racing away from that whole Petigru Park area yesterday afternoon."

Theodosia held up a hand. "I *heard* that, kind of a high-pitched revving noise. I didn't make the connection at the time, but now that you say motorcycle, that must have been it. The killer on his bike, racing away from the scene of the crime."

"The scene of the murder," Riley said. "Claxton's death has officially been ruled a homicide by the powers that be."

"I assumed it would," Theodosia said. "I'm also sure there are hundreds of motorcycles in Charleston. Maybe even thousands."

"Yes, but we have an eyewitness who saw and remembered a partial plate number—nine five three. A couple of the numbers match the license plate on Ben Sweeney's motorcycle. So I have to ask. Was Ben hanging around your tea party yesterday?"

"Are you asking if he was at the tea itself or somewhere in the vicinity?" Theodosia suddenly didn't like where this conversation was going.

"There. Nearby. Anywhere."

"I don't know."

"Then I'd better talk to Haley," Riley said.

Theodosia held up a finger. "Just a minute. Are you here in an official capacity?"

"It's a murder investigation, sweetheart."

"I'll take that as a yes."

"So will you please get Haley?"

But when Theodosia went into the kitchen and explained Riley's visit to Haley, she was visibly uncomfortable.

"Do I have to talk to him?" Haley asked, her eyes widening in alarm. She was dressed in a white chef's jacket over a black T-shirt and leggings and had bright yellow Crocs on her feet. What she called her cookin' shoes. At the moment she'd just finished working her magic in their postage-stamp-sized kitchen and put double batches of apple scones and lemon tea bread into her oven.

"I think the sooner you do, the quicker this mistaken identity thing, which I assume it is, will be cleared up," Theodosia said.

Haley considered Theodosia's words, then wrinkled her nose and said, "Awright."

But when they stepped from the kitchen into the tea room, Haley said, "Can Theodosia stay with me while we talk?"

"I suppose," Riley said.

"Let's go in my office, then," Theodosia suggested. "Where we can have some privacy."

They all trooped down the hallway into her office. Theodosia took a seat behind her desk, Haley lurked directly behind her, and Riley sat across the desk from them on an oversized cushy chair.

"I'm only here to ask a few basic questions," Riley said.

"About Ben," Haley said. Her eyes roved around Theodosia's office, taking in the crates filled with tea tins, stacks of hats, and shelves full of extra tea cozies and jars of jam. Looking everywhere but directly at Riley.

"That's right," Riley said. "Was he at the tea yesterday?"

Haley shook her head. "No. And Ben didn't have anything to do with the murder either."

"You seem awfully sure of that," Riley said.

Haley folded her arms across her chest. "I am."

"The witness, whoever it was, could have transposed the numbers on the license plate, right?" Theodosia said. "I mean, you said they only saw a partial number?"

Riley ignored Theodosia and continued to focus on Haley. "Do you know who was running against Osgood Claxton for a seat in the legislature?"

Haley looked puzzled. "Um, no. I'm not really into politics."

"It's a man named Lamar Lucket," Riley said.

"Never heard of him," Haley said.

"What does Lucket have to do with Ben? Or with Haley for that matter?" Theodosia asked.

"The reason I ask," Riley said, once again addressing Haley, "is because your friend Ben once worked as a volunteer on one of Lucket's campaigns."

"So what? That doesn't mean anything," Haley said. But she suddenly looked unsure of herself.

"Have you ever heard Ben say anything negative about Osgood Claxton?" Riley asked.

"I've never heard Ben say anything negative about anyone," Haley said in a rush. Her cheeks had colored bright pink and she looked like she was ready to cry.

"Really," Theodosia said. "I think we've covered everything you came in for. So if you'd kindly let us get back to work . . ."

"Okay," Riley said in a reluctant tone. "But this might not be over. There could be a few more questions."

"We're not worried," Theodosia said. Even though Haley looked scared to death.

The Indigo Tea Shop was busy all morning. Neighboring shopkeepers dropped by for their de rigueur cuppa and to commiserate about yesterday. Multiple groups of tourists found their way in, perhaps drawn by the charm of the shop—the brickwork, leaded windows, hunter green awnings, and rounded door looked like it might lead to an Alice in Wonderland–type adventure.

And it kind of did. Because the interior of the tea shop was just as intriguing as the exterior. With a touch of country

French and a smattering of Olde England, the Indigo Tea Shop was a jewel box of a shop. Blue toile curtains were artfully swagged on wavy leaded windows, while faded Oriental carpets made cozy statements on pegged pine floors. There was a small wood-burning fireplace and a French chandelier that imparted a warm, almost hazy glow—Drayton always referred to it as Rembrandt lighting. In the far corner, antique highboys held retail items that included tea towels, tea cozies, tins of tea, Theodosia's proprietary T-Bath lotions and moisturizers, and jars of DuBose Bees Honey. A velvet celadon green curtain separated the café from the back half, and brick walls were hung with antique prints and twisty grapevine wreaths decorated with miniature teacups.

Of course, the shop hadn't magically sprung to life. Theodosia had scrimped and saved, then tossed in some 401k money from her previous marketing job to nail down the small, historic building as her very own. Drayton had come on board as her tea sommelier. And Haley, casually answering a want ad, had suddenly found her baking skills (and her grandma's recipes) in high demand.

The rest of the tea accoutrements had come about organically, with Theodosia sifting through flea markets, antique shops, and tag sales to find the perfect vintage teacups, teapots, goblets, and silverware.

After several years together, Theodosia, Drayton, and Haley had become a confident, carefully coordinated team that never failed to delight visitors and neighbors with their baked-from-scratch scones and muffins, dazzling array of fine teas, extraordinary catering, and ever-popular special event teas. They'd all come to realize that family didn't always have to mean blood relatives.

"Thanks," Haley said when Theodosia popped in to grab a

plate of apple scones and of bowl of Devonshire cream for a table of guests. "It's kind of scary when the cops question you."

"Not to worry," Theodosia said. "Especially since it was just Riley."

"Still, he seemed pretty serious. A little intense, in fact."

"Just hang in there, I'm sure this will all blow over soon."

Theodosia dropped her scones off, then stopped at the front counter to grab a pot of tea. Most of the tables were occupied and the tea shop was fairly buzzing.

"I'm thinking of brewing a pot of Ti Quan Yin for lunch," Drayton said. "It's such a remarkable spring floral tea."

"Go for it," Theodosia said.

"As for the Ceylonese silver tips . . ." He indicated the teapot in Theodosia's hand. "Maybe let it steep an additional minute." He closed one eye, thinking. "Make that two."

"Gotcha," Theodosia said. She lifted her shoulders, trying to unkink her neck, and said, "Busy morning."

"Has everyone been gossiping about Claxton?" Drayton asked.

"It's all they're talking about. I'm getting tons of questions, some not all that subtle."

"Just be noncommittal," Drayton said. "This will all be forgotten in a day or two."

"That's exactly what I told Haley."

"Right. I mean the man's deceased. What more could possibly happen?"

A loud CLUNK rattled the tea room, then a sharp WHAP sounded as the front door opened and bounced hard against the inside wall.

"I say," said an exasperated Drayton. "There's no need for . . ."

That's when Holly Burns and Jeremy Slade burst into the tea shop. They glanced about, twitching with anxiety, fairly jittering on the balls of their feet. Neither one appeared to have slept last night and both looked as if they were carrying the weight of the world on their back.

"Theodosia!" Holly quavered when she spotted her friend standing at the front counter. It was such a sad, plaintive cry that every head in the tea shop turned to look.

5

~❦~

"Holly?" Theodosia's footsteps snapped like castanets on the pine floor as she hurried over to intercept Holly and Jeremy. "What's going on?"

"You won't believe it," Jeremy said. The expression on his face was one of pure anguish.

"We're in big trouble," Holly said. Her eyes blazed, her teeth practically chattered with pent-up anxiety.

"By that she means the gallery," Jeremy echoed.

"Wait one," Theodosia said. She quickly delivered her pot of tea, then came back, grabbed Holly's hand, and guided them both to a nearby table. Once Holly and Jeremy had collapsed into chairs, Theodosia did a quick check of the tea room. When it appeared she had a few moments to spare, Theodosia sat down and said, "Start from the beginning. Tell me everything."

"Things couldn't be worse," Holly said. Her shoulders sagged, the corners of her mouth twitched. "Several of the big-name artists we signed have suddenly decided to pull out."

"Not only that," Jeremy said, "but three major customers canceled their orders and are demanding full refunds."

"This could ruin us," Holly cried. "Yesterday the Imago Gallery was starting to gain some much-needed traction in the community, today we're making headlines and losing business because of a murder!"

"It's guilt by association over a murder we had nothing to do with," Jeremy said.

Theodosia listened as they spun out their tale of woe. And the more they talked, the more serious the situation at the gallery sounded. Artists *were* abandoning them in droves, fearing their little gallery would be deemed culpable in Claxton's murder.

"And your financial investment?" Theodosia said, turning to Jeremy. "The money you put in, that's in jeopardy as well?"

"Absolutely," Jeremy said. "When I invested in the Imago Gallery it was to help relaunch it. To try and attract a higher caliber of artist as well as more upscale and qualified buyers."

"And to stage events and jazz up our marketing and PR campaigns," Holly added.

"Who knew that a single disruptive act could throw our gallery into complete and utter chaos?" Jeremy said. "I mean, the press has been having a field day with Claxton's death."

"And with us," Holly cried.

"You can't let the media define you," Theodosia said. "You need to take charge and do immediate damage control. Figure out a strategy to mitigate all the bad press."

"That's why we thought of you," Holly said. "You have a background in marketing. You must have had clients who needed crisis management at one time or another, right?"

But Theodosia was shaking her head. "Not a worst-case scenario like this. I'm afraid I don't have that kind of hard-edge experience."

Jeremy shot Holly a nervous look. "Ask her," he hissed.

"Ask me what?" From the looks they'd exchanged, Theodosia knew something was brewing. And it wasn't a pot of tea.

There was a pregnant pause and then Holly said, "Even if you can't help us media-wise, we still need your smarts."

"You might be our only salvation," Jeremy added.

"Excuse me?" Theodosia said. Had she heard them correctly? Their salvation?

Jeremy flashed another look at Holly, then turned his gaze directly on Theodosia. "Holly tells me you're some kind of neighborhood detective. That you've managed to solve quite a few crimes."

"Solved actual *murders*," Holly said with emphasis.

Theodosia picked abstractly at her apron. "Oh, I don't know about that. It was more like noticing a few strange inconsistencies and pointing the police in the right direction."

But Holly was shaking her head. "No, Theo, you're being far too modest. That fashion show woman who got killed a while back, you were instrumental in figuring out who shot her."

"And almost got killed in the process," Drayton mumbled, loud enough for them to hear.

Theodosia glanced over at Drayton, who was still standing behind the counter, looking innocent as he measured scoops of jasmine tea into a Brown Betty teapot.

"Drayton, if you want to be part of this conversation, why don't you come over here and sit down," Theodosia said.

Drayton raised both hands in a benign *no thanks* gesture and shook his head.

"Okay then," Theodosia said. It looked as if Drayton preferred to kibitz from afar. "So you're asking . . . wait, what are you asking?"

"For your help," Holly said. "We need someone like you

who's influential in the neighborhood and . . ." She ducked her head and glanced around the tea room. "And who hears things. You know, gossip, street news, rumors."

Theodosia knew it was more than that. "You're asking me to try and figure out who killed Osgood Claxton, aren't you?"

They both nodded.

Theodosia took a few moments to consider their request. Obviously, her head was still spinning with information that Riley had given her last night. About Claxton's contacts, dirty tricks, and misdeeds. How he was connected. But knowing the man's background was a far cry from ferreting out actual suspects. "I'm not sure I can do that," she said.

Holly reached over and grabbed Theodosia's hand. "You can. I know you can."

"Even if you just look into things in a tertiary way," Jeremy implored. "It would be a great help."

"You realize," Theodosia said. "Claxton was a bad guy."

"We're familiar with many of the rumors," Jeremy said. "Which is why we came to you. Yes, the police are working the case but . . . who knows? With all of Claxton's past connections and influence, maybe they won't work it so hard, so diligently?" He tilted his head sideways in a questioning gesture. "Maybe they don't want to uncover skeletons in the attic?"

Theodosia nibbled at her lower lip. Jeremy could be right about that. Maybe some folks in city government had benefited from a few of Claxton's deals. So the wheels of justice might turn painfully slow. On the other hand, the idea of getting involved . . . well, she had to admit it gave her a tingle. Intrigued her and pulled at her sense of adventure.

"Why was Claxton at the tea?" Theodosia asked.

"He came as someone's guest," Holly said.

"Their plus-one," Jeremy said, rolling his eyes.

"If I were to do anything, anything at all," Theodosia said, "the first thing I'd want to check would be your guest list. I'd need to see who all was in attendance yesterday."

"It's yours," Holly said, practically pouncing. "If you could drop by the gallery later today, I'll print out a list for you."

"Around four-ish?" Theodosia said.

Holly nodded. "Perfect."

"I'd also like a list of the artists," Theodosia said.

Jeremy looked suddenly nervous. "That's kind of confidential. We have certain agreements in place . . ."

"*Had* certain agreements," Holly interrupted, tapping an index finger against the table. "Now those artists are abandoning us like rats from a sinking ship. No, if Theodosia's willing to step in and help, we need to give her everything. Open the kimono, so to speak."

Jeremy lifted both hands and said, "Okay. She gets complete and total access."

"Oh." Holly was about to add something else, then her jaw bunched and her mouth snapped shut.

"What?" Theodosia asked.

"Nothing," Holly said as her eyes skittered away.

"Something," Theodosia said.

Holly grimaced. "I was just thinking . . . I hope Booker didn't do anything crazy."

"Booker?" Drayton said. Clearly, he was still listening in on the conversation.

"Who's Booker?" Theodosia asked.

Holly looked across the table at Jeremy with widened eyes, silently urging him to speak up.

Finally, Jeremy sighed and said, "Thadeus T. Booker. He's one of the artists Holly recently signed to the gallery. Booker's what you might classify as an outsider artist. He's remarkably talented but a trifle eccentric. He smokes a little weed and has been known to carry a knife."

"And why would you think Booker might have done something crazy?" Theodosia asked.

"Because he's just plain off the chain," Holly said. "Booker talks about painting in blood and doing crazy street art. Sometimes he'll sneak out at two in the morning and work all night, creating some kind of weird giant mural on the side of a building. Without the building owner's permission, of course."

"Booker incorporates words and numbers along with rather startling images," Jeremy said. "He refers to it as guerrilla art."

"I think I'd like to talk to this Booker," Theodosia said.

"No, you don't," Drayton murmured under his breath.

"Where would I find him?" Theodosia asked.

"Last I heard he was hanging around the colleges, working on street paintings. The coffee shops and tattoo parlors are big fans of the stuff he does, the graffiti stuff and the phantom art," Holly said.

"What's phantom art?" asked Theodosia.

"It's when Booker does a painting, signs it, and disappears," Holly said.

"Interesting," Theodosia said. *Very interesting indeed.*

Twenty minutes later, Theodosia was in the kitchen, nibbling an apple scone. Haley had just pulled a pan of blond brownies from the oven and was mixing up a bowl of chocolate frosting, whipping it into a frenzy with her wire whisk.

"My mulligan soup should make a nice starter today," Holly said. "It's chockablock full of beef brisket, gold potatoes, and carrots, and should go well with my lemon poppy biscuits."

"Terrific," Theodosia said. "What else do we have on the menu?"

"Seafood salad, caramelized onion and cheddar quiche, cucumber and cream cheese tea sandwiches with blackberry jam, and crab salad on brioche tea sandwiches. Plus, we've still got plenty of scones and tea bread from this morning."

There was a soft knock on the door jam and then Drayton poked his head in.

"Theo," he said. "We're getting busy."

The Indigo Tea Shop was busy all right, but nothing Theodosia couldn't handle. She took orders, ran them into the kitchen, then swooped back out to grab pots of freshly brewed tea from Drayton. It was a ballet of sorts, the dipping, swooping, and pouring, but it energized Theodosia. Reminded her just how much she loved her cozy little tea shop. How important owning a small business was to her own self-worth.

At one fifteen, Bill Glass, the photographer and publisher, sauntered in. He saw Theodosia standing at the front counter, touched two fingers to his forehead, and shot her a mock salute. Today Glass wore a faded denim jacket, saggy jeans, and a pair of scuffed loafers. A Nikon camera was slung around his neck.

"There she is, the Angel of Death herself," Glass said.

Theodosia gave him a quick glance. "Don't you have to be somewhere?" she asked. Her words were polite but firm.

"What are you talking about?" Glass smirked.

"Shouldn't you be sneaking through the bushes at the Country Club of Charleston or intruding on a meeting of the Junior League? Trying to get a compromising shot for your little rag of a paper?" Maybe she could shame him into leaving?

"I could, but it wouldn't be half as exciting as yesterday. That was a real pip of a tea party, huh?" He came closer, banged the flat of his hand down on the counter, and said, "How often do you get a front-row seat at a genuine murder!"

Drayton set an indigo blue paper cup on the counter and said, "Let me pour you a cup of Darjeeling to go."

"To go?" His face darkened. "You're asking *moi* to leave?"

"If you would," Drayton said.

But Glass was never one to take a hint, not even a heavy-handed one. Instead, he stuck around like flypaper, noisily slurping his tea, making the occasional rude comment.

Theodosia racked her brain as to how to get rid of him. Maybe she could pretend to close early? No, that wasn't going to work, there were too many customers. Then she was struck by a peculiar notion. Maybe Glass, with his intrusive picture taking, had been a kind of witness.

"You took a lot of pictures yesterday, right?" Theodosia asked Glass. "At our Honeybee Tea?"

"Sure did," Glass said. "Got some real doozies."

"Show me, will you?"

Glass held up his camera for her to look and clicked through at least three dozen pictures. Over his shoulder, Theodosia squinted at them as best she could.

"Seen enough?" Glass asked.

"Those are pretty interesting," Theodosia said. "Is there a chance we could download them to my computer?"

"If you've got a USB cable, it shouldn't be a problem."

So they went into Theodosia's office, fussed around, and did exactly that.

Seeing the photos on her large computer screen made all the difference in the world for Theodosia. "These are good," she said as she studied them.

"Of course they're good," Glass said. "I shot them."

"What I meant was . . . they give an excellent documentation of the event. Who was there, the interaction between Claxton and the beekeeper. I'm impressed you managed to keep shooting even when that toxic smoke started drifting across the tables."

"I kept clicking away until I couldn't see anymore. Man, it was hairy, like being back in a war zone."

"When were you ever in a war zone?" Theodosia asked.

"When I was younger," Glass mumbled. "Did some shooting for the Associated Press."

"Sure." Theodosia didn't want to argue with Glass. She wanted to keep the photos he'd taken so she could go through them again with a careful, more discriminating eye. Who knows? She might learn something. "Listen, can I keep these photos for now?"

"I suppose. It's not like you're going to try and sell them or anything." He gave her a cautious look. "Are you?"

"No."

"Okay then. But I don't know what you think you'll find. I scanned through all of them and didn't see any big revelation. It's not like I caught the killer's bare face before he climbed into his beekeeper suit."

"I wish you had."

Glass looked mournful. "Hey, *I* wish I had. Then my shots would be on the front page of the *Post and Courier.* Maybe even on Fox News and CNN."

Theodosia studied the last few pictures, then tapped a finger lightly against the computer screen. "Did you give these photos to the Charleston police? To the investigators who are working the case?"

"Um, the ones on my other camera, the Leica, yeah, I did."

"But not these images," Theodosia said.

"No. Do you want me to? Turn them over to the police, I mean?"

"Why don't we keep this between us for the time being, okay?"

"I guess." Glass shifted from one foot to the other. "What do you think you're going to find?" He sounded curious, edgy.

"Not sure," Theodosia said. "Finding anything meaningful is kind of a snipe hunt at this point."

Glass nodded. "Tell me about it."

6

By midafternoon, things had settled down to a dull roar. Lunch, which had drawn a surprisingly good crowd, had ended, and now there were four tables of guests enjoying afternoon tea.

Theodosia served pots of gunpowder green, Earl Grey, and cinnamon spice tea, as well as cream scones and Haley's famous lemon poppy biscuits. Then, keeping an eye on her customers, she wandered back to the front counter. Drayton had his Montblanc pen out, jotting notes in one of his Moleskine notebooks. His tortoiseshell glasses were poised halfway down his nose.

"Figuring out your unpaid taxes?" Theodosia asked.

"Um, no," Drayton said, glancing up and looking startled. Then, "Don't frighten me like that. You know how I am when it comes to personal finances. I tend to go a bit rigid."

"We all do. That's why we've got Miss Dimple." Miss Dimple was their bookkeeper, sometimes server, and crackerjack preparer of income taxes. She kept them all on the straight and narrow.

"Actually I was working on ideas for a couple of event teas."

"I'm glad somebody's on top of this," Theodosia said.

"What would you think about a Fox and Hounds Tea? You know I scored several pieces of Old Britain Castles dinnerware. Or how about a Secret Garden Tea?"

"Both ideas sound fabulous and a little offbeat," Theodosia said. "Kind of like tomorrow's Wind in the Willows Tea. Which is a fun, almost eccentric theme that I'm glad we took a chance on."

"Are you kidding? We're practically sold out," Drayton said. "There's maybe two or three seats left."

"Thanks to your enterprising nature. I know you've been hustling tickets to everyone who's come in here."

Drayton lifted a shoulder. "Word-of-mouth selling is just good business. As you always like to point out, making a profit trumps simply making a living."

"It's amazing how many small businesses don't understand that," Theodosia said. "They're afraid to do a little marketing or put on their sales cap and ask for the order."

"So." Drayton gazed at her. "You intend to insert yourself in the Claxton murder?"

"Not necessarily. I see it more as lending a hand to Holly and Jeremy."

"Semantics," Drayton said. "I think you're juggling words."

"You'd prefer I juggle suspects?"

"No! I don't think you should get involved at all. Claxton's murder didn't just happen, it was premeditated. Someone planned it out quite methodically." His brow furrowed. "The thing is, someone *knew* Claxton was going to be attending our tea."

"You make a good point," Theodosia said. "Someone had firsthand knowledge."

"But who?"

Loud footsteps sounded in the back hallway.

"Sounds like storm troopers. Or is that Haley stomping around in those weird crocodile shoes?" Drayton asked.

"Crocs. And that's not Haley," Theodosia said.

"Then who? Our back door is supposed to remain locked."

Haley suddenly parted the curtains, peeked out at them, and said, "I unlocked it. Ben's here."

Drayton's eyebrows shot up again.

"Just who I wanted to talk to," Theodosia said. She hurried into the back hallway and called, "Ben?"

Ben Sweeney was standing there munching a cream scone. He was blond with longish hair and a slightly scruffy beard that seemed to be all the rage among young twentysomething guys. The way he was dressed—black AC/DC T-shirt and ripped jeans—made him look more like a garage band freak than someone who was working toward his master's degree.

"Oh hi" was Ben's muffled reply as he continued to chew. "I just came by to pick up Haley."

"I'll be ready in two shakes," Haley called to him from the kitchen. "Just gotta package up the leftover tea bread and flip the switch on the dishwasher."

"Have the police talked to you?" Theodosia asked Ben. "About your motorcycle?"

Ben stuffed another bite of scone in his mouth and said, "Yeah. I told 'em it wasn't me. That I was at the library."

"Did you know Osgood Claxton?"

Ben swallowed hard, shook his head, and said, "Nope."

"What about his political opponent, Lamar Lucket? Rumor has it you once worked on one of Lucket's campaigns."

Ben's brows pulled together. "That jerk?" He let loose a derisive snort. "It was a couple of years ago and it was part of a volunteerism project for an undergraduate poli-sci class."

"That's it?" Theodosia said.

"Hey, I wouldn't recognize either one of those guys if I ran into them on the street. If I ran *over* them."

"I'm ready!" Haley cried as she squirted out the door of the kitchen and planted herself firmly between Ben and Theodosia.

Ben put an arm around Haley's shoulder. "Then let's bounce," he said.

"Have fun, you two," Theodosia said as they careened through her office and out the back door.

"That was Ben?" Drayton asked when Theodosia returned to the tea room.

"Yup. I asked him if he knew Osgood Claxton and he said no."

"How about the fellow who was running against him, Lucket?"

"Ben claimed the only reason he volunteered on the man's campaign was to fulfill a class requirement."

"Do you believe him?" Drayton asked.

"About ninety-eight percent," Theodosia said.

"And the other two percent?"

"Still up in the air."

It was after four by the time Theodosia arrived at the Imago Gallery. From outside, she could see pinpoint spotlights shining through the windows. But when she pushed her way through the front door, the place looked deserted. Well, devoid of people anyway. Still, light cascaded down on colorful paintings that were hung on stark white walls, and a few good-sized metal sculptures—one resembling a strangled bird—were perched on blocks of white Lucite. At the same time, more than a dozen canvases were leaned up against a counter and narrow wooden crates were stacked nearby, as if paintings were about to be packed up and shipped out.

"Anybody home?" Theodosia called out as she walked across their uber-trendy gray industrial carpeting.

"Hello?" a voice echoed from the back. It was a man's voice, deep and resonant. Theodosia wondered if it might be one of the artists who'd stopped by to pick up their work. Or maybe pick up a check?

Seconds later Philip Boldt appeared. Besides his appearance yesterday, Theodosia had met Philip a few times, mostly when he filled in as bartender at one of Holly's art openings. But Philip was actually a budding restaurateur. Right now he ran what he called a ghost kitchen over on Cumberland Street. Ghost because he was only doing a takeout business on food until he could get his entire restaurant up and running.

"Philip," Theodosia said. "How are you?" Philip was slight to the point of being skinny, which was made even more apparent by the tight T-shirt and black jeans he wore. His dark hair was scraped back into a small man bun which seemed to emphasize his long face, slight hawk nose, and dark eyes.

Philip shrugged. "Not great. Mostly because Holly's pretty upset. As for Jeremy Slade . . ." He rolled his eyes. "You can imagine how he's feeling right now. Seeing his investment trickle away through no fault of his own. Or ours, for that matter."

"Maybe it's not as bad as all that," Theodosia said. She liked to see the upside of things. Often felt that situations others deemed hopeless could still be salvaged.

"Oh, it's bad," Philip said. "Really bad. Wait until you talk to Holly."

I already have, Theodosia thought to herself. Then said, "Holly's here, right?"

"Yup, let me run back and grab her."

Philip disappeared into the back office, closing the door behind him. There was a quiet exchange of words—Theodosia couldn't hear what was being said—and then Holly came flying out like a little dust devil, dark hair flying, jewelry clanking around her. Philip followed behind in her footsteps.

"Theo," Holly cried, practically breathless. She reached forward, grabbed both of Theodosia's wrists, and said, "You're not going to believe what just happened."

"What just happened?" Theodosia asked. For a quick moment she hoped it might be good news. That the police had developed a serious lead. Or they'd taken someone into custody.

Didn't turn out that way.

"I'm being sued!" Holly cried. Now she released Theodosia and threw her hands up in the air. "By no less than Osgood Claxton's wife!"

"The court served Holly with papers an hour ago," Philip put in.

"Not only that," Holly continued, her voice rising in pitch. "She's his soon-to-be *ex*-wife!"

"Why on earth are *you* being sued?" Theodosia asked. "You didn't do anything. The murderer was an unknown outsider. I can't imagine you can be held responsible for Claxton's death. It seems . . . preposterous."

"Well, I haven't read through all the paperwork," Holly said. She touched a hand to her head, scrubbed at it, then twisted a hank of hair. "Because my reading comprehension is horrible. I'm just not oriented that way, I'm a *visual* person." She looked to Philip for confirmation. "Aren't I, Philip?"

"You are," he agreed. "You're extremely visual."

"But this lawsuit raises the stakes even higher," Holly said to Theodosia. "Which means we need your help more than ever."

"Wait. What?" Philip said.

"Theodosia's agreed to help us," Holly said. "Generously agreed. She's going to run a . . . gosh, what would you call it?" Her mouth worked furiously as she managed an anxious smile. "A kind of shadow investigation. While the police are looking for suspects, Theodosia's going to snoop around and see if she can figure out what happened."

"She can do that?" Philip looked startled as he gazed from Holly to Theodosia. "You can do that?"

"I can try," Theodosia said. "Maybe spot some sort of discrepancy that the police missed." She raised a hand, made a fluttering gesture. "I don't know. Holly asked for help, I said yes. It's as simple as that."

"Well," Philip said, rocking back on his heels and nodding. "I like that. And I happen to know you're one smart cookie, so your offer to help is really quite generous."

"It is, isn't it, dear?" Holly grabbed Philip's arm and pulled him close.

"For sure," Philip said. "Job number one is keeping the Imago Gallery afloat. So anything you can do . . ." He gazed at Theodosia with a thoughtful, almost hopeful expression on his face. "But how do you even *start* with something like yesterday's murder? How do you sort through all the craziness?"

"I'll begin with the basics," Theodosia said. "Study the guest list, look at the list of artists. See if anything jumps out at me."

"And then what?" Philip asked.

"Then I'll dig deeper and ask a few questions. If I actually discover something worth pursuing, I probably have to hand it over to the investigators," Theodosia said.

"Sounds good to me," Philip said, his enthusiasm growing by leaps and bounds. "Wow, thanks so much for putting your smarts to work on this. Since people are actually returning paintings and canceling orders for commissioned work, today's been another disaster for Holly." He gazed at Holly, who nodded and managed a frazzled half smile. "So anything, really anything you can do to help, would be a step in the right direction."

"Let me get those lists for you," Holly said as she headed back to her office.

Theodosia glanced around, then reached a hand out and touched a large canvas that was leaning up against the counter. From what she could see, it was a blue-and-green abstract painting with a small red sticker in one corner. "This painting's been sold?" she asked Philip.

Philip made a lemon face. "It was. Until Holly got a call from the buyer saying they were no longer interested."

"Sad," Theodosia said.

"Unfair," Philip said.

"Here are those lists." Holly returned to hand over three sheets of paper, still warm from the printer. "The first two pages are our guest list from yesterday, the third sheet details the new artists we signed up."

"And how many of those artists have pulled out?" Theodosia asked.

"Five called to tell me they're going to seek representation elsewhere," Holly said, "so I put little ticks next to their names and contact information." Her mouth twisted in a grimace. "'Seek representation elsewhere.' Those words sound so benign, yet they're slowly killing me." She looked around the gallery. "Killing my dream."

"I'll get to work on this right away," Theodosia said.

"Can't be easy to find a killer," Holly said.

"You know what?" Philip said. "If I had to put money on

anyone as the guilty party, it'd be Lamar Lucket, Claxton's political opponent. From what I know, the guy's a snake."

"Why do you say that?" Theodosia asked.

"Well, being a restaurant owner I naturally hear things from my friends in the hospitality industry," Philip said. "And most people don't have a positive opinion of Lamar Lucket. He's apparently difficult to deal with and notoriously hard on his staff."

"That's what I've heard, too," Holly said.

"But is Lucket a killer?" Theodosia asked.

"Hard to say," Philip said. "But if Lucket *is* involved, there's always the chance he didn't do the hit himself, that he hired someone. But I know Lucket was the main dude who was running neck and neck against Claxton."

"Who do you think would have been successful?" Theodosia asked. "Who would have won the election?"

Philip screwed up his face, as if he were deep in thought. "Hard to say. Both Claxton and Lucket played dirty and I think the polls had them at even odds."

"What about now?" Theodosia asked.

"Now?" Philip said. "Since it's too late in the game to find a suitable replacement for Claxton, Lucket's a shoo-in."

"Yeah," Theodosia said. "That's what I think, too."

7

"You're still here," Theodosia said. She'd hurried back to the Indigo Tea Shop, hoping to catch Drayton, and here he was, still fussing about with a self-satisfied look on his face.

"Teapots are wiped out, floors are swept, and I was just about to lock up," Drayton said.

"Wonderful. Now I have a proposition for you."

"Uh-oh." Drayton touched his bow tie in a nervous gesture. "Does this have anything to do with the murder of Osgood Claxton?"

"How did you guess?"

"Because you just came from the Imago Gallery and have that thrill-of-the-hunt look on your face."

"Well , . ." He had her there.

"Okay, I'll bite," Drayton said. "What exactly does your proposition entail? Please tell me we're not going to break into the county morgue and spirit away Claxton's body or something equally dreadful."

"Nothing that grisly. But . . . if you had to pull a name out of your hat, someone who probably wanted Claxton out of the way, who would it be?"

"Is this a trick question?" Drayton asked.

"No, it's for real."

"Okay. Then perhaps . . ." Drayton finger walked up his lapel and touched the edge of his bow tie again. "Off the top of my head I'd probably have to say it was the politician running against him."

"Lamar Lucket."

"Whose name reminds me of a country-western singer."

"Actually, Lucket is a hotelier," Theodosia said. "Besides being a political candidate, he owns that new boutique hotel over on Spring Street."

"Of course, the Ayung Hotel. I read about it in *Charleston Magazine*. It's named after a major river in Bali, Indonesia. The atmosphere is supposed to be extremely tranquil and Zen."

"So you'll go with me?"

Drayton shrugged. "I suppose a little tranquility couldn't hurt."

They locked up the tea room and climbed into Theodosia's Jeep, which was parked in the back alley.

"Is this just for a quick drink or are we going to have dinner?" Drayton asked as they drove.

"Let's play it by ear," Theodosia said.

He tapped his fingers against the dashboard. "Works for me."

The Ayung Hotel was unlike anything they'd seen before in Charleston. The lobby featured a floor-to-ceiling living wall of green plants, a koi pond, gigantic marble elephants, carved dragons, Balinese Barong masks hung on the walls, and a teak-wood floor. The furniture was all hand-carved teak with embroidered pillows.

"Listen," Drayton said as they stood in the lobby.

"What?" Theodosia said. And then she heard it. A soft cacophony of pattering water, wind chimes, and gamelan music. Gentle music for the soul.

"I feel like I've been magically transported to Bali," Drayton said in a reverent tone.

"Lovely, really lovely. But let's not forget why we're here." Theodosia headed for the front desk, where a woman in a yellow silk sari was tapping away at a computer.

"Excuse me," Theodosia said. "Where would we find Mr. Lucket's office?"

The woman lifted a hand. "It's right down this corridor, but I'm afraid he isn't available at the moment."

"Oh." Theodosia let her disappointment show through.

"He's meeting with his campaign people right now, but I happen to know he should be done in ten or fifteen minutes. Who shall I say is inquiring about him?"

"Theodosia Browning."

"The desk clerk dutifully wrote down Theodosia's name, then said, "Perhaps you'd care to wait in our lounge?"

"We'll do that," Theodosia said.

"The Nusa Dua room," the desk clerk said. "Just across the lobby."

"*This feels quite* authentic," Drayton said as they sat down at a rattan table in a small restaurant that was all ferns, bamboo plants, draped fishnets, and low lighting. "Like being in old Java." He glanced around. "Except for that carved wooden mask with the bulging eyes and angry grimace. Makes me feel like I washed up on a desert island where the locals aren't all that friendly."

Theodosia handed Drayton a menu that featured colorful photos of drinks with names like Tiki in the Jungle, Tiger Shark, Mr. Bali Hai, and at at least twenty other tropical themes. "Take a look at these cocktails," Theodosia said. "Maybe you'll change your mind."

Drayton smiled faintly as he perused the drink menu. "So there is an upside after all."

"And there's food," she said. "What do you think about ordering the grilled octopus?"

"Pass."

"Tuna tartare?" Theodosia asked.

"That might be a bit experimental for my palate."

"How about the sati babi?"

"Which is?" Drayton said.

"Really just a pork satay."

"Better. Oh, and maybe an order of their Friki Tiki Beans. And I wouldn't mind coconut shrimp."

They ordered flower mojitos and three small plates to share, which all proved to be delicious. Then, some twenty minutes later, Lamar Lucket came striding into the restaurant.

Lucket was one of those men who projected a good deal of bluster and swagger. Not the kind of man you'd want to get involved with, but probably the perfect temperament for politics. He looked fearless, harsh words probably rolled right off his back. He was also tall and rail thin with an olive complexion, silver hair swept back from his high forehead, probing eyes, and thin lips. Lucket wore a double-breasted gray pinstripe suit that was probably Armani and cost several thousand dollars. Even so, Theodosia thought he looked like a mafioso type. Or a wheeler-dealer politician, which he pretty much was.

Following on Lucket's heels was a frazzled-looking woman in a tight black skirt suit. She had thin, hunched shoulders, frizzy blond hair, and carried a briefcase as well as an enormous stack of papers that threatened to slip away from her. She basically looked as if she had too much on her plate.

"Lamar," the woman called as she struggled to keep up with him. "The election's in six weeks! We need to huddle with Alex. Talk about publicity and what to do when the opposition throws another candidate at us—which you know they will. Try to work out a few strategies!"

But Lucket was unfazed. "All in good time, Clarice," he said as he held up a hand to back her off. "Besides . . ." He grinned. "I see only smooth sailing ahead."

He seemed jubilant as he walked through the restaurant, Clarice following in his footsteps as he handed out campaign buttons to all the customers. The buttons were a take on the old *I Love New York* theme. Only Lucket's buttons featured a capital I, then a heart, then the words A WINNER. Underneath that read, LAMAR LUCKET.

When Lucket swung by their table, Theodosia said, "May we have a word, please?"

Lucket stopped and gave Theodosia and Drayton the once-over. "You're the people who wanted to speak with me?" He handed them each a large button.

"Please," Theodosia said.

"If you have a moment," Drayton said.

Clarice blew a puff of hair out of her face. "Mr. Lucket's awfully busy," she said in a dour tone.

Lucket favored them with a practiced smile. "You're campaign donors?"

"Not exactly," Theodosia said.

Lucket's smile faded. "Then what?"

"We're looking into the death of Osgood Claxton," Theodosia said.

"That's it, we're done here," Clarice snapped.

"So you're investigators?" Lucket said. He sounded mildly interested.

"Private investigators," Theodosia said, even though it was a little white lie.

"Well, I don't know what to tell you," Lucket said. "Somebody up and shot the poor jerk. At least that's what it said in the newspapers."

"Maybe not the jerk part," Drayton said.

Lucket looked thoughtful. "Well, no. But, unfortunately, these things can be the norm in politics today. You get a few crackpots who decide to take matters into their own hands . . ." He paused when he noticed they were studying him closely. "Wait a minute, you're not trying to insinuate that *I* had anything to do with Claxton's death, are you?" He sounded deeply offended.

"Lamar was at a campaign rally when it happened," Clarice said in a shrill voice.

Theodosia ignored Clarice, who was beginning to irritate her. She reminded her of a small, yappy dog that wouldn't quit nipping at your heels. So Theodosia focused only on Lucket. "Not at all," she lied. "We're certainly not impugning your reputation. But since you and Claxton ran in the same political circles, I thought perhaps you might offer a few insights."

"Concerning who killed him?" Lucket said. He looked both interested and flattered.

"That's right," Theodosia said. "Surely you must have a few ideas. By now you and your team must have kicked around the circumstances of Claxton's death and wondered who could be responsible."

Lucket shook his head. "Not really, other than to say 'How crazy was that?' Besides, word on the street was the shooter was some guy on a motorcycle. Probably one of those scruffy biker types wearing club colors."

"That suspect didn't pan out," Theodosia said.

"Then I don't know." Lucket put a hand to his face and tapped an index finger against his lower lip. "As far as suspects go, nobody in local politics jumps out at me. Most of them are too chicken-livered to pull a crazy stunt like that. But . . ."

"Yes?" Theodosia said.

Lucket looked around hastily, as if to make sure nobody was listening. "If anyone wanted Osgood Claxton dead, buried, and forgotten, it would be Mignon Merriweather, his soon-to-be ex-wife."

"What makes you say that?" Theodosia asked.

"Because of the money involved," Lucket said. "You realize Mignon and Claxton were still in the early stages of divorce. They hadn't yet sat down to haggle over who gets what and split the assets. Now, because Mignon is technically still Claxton's wife, she inherits it all."

"Is there a lot to inherit?"

"I'd have to say . . . yes. A good amount. Claxton was a sly devil. Had his sticky little fingers in all sorts of different pies, raked in a pile of money over the years. Heck, he probably has stacks of fifty-dollar bills stashed in safe deposit boxes all over Charleston. Or maybe he wised up and stuck it offshore in the Cayman Islands."

"One final question," Theodosia said.

"Gotta make it quick," Lucket said.

Theodosia fingered the button Lucket had handed her. "Did you have your campaign buttons made before Claxton was murdered or after?"

"Doesn't matter. I was always fated to win." Lucket stared at her in the faint glow of an illuminated blowfish and gave a wolfish smile.

Theodosia dropped Drayton at his home, then drove to her own little home in the Historic District. She parked in the back alley and let herself into her backyard through the wooden gate. Took a look at her tiny fish pond, where a new crop of goldfish lazed around. Breathed a deep sigh of contentment as she admired the magnolia trees, banana shrubs, and purple iris that had recently bloomed.

She was delighted to finally be home. At her lovely, quirky little cottage that had been given the charming name of Hazelhurst by its original builders. True, it was much smaller than all the mansions surrounding it, but it was hers—lock, stock, and barrel. Constructed in the Queen Anne tradition, also known as Hansel and Gretel style, the exterior was configured in a slightly asymmetrical design, and had cedar shingles that replicated a thatched roof. There were also arched doors, a blip of a two-story turret, and curls of lush green ivy meandering up the sides of the house. It was your basic picture-perfect cottage.

Inside, Earl Grey was waiting in the kitchen.

"Rrowr?" The dog stared at her anxiously as she came through the door, then thumped his tail.

Theodosia dropped her purse and keys on the kitchen counter. "How you doin', buddy?" She gave his ears a tug and delivered a kiss on his muzzle. "You want to go for a quick spin?" It was their routine to take a nightly jog. Even though Earl Grey had a dog walker who stopped by in the afternoon, he loved nothing better than running with his favorite human.

"Yowwr." Earl Grey gave a quick shake, starting at his

nose, working down to his tail, setting everything in motion at once.

"Okay, let's do it." Theodosia ran upstairs, did a quick change into workout gear and tennis shoes, then grabbed a leash and was out the back door with Earl Grey beside her. They sped through her back garden, danced through the gate, and ran down the dark alley.

Theodosia always found it exhilarating to run at night. Old-fashioned streetlamps with yellow globes threw little stepping stones of light. Wrought-iron gates that surrounded historic buildings and homes were closed and sometimes locked, so they reminded her of miniature fortresses. Fog drifted in from Charleston Harbor, dampening the air, tamping down noise, and making everything appear slightly soft and ethereal. The darkness was also a kind of cover for Theodosia, which meant she could jog down Charleston's hidden lanes and alleys without any prying eyes on her. Many were marvelous old passageways that dated back to the seventeen hundreds, with names like Stoll's Alley, Longitude Lane, and Philadelphia Alley, though Theodosia preferred its more sinister name of Dueler's Alley.

These narrow, cobblestone gems were lined with row houses, statuary, and hidden doorways set into high brick walls. Shaded by canopies of palm trees and live oaks, they were private during the day—hardly any tourists ever found them—and deliciously spooky at night.

But as Theodosia jogged along this quiet evening, Earl Grey keeping pace with her, she decided upon a different route. So she headed over to Archdale, zigzagged over on Beaufain Street, then headed down Glebe Street into the area where the College of Charleston was located.

Because she had an idea. One that had been planted in her

brain this morning when Holly had mentioned that the graffiti artist Booker had been working in that area.

She ran past Bennie's Bagels and the Wash Tub Laundry, then turned down Lebeau Street. A few students were out strolling, but there was no sign of anybody painting murals. Maybe she was too early? Maybe Booker wasn't working tonight? Feeling a little foolish, Theodosia doubled back to Glebe Street and headed down one of the dark alleys. She jogged behind a pizza parlor—she could tell by the aroma of cheese and sausage emanating from the half-open back door—and behind a Thai restaurant (spices perfumed the air here). Dumpsters sat in shadows and trash cans overflowed. At one point a striped cat strolled out from behind a stack of cardboard boxes and flicked its tail at her.

Earl Grey turned a baleful look on Theodosia, as if to say, *It's a cat. Could make for an exciting chase.*

"Be good," Theodosia told him. And as she continued down the alley, her eyes beginning to adjust to the intense darkness, she suddenly found what she was looking for.

Because up ahead was a large shadow. A man who, in profile, looked like he was big enough to be a professional wrestler, was dipping a paintbrush into a pail of paint, then applying it to the brick wall in front of him.

Is that you, Booker?

8

Her heart beating faster, Theodosia slowed to a walk. And crept closer until she could see what was going on. Yes, it was definitely someone painting a mural on the back of a building.

Feeling fairly brave now, Theodosia approached the man. As she drew closer she stepped into a small circle of light thrown by an overhead streetlight. Now she could see the design on the brick wall. It was a black-and-orange tiger, looking fierce as it curled around, trying to grab its own tail. It was surrounded by numbers, symbols, and a few crudely painted faces all showing bared teeth.

"I like your painting," Theodosia said by way of an opening line. "It reminds me a little of Basquiat."

Booker glanced over at her. "Basquiat was a tortured soul, I'm just a starving artist."

"You're one of Holly's artists," Theodosia said. "Right? You go by the name Booker?"

"Yeah," Booker said as he shot her a sideways glance. His features were squared off and blunt, and he was linebacker big with wide shoulders, plenty of muscle, and dirty blond hair. His plaid work shirt was spattered with paint and there were drips and drabs on his jeans and motorcycle boots. Curiously, his voice was soft and slightly high-pitched. "You know Holly?"

"She's a friend of mine."

"That's nice. And who are you?" Booker continued to paint.

"Theodosia Browning. I own the Indigo Tea Shop on Church Street. In fact, I'm the one who catered Holly's tea party yesterday."

"I read about that fiasco in the *Post and Courier*. Bunch of poison gas got sprayed all over Petigru Park."

"I don't believe they've determined the exact nature of the material."

In the faint glow from the overhead sodium light, Booker turned and gave a mirthless grin. "It couldn't have happened to a nicer guy."

"That's pretty harsh," Theodosia said. "After all, the man was basically murdered in cold blood. So why would you even say that?"

Booker dipped a brush into a can of black paint that sat at his feet. Then he carefully outlined an image of a screaming head. "Probably because we have a history together."

Theodosia's internal radar started to ping. "Excuse me?"

She tried not to betray her excitement that Holly and Jeremy's suspicion could have been right on. That this guy Booker might actually be a little crazy or maybe even a viable suspect.

"You said you have a history together. Care to elaborate on that?"

Booker finished outlining the head. Then he reached down and picked up a jean jacket that was lying on the ground and put it on. It was spattered with paint and looked like something Jackson Pollock might have created. Or even worn. Finally, he said, "Osgood Claxton was one of the proverbial fat cat politicos that helped run the City of Charleston. He held a lot of offices, sat on a lot of committees."

"So I've heard," Theodosia said, hoping to keep him rolling.

"One of the committees he served on was the Charleston Arts Board. Every year they award grants to deserving artists— fellowships, they call them. I applied for one of those grants three years running, completed all the paperwork, submitted photos of my work. But it was no dice. I'd come close, was actually a finalist once, but then I'd be told that my work wasn't compatible with their stated mission or my paintings were too aggressive and in-your-face."

"Okay." Theodosia knew Booker was working up to something.

"Then last year I scored the golden ticket."

"You got the grant," Theodosia said.

Booker's face turned dark. "For all of two minutes. There I was, floating on cloud nine, dreaming about not having to live hand to mouth for a while. Then, pop, my grant—my eighteen thousand dollars—was jerked clean away from me." He turned toward her, lips curled back, teeth bared. "Care to guess who was responsible?"

"Osgood Claxton?" Theodosia said in a small voice.

Booker nodded. "You got it, lady. Claxton deemed my work degenerate. Which is exactly what the Nazis said about paintings by Picasso, Cézanne, and Dalí."

"That's why you lost your grant?"

"I lost it because Claxton made a big, hairy stink to the committee and basically browbeat them into rescinding my award."

"Unfair."

"Absolutely, it was. But it happened. Claxton appointed

himself the Reich Minister for Public Enlightenment just like Joseph Goebbels did in the forties. So you see, Miss Theodosia, whether Osgood Claxton was poisoned, shot, or hung by his thumbs and devoured by jackals, I'd say he got exactly what he deserved."

"Death," Theodosia said. "And you see that as karma?"

"Sometimes there's order in the universe, sometimes you have to make it happen yourself."

Theodosia stood there, trembling at such harsh words. Wanting to ask Booker straight out if he was the one who'd murdered Osgood Claxton, if he'd tried to restore order to the universe. But she was too afraid. Because this man, this very large man, was not only clouded with rage, he clearly had a taste for revenge.

Her concentration was broken when Earl Grey tugged on his leash.

"You have a dog," Booker said, suddenly noticing Earl Grey. "Nice."

"Who's probably ready to go home."

"You live around here?"

"Close enough," Theodosia said. She wasn't about to give Booker a hint as to where she lived.

"Well, good night, lady," Booker said. "Sleep well while I continue to work on my mural here."

"Good night," Theodosia said. She turned and jogged back down the alley. Then, with a look over her shoulder to make sure Booker wasn't following her, turned down Glebe Street and headed for home.

When Theodosia and Earl Grey arrived home, she locked the door, checked it twice, then grabbed a bottle of Fiji water out of the fridge. As she took a few sips, she realized she still felt nervous and a little scared. Booker was a guy who seemed to have an anger management problem. Maybe he was even a killer.

As Theodosia turned out the lights and headed upstirs, she wondered if Booker could have pulled on a beekeeper's suit and gone after Claxton. Was he the one who'd threatened her yesterday when she'd chased after him? Maybe, but tonight he hadn't shown an ounce of recognition. On the other hand, he could be a great actor. Lots of people were skilled at concealing their true nature. And if Booker was a killer then he could also be a sociopath, capable of great deception.

Earl Grey curled up on his overpriced L.L.Bean dog bed while Theodosia stepped into the shower, dialed it up hot, and let the spray wash away some of the psychic dust she'd accumulated during the course of the day. Then, when she felt a prune situation coming on, she stepped out and wrapped herself in a thick terry-cloth robe.

Early on, she'd converted her entire upstairs into a bedroom-bathroom-reading-room kind of loft. One that was both girly and relaxing. The walls were covered with Laura Ashley wallpaper, the comforter on her four-poster bed done in a matching print. There was a plump marshmallow-soft chair in her reading room and a vanity scattered with jewelry, bottles of Chanel and Dior perfume, an antique comb set, a ceramic leopard, her journal, and a Jo Malone candle. And she'd finally splurged and bought that pair of antique Chinese ginger jar lamps she'd been coveting for a long time. They lent the perfect touch—and soft illumination—to what had become a kitchy, creative, relaxing space.

Theodosia piled up four pillows on her bed, climbed in, then grabbed the two lists that Holly had given her. She scanned the guest list first and saw a few prominent names, movers and shakers, descendants of old Charleston families, most of whom resided in the Historic District.

Could any one of these people have masterminded Claxton's death? Sure they could have. Prominent people, wealthy businessmen, had manipulated history for decades.

Theodosia switched to the list of artists. She recognized two or three names, mostly because they were fairly well-known in the community. They donated pieces of work for charity auctions, created pieces for public buildings. She doubted a prosperous artist would even be interested in a man like Claxton.

But then there was Booker. Angry, a chip on his shoulder, and from the looks of him definitely not prosperous.

Theodosia grabbed her phone and called Riley.

"I need to tell you about Booker," she said when he answered.

"Booker." Riley repeated it slowly as if testing the word. "Is that someone's name or an occupation?"

"It's the name of an artist," Theodosia said. "Thadeus T. Booker. Actually an artist that Holly represents at the Imago Gallery."

"And what's so special about this Booker guy?" Riley asked. "Wait, did you buy one of his paintings?"

"No. But the reason I bring him up is because Holly and Jeremy were acting a little hinky about him."

"Hinky how? In what context?"

"Hear me out. When they stopped by the tea shop today, Claxton's name immediately came up in conversation."

"Okay."

"And as we talked about suspects, Holly and Jeremy exchanged these kind of furtive glances and Holly said she hoped Booker hadn't done anything crazy."

"That doesn't sound good."

"No, it doesn't."

"What else did they say?"

"Well, they might have mentioned that Claxton was instrumental in rescinding a major arts grant that Booker had been awarded." She wasn't about to tell Riley that she'd stood in a dark alley and got that information directly from Booker himself.

"So I need to look into this guy."

"I think so, yes."

"Thadeus what?"

"Thadeus T. Booker," Theodosia said. She paused, then said in what she hoped was a casual tone, "I was also wondering if you're looking at Mignon Merriweather, Claxton's soon-to-be ex-wife?"

"Why are you asking about her?"

There was something in Riley's tone that told Theodosia she'd hit a nerve.

"So you *are* looking at her."

Then he was back to his smooth-casual detective voice. "Sweetheart, we're looking at all sorts of people. Which means you don't have to."

"But I . . ."

"I know. You were there. We've established that. You chased after the big bad man . . ."

"So you know about that?" Theodosia said.

"Of course, and I'm not one bit happy about it. That said, you've done your civic duty and can now take a rest. Let *me* worry about chasing down Claxton's killer. Okay?"

"I was just asking a few questions."

"And that's great. Helpful even. Just don't get too involved, okay?"

"Sure," Theodosia said.

"Why do I not believe you?" Riley asked. Then he sighed

and said, "Let's do something fun this week. Maybe go out to dinner. Someplace cool like Saracen or Poogan's Porch. How would that be?"

"Love to," Theodosia said.

"Wednesday night, mark it on your calendar."

"Got it."

"Okay then, sleep tight and sweet dreams."

"Good night." Theodosia hung up and snuggled in bed. Turned out the lamp and burrowed under the covers. But it was a long time before she fell asleep. And when she did, she dreamed about a man chasing after her with an enormous can of paint that morphed into a bee fogger.

9

Tea kettles sang their chirpy songs and steeping teapots released puffs of aromatic steam as Theodosia bustled about the tea shop this Tuesday morning. It looked to be a busy day. Their regular morning tea service always kept them hopping, and they also had to get ready for their special Wind in the Willows Tea luncheon. Thanks goodness Miss Dimple was coming in to help.

But for now, Theodosia set the tables with pale yellow placemats, put out the Chantilly silverware, and added Dainty Blue teacups and saucers by Shelley. She grabbed tea lights and sugar bowls, then ran into the kitchen to grab plates of thinly sliced lemons and small pitchers of cream.

There. She gazed around the tea shop. What else to do? Well, she could tell Drayton about last night. Get his take on what she learned talking to Booker.

Theodosia inched up to the counter, where Drayton was busy pulling down tins of tea. He looked like an alchemist getting ready to brew up some magic.

"Do you remember when Holly and Jeremy were in yesterday and they mentioned an artist named Booker?" Theodosia said.

"The fellow they worried might have done something crazy?" Drayton said without looking up. He obviously did remember the conversation.

"Exactly. Well . . ." Theodosia hoped Drayton wouldn't pop his cork over what she was about to tell him. "I ran into Booker last night."

Now Drayton lifted his head and stared at her. "You *ran* into him? Pardon me while I step outside and scream at the universe."

"No Drayton, hear me out."

Drayton tilted his head in her direction. "Why do I think you're going to give me an abridged version of the story? Let's start with the actual facts. Such as perhaps you *sought him out?*"

"That's one way to put it."

Drayton's brows knit together in worry. "Tell me you didn't really talk to the man."

"I did really."

"Will you never learn?"

"Actually, I learned quite a lot. It seems that Booker despised Osgood Claxton because Claxton used his political power to yank an arts grant away from him. A grant worth eighteen thousand dollars."

"Hmm?" Drayton looked slightly more interested now. "Therein could lie a motive I suppose."

"That's what I thought."

Drayton measured six scoops of tea into a pink floral teapot and poured in a steady stream of hot water. "So Holly was right about this Booker character being a little crazy."

"Booker was kind of drooling with glee over Claxton's murder. He said it couldn't have happened to a more deserving guy."

"That's dangerously close to a confession. I hope you shared that information with Riley."

"I did and Riley said he'd look into it."

"So now you don't have to," Drayton said.

Theodosia tapped a finger against the lid of a glazed green teapot. "That's exactly what Riley said."

Drayton smiled. "Great minds think alike."

"But it's still fascinating. To know that Booker had a grudge against Claxton and could have been the killer."

"Actually, it's terrifying. And if I *never* have to make the man's acquaintance I'll be deliriously happy."

DING DING.

Theodosia and Drayton both glanced toward the front door at the same time.

"Customers," Drayton said, while Theodosia was already speeding to the door, a smile on her face, to welcome them in.

The tea shop got busy then, with Theodosia taking orders for cinnamon scones and banana bread and Drayton brewing pots of Keemun and Irish breakfast tea. Haley also had a pan of chocolate muffins in the oven, so a lot of customers were fizzing with anticipation.

As business and buzz hit an all-time high around ten fifteen, Delaine Dish came steaming into the tea shop like a schooner under full sail. She looked sleek as a cat in her black skirt suit and saucy hat to match as she stopped to whisper greetings to a couple of customers she knew, then grabbed Theodosia and quickly pulled her aside.

"I wanted you to know that, besides my aunt Glorene, who's here for a visit, hopefully a short one, I'm bringing another guest—a lovely new friend—to today's tea luncheon." Delaine delivered her message in one long breathless sentence.

"Wonderful," Theodosia said. She was busy clearing a table, piling teacups and saucers into a blue plastic tub. "The more the merrier."

Delaine was the owner of Cotton Duck Boutique and a fixture on Charleston's social scene. She was also a dedicated fashionista, semi-professional gossip, and a type A personality who always acted as if she'd just overdosed on Ritalin.

"The thing is, my friend's been recently widowed." Delaine reached into her Chanel bag, pulled out a linen hanky, and daubed at her eyes even though there weren't any actual tears. With her heart-shaped face, fair skin, and pouty lips, she was pretty. Beautiful, even. But she was also tricky and didn't always give you the full story.

Theodosia stopped fussing with her dishes. "I'm sorry to hear that. When did your friend's husband pass?"

Delaine wrinkled her nose as she twisted the hankie in her hands. "Sunday?"

Theodosia narrowed her eyes and stared pointedly at Delaine. Was there a piece of critical information Delaine was leaving out of this conversation? Clearly there must be.

"Don't look at me like that," Delaine pouted. "It feels so accusatory, like I've committed some sort of heinous crime."

"Delaine," Theodosia said in a firm, no-nonsense voice, the same one she used when disciplining Earl Grey. There was a strange vibe radiating off Delaine and it rattled Theodosia. Made the tiny hairs on the back of her neck stand up. "Just come right out and tell me. Who's the widow?"

The rakish feather on Delaine's hat bounced as she said, "Mignon Merriweather Claxton."

"Osgood Claxton's *wife*?"

This wasn't what Theodosia needed right now.

"What are you up to, Delaine? Why would you bring her *here* when we just hosted the tea where her husband was *murdered*?"

Delaine's gloved hand touched Theodosia's arm. "He was Mignon's soon-to-be *ex-husband*, dear."

Mignon, Theodosia thought. *The one Lucket said loved money so much. And who, heaven forbid, could have also killed Claxton. Or paid to have him killed.*

Then Theodosia's gentle, more trusting nature took over and she shook her head. No, she wasn't here to judge. "It doesn't matter what their marital status is or was," Theodosia said. "Today's luncheon might pose an uncomfortable situation for Mignon. It could trigger unhappiness. Tears, even. Why would you want to do that to the woman?"

"I don't want to upset her," Delaine argued. "I want to be kind to her. Show her some compassion."

Theodosia knew that compassion wasn't exactly Delaine's strong suit. Fact was, Delaine was vain, egotistical, and self-centered. She threw barbs behind people's backs, showed no mercy to men she dated, and had the attention span of a mayfly. It was only when dogs and cats were concerned that Delaine displayed an ounce of compassion.

"What do you want me to do, Theo? *Un-invite* Mignon?" Delaine's green eyes glittered, her mouth pulled tight.

"No, that would be rude. Just . . . okay . . . bring Mignon along. But please be prepared to deal with some hurt feelings on her part."

"You'll like her," Delaine said, upbeat again now that she'd gotten her way. "Mignon's a lovely person. Bouncy and smart and an entrepreneur to boot." She held her thumb and index finger together. "She's this close to opening a gorgeous new boutique."

For some reason, the word *boutique* caught Theodosia's attention. "What did you say?"

"I was referring to Mignon's boutique. It's this really lovely old world shop called Belle de Jour. In fact, she's just back from Paris where she was shopping the flea markets and some of the more upscale *marchés*. As you well know, it costs a bloody fortune to stock a boutique."

"Interesting," Theodosia said.

"Isn't it?"

But Theodosia's interest came from a slightly different angle. She was suddenly curious about the bloody fortune Mignon had spent in Paris. And a little suspicious as well. Could Mignon have dipped into Claxton's personal fortune, got into trouble for doing so, then had him killed? Money was a powerful motivator when it came to murder. In fact, it was right up there on the FBI's list of reasons for criminality along with revenge, political ideology, pride, and jealousy.

"Well, ta-ta," Delaine said. "See you in a bit. Say now, you're still coming to Cotton Duck tomorrow, aren't you? For my fabulous trunk show—or should I saw trunk *shows* since I have three ultra-fabulous designers coming in?" She smiled widely. "Remember? You promised!"

Theodosia gave a quick nod. "Wouldn't miss it for the world."

Even though I have better things to do. And right now I'd better grab those teapots off the counter before Drayton gives me the evil eye for letting his tea steep too long and release tannins.

But things have a way of working out, and by the the time Miss Dimple came flying into the shop, Theodosia had everything under control.

"Hey, pretty lady," Theodosia called to Miss Dimple.

Their still-spry octogenarian bookkeeper grinned at her from under her cap of pink-tinged curls and sped to the front counter. "I was thrilled when I got your call," she said. "You know how much I love coming in to help serve. Makes for a fun break—sometimes tallying columns of numbers and making out payroll checks gets a little old."

"We love having you, dear lady," Drayton said, which made her smile even more. In Miss Dimple's eyes, Drayton was the perfect Southern gent who could do no wrong.

"What do you want me to do?" Miss Dimple asked. She was plumpish, barely five feet tall, and sharp as a tack. She spoke in a breathy voice and used old-fashioned phrases such as *my heavens* and *bless me.*

"Make the rounds with seconds and tally up checks," Theodosia said. "Most of our morning tea customers are getting ready to leave, so then we can clear the tables and kick it into high gear. Do some decorating."

Miss Dimple blinked as she gazed around the tea shop, which was about three-quarters full. "And you're hosting a Wind in the Willows Tea at noon? Did I get that right?"

"You did indeed," Drayton said.

"So cute and inventive," Miss Dimple marveled. Then she grabbed a teapot in one hand and a pitcher of ice water in the other and took off.

Theodosia had thought long and hard about the decor for their Wind in the Willows Tea. So she'd gone to a craft shop and bought all the packages of dried moss that she could find. Now, with the tables finally cleared, she was ready to see if she could bring her vision to fruition.

First, she placed a carpet of green moss on each table. This was followed by a crystal vase filled with yellow daffodils. Then she added a few *Wind in the Willows* picture books, followed by an array of plush animals that she'd borrowed from Leigh Carroll, the owner of the Cabbage Patch Gift Shop.

"It's Mr. Toad," Miss Dimple said, suddenly snatching up one of the plushies. "He's my favorite. But I see you've got the entire cast of characters on display." She touched a hand to her ample chest to express her joy. "I love it."

"We're not done yet," Theodosia said. "I managed to borrow a bunch of Royal Albert plates from Miss Hattie's Antiques." She set down her stack of plates on one of the tables and handed the top plate to Miss Dimple.

"This is amazing," she exclaimed. Who would have guessed there are actually *Wind in the Willows*–themed plates?"

"Probably because the book is that much loved."

As Miss Dimple set out the plates, cups, and saucers, Theodosia added stalks of dried lavender tied with ribbons and small boxes of Walkers shortbread cookies as favors for her guests. Then she stood back to admire her handiwork.

"Yes," she declared, a glow of satisfaction lighting her face, "this will do nicely."

At the stroke of twelve noon (or eleven fifty-four, per Drayton's perpetually slow-running watch), their guests began to arrive. There were two couples who'd come from the nearby Featherbed House B and B (on the recommendation of Angie, the proprietor) and a mom with two daughters who were interested in learning more about tea service. There was a flock of tea regulars, as well, that included Jill, Kristen, Judi, Jessica, Monica, and Linda.

Theodosia greeted everyone with a warm hello and gently handed them off to Miss Dimple, who escorted them to their various tables.

As the trickle of guests began to slow and Theodosia was about ready to give up on Delaine, there was a high-pitched, boisterous cry. Then Delaine burst through the door, all the while delivering a loud, running commentary to her two guests about the history of Church Street and wasn't it *extraordinary* that a historic old building had been converted into such a *charming* little tea shop?

Then Delaine looked up and shouted, "Theo!"

Theodosia squared her shoulders as she went to greet Delaine. But Delaine was already babbling away.

"Theo, this is my dear, dear aunt Glorene, who's come for a visit, a short visit." Delaine glanced sideways at the sixty-something, silver-haired woman as if delivering a coded message.

"Lovely to meet you," Theodosia said.

"And this . . ." Delaine almost shoved her other guest forward. "This is Mignon Merriweather Claxton."

"Mrs. Claxton," Theodosia said, extending her hand. "You have my deepest sympathies."

"Thank you," Mignon purred back but with a twinkle in her eye. "How very kind of you."

Theodosia studied Mignon as she led the three women to their table. Mignon had to be a good ten years younger than her recently deceased husband and a few inches taller. Her reddish-brown hair was swept up in an artfully messy topknot that complemented her oval face, her lips were full and voluptuous. Most interesting of all, Mignon's hazel eyes were slightly canted, which gave her an exotic, almost predatory look. She wore a preppy-looking navy cashmere jacket that was nipped at the waist, cream-colored slacks, and high-heeled Gucci sandals.

There's some money there, Theodosia decided. Then she shook her head to dispel that thought and stepped to the center of the room.

"Ladies and gentlemen," Theodosia said as the buzzing room suddenly quieted down. "Welcome to our first ever Wind in the Willows Tea."

There was a spatter of applause and more than a few comments.

"Love your table decor."

"These plush animals are adorable."

"And look at the plates!"

"As you all know," Theodosia continued, "*Wind in the Willows* was written by the British novelist Kenneth Grahame. Published in nineteen-oh-eight, the book features Mole, Rat, Mr. Toad, and Mr. Badger, who all live in a pastoral version of Edwardian England. This book is much beloved by many generations and has been countlessly reprinted, translated to TV and movies, and was even adapted as a musical in twenty-fourteen by Julian Fellowes, the creator of *Downton Abbey*."

This time the applause was even greater.

"So it only stands to reason," Theodosia continued, "that the Indigo Tea Shop, with our love of all things tea and British, would draw keen inspiration from this wonderful book and reflect it in today's menu."

Now Theodosia had them on the edge of their seats.

"For our starter today we'll be serving Mr. Badger's favorite English crumpets accompanied by Devonshire cream and elderberry jam. Our second course consists of Mr. Toad's smoked trout tea sandwiches with English mayonnaise. And our main course will be Mole's cheddar and sausage Scotch eggs with garden greens and a citrus dressing. For dessert we hope to delight you with Rat's ginger beer cupcakes."

Theodosia crooked a finger and Drayton hurried over to join her.

"For our tea today, we'll be serving our special Wind in the

Willows house blend," Drayton said. "A delicate combination of black tea highlighted with bits of peach, apple, and sunflower."

From there on, Theodosia and Drayton had their guests practically eating out of their hands. Miss Dimple and Haley hustled out with fresh-baked crumpets while Theodosia and Drayton poured steaming cups of tea.

"They're loving it," Drayton whispered to Theodosia as he slid past her some ten minutes later.

"Why wouldn't they?" she replied.

"Do you see how they're going for the smoked trout tea sandwiches?"

"And you thought smoked trout might not fly," Theodosia said.

"Well, I was wrong. And happily so."

"Just wait until we wow them with our . . ." Theodosia stopped dead in her tracks as a terrifying CRASH at the front door suddenly reverberated through out the tea room.

Conversation stopped.

Heads swiveled.

And Drayton spun on his heels, looking worried and alert. "What on earth?" he cried.

Startled by the commotion, all the guests turned to look at the large man in paint-stained overalls with flyaway hair who'd come skidding in. And as he looked around, a deep scowl darkened his face.

"Booker," Theodosia said under her breath.

10

Incensed by his rudeness, Theodosia flew across the tea shop, grabbed Booker by the arm, and pinched him hard, which not only brought a look of shock to his face, it stopped him cold.

"What do you think you're doing?" Theodosia hissed. "Coming into my tea shop and being so disruptive!"

Booker's jaw went slack as he stared at her.

"In front of all these people," Theodosia continued.

"People?" Booker's growl suddenly morphed into a high squawk.

"Look around. You see those faces staring at you? Wondering what you're doing here? They're curious because you've been intrusive and impolite."

Booker tamped his anger down and swallowed hard. "I didn't mean . . ."

Theodosia tugged on his arm again and pulled him outside. Once they were on the sidewalk, in the clear light of day and away from prying eyes, she said, "What's your problem? Why would you come storming in like that and frighten all my guests?"

Booker stared at her with red-rimmed eyes and a down-turned mouth. "Because I got a bone to pick with you."

"I can't image what that would be," Theodosia said.

"Oh yeah?" Now Booker was fired up again. "How about two cops showing up at my door this morning and basically jerking me out of bed to question me!"

"Uh-huh." Theodosia was really thinking, *Uh-oh.*

"And since *you* were the one who asked all those nosy questions last night, I figured you were the one who sicced the cops on me."

"I didn't single you out, if that's what you mean," Theodosia said. She knew it was a little white lie—oops, those lies could start to pile up—and didn't feel good about it. Because she *had* mentioned Booker's name to Riley last night. On the other hand, Booker could be a viable suspect, so talking to Riley had been a good thing. From her point of view, anyway.

Booker took a step back from her. "You didn't?"

"I would never tell the cops to jerk you out of bed."

"Somebody did."

"Well, you do have a history with Claxton," Theodosia said. "About him nixing your grant. There must be other people who know about that."

Booker looked down at his scuffed work boots and studied them for a few moments. "I guess."

"Then are we cool? Tranquility restored?" Theodosia asked.

He shrugged. "For now."

"No more pop-in visits like this one, okay?" She glanced down the street, where a motorcycle was sandwiched between two SUVs. "Just . . . try to walk in like a normal human being if you want a scone and a cup of tea."

"I don't drink tea."

Theodosia gave a faint smile. "Maybe you should." She turned away from him, raised a hand to signal farewell, and walked back inside the tea shop.

"Everything okay?" Drayton whispered as he brushed past her carrying a teapot.

"Seems to be now," Theodosia said. "Were our guests upset and wondering what that crazy interruption was all about?"

"Only for about two seconds. Then Haley and Miss Dimple brought out the Scotch eggs and salads and everyone basically went facedown."

"Thank goodness." Theodosia grinned as she pantomimed wiping beads of sweat from her brow.

"But you know what I was thinking?" Drayton said.

"I do. That this was like shades of our Honeybee Tea. But, thankfully, no one got killed."

"Not yet, anyway," Drayton said in an ominous tone.

An hour and a half later, a few guests still lingered at their tables while others busily checked out the tea gifts Theodosia had for sale. The tea cozies were the most popular item—cute quilted cozies with cats and pandas and even pink mice that snugged over teapots. Then there were her proprietary T-Bath products—the Chamomile Calming Cream, Lavender Love Moisturizer, and Rose Petal Feet Treat. But a couple of Theodosia's grapevine and miniature teacup wreaths were also lifted off the brick wall and brought to the front counter.

Theodosia wrapped everything in sheets of indigo blue tissue paper, then packed it in boxes as best she could. As she handed a blue bag to one customer, she noticed that Mignon Merriweather Claxton was still here. Or rather, Mignon had just gotten up from her table—even though Delaine and her aunt had long since departed—and was headed in her direction.

"Mignon," Theodosia said as she approached.

"Lovely, simply lovely," Mignon said. "I don't know when I've had a more pleasant tea. And that includes a few trips to Paris where I enjoyed tea at Mariage Frères and Ladurée."

Which gave Theodosia the perfect opening.

"Delaine mentioned you'd recently returned from a Paris buying trip."

"For my new boutique, Belle de Jour, over on King Street. The building is a former woodworking studio, so I retained the old heart-pine floors and a couple of workman's trestle-top tables—so perfect for displays. Of course I painted the interior walls an eggshell color and am stocking the place with a raft of antiques I picked up in Paris. Old signs, music boxes, some lace, antique French champagne glasses, lots of jewelry."

"And you'll have new merchandise, too?" Theodosia asked.

"Tons of it. We're talking perfumes, French milled soaps, select cosmetics from the Bourjois line, French macarons, Isabel Marant T-shirts . . . well, you get the idea. Oh, and I'll be carrying a line of hand-sewn lingerie called Ballerina." She dimpled prettily and winked. "I think you'd love some of the pieces."

"Your shop sounds delightful," Theodosia said. "Just what Charleston needs. We've got plenty of touristy shops that carry T-shirts and pepper sauces, but we can always use another high-end shop."

"Trying to open a retail shop, figuring out how to market it . . . has been a crazy experience," Mignon said. "The learning curve has been fairly steep and merchandising the shop . . . well, it's been expensive beyond my wildest dreams. I've run through almost all of my personal funds. Thank goodness I still stand to inherit Osgood's money and insurance benefits.

But the high cost of doing business is also the reason I filed a heavy-duty lawsuit against the Imago Gallery. I'm hoping to collect on Osgood's wrongful death."

"Holly told me about your lawsuit," Theodosia said. "She's pretty upset that you're holding her responsible for your husband's death."

"Actually, he was almost my ex-husband." Mignon lifted a hand and made a fluttery motion. "Though our relationship was finished long ago."

"But you're still suing." Theodosia tried to keep her tone nonjudgmental because she wanted to hear more.

"Of course."

"The man who came charging in here before, the artist named Booker, do you by any chance know him?"

Mignon shook her head. "Should I?"

"He's one of Holly's artists and he knew your husband."

"How so?"

Theodosia quickly explained how Claxton had influenced the State Arts Board and had Booker's grant pulled from him.

"Wait a minute." Eyes wide, color flaring in her cheeks now, Mignon held up a hand. "Do you think this Booker character was holding a grudge? Is it possible *he's* the one who murdered Osgood?" She looked horrified.

"The thought had entered my mind. But now that I give it a little more consideration . . . well, I don't know."

"But it's possible?" Mignon said.

"I'd say fifty-fifty."

"Have you told the police this same story about Booker?"

"I did. Which is what prompted him to come storming in here."

"He thought you pointed a finger at him?" Mignon asked.

"Something like that," Theodosia said.

Mignon was quiet for a few moments, then said, "If you're really on the hunt for suspects . . ." Her tone sounded casual but Theodosia could feel ramrod steel behind it.

"What?" Theodosia asked. "Do you have someone in mind?"

"Ginny Bell," Mignon said, a hard look crossing her face. "She's the woman Osgood was having a relationship with for the last three years."

This was news to Theodosia. "Seriously?"

Mignon cocked her head to one side like a curious magpie. "Oh my, yes."

"And you think this Ginny Bell could have murdered him?" Theodosia was both surprised and curious.

Mignon took Theodosia by the elbow and pulled her into the nook next to the stone fireplace. "Ginny Bell is a treacherous Jezebel," she snarled. "The woman tried her hardest to get her hooks into Osgood and rip us apart. Which she eventually did, of course. Osgood, may his soul rest in purgatorial bliss until the end of time, was flattered and tickled pink to carry on with Miss Bell, though he never in a million years would have married her."

"I'm sorry, but I was under the impression that the two of you were in the process of getting a divorce," Theodosia said. "So maybe he *was* going to marry Ginny Bell."

"No, no, don't believe that for a minute. In fact, they'd actually called it quits a few months ago." Mignon paused. "And it did not end on friendly terms."

"Really."

Mignon lowered her voice. "I heard—mind you, this was through the gossip grapevine—that Ginny Bell was absolutely furious with him. Like losing-her-mind-getting-revenge furious."

Theodosia digested Mignon's words for a few moments. "Excuse me, you're implying that Ginny Bell had an axe to grind? That *she* might have killed him?"

Mignon held up an index finger. "I didn't say that."

"Not in so many words. But that's what you meant, right?"

"Okay, I suppose that *is* what I meant."

"Do you have any evidence?"

"If I did, I'd have gone running to the police immediately," Mignon said. "Because I love the idea of putting Ginny Bell's scrawny butt in Graham Correctional Institution for the next twenty years."

Once the guests had all left, Theodosia cleared tables with Miss Dimple, then sidled up to the front counter where Drayton was wiping out teapots.

"Did you by any chance overhear the exchange I had with Mignon?"

"The outraged soon-to-be ex-wife?"

"So you did hear us."

"Bits and pieces of your conversation," Drayton said. "I take it her angry words set your head to spinning?"

"Mostly they got me thinking. First we had Lamar Lucket pegged as a possible suspect. Then Lucket pointed his finger at Mignon as the killer. Now we have Mignon pointing a finger at this Ginny Bell person. It seems like any one of them could have had a good reason to kill Claxton."

"Or maybe Booker did it after all," Drayton said.

"Right. Or maybe Booker. Confusing."

"Nothing's ever cut-and-dried," Drayton said.

"The thing that worries me is that Mignon says she's almost out of money. And that she's counting on the insurance money from Claxton's death as well as winning a lawsuit against the Imago Gallery."

"Counting her chickens before they're hatched," Drayton said. "Which sounds kind of fun and frivolous but is really rather foreboding."

"I know. What if Mignon was the one who killed Claxton?"

Drayton picked up a clean cloth and wiped out the inside of an oxblood red teapot. "It wouldn't be the first time a woman killed her husband so she could collect the insurance money. It's almost Shakespearean, except for the fact they probably didn't have insurance back then."

"But they had money."

"Point taken."

"Remember that horrible woman a few years ago? Anastasia something from Goose Creek?" Theodosia said.

"Anastasia Goddard."

"She ran over her husband's head with a lawn mower and ended up killing him. Then claimed it was accidental so she could collect the insurance."

"Last Sunday was no accident," Drayton said. "It was cold-blooded murder."

"Premeditated murder," Theodosia agreed. "I mean, it couldn't have been easy to figure out what kind of toxin to use. And whoever did it intentionally targeted Claxton, disorienting him and almost knocking him out so they could finish him off with a gunshot."

"While not killing the people around him," Drayton said, rolling his eyes as he recalled his own brush with the toxic gas. "Just obscuring the scene and making them sick."

"So who hated Osgood Claxton enough to kill him?"

"Everybody." Drayton poured a cup of Moroccan mint tea for Theodosia and slid it across the counter to her.

"It's one thing to hate someone and another to go so far as to *kill* them. That takes a determined, stone-cold killer." Theodosia took a sip of tea.

"Like Mignon?" Drayton said.

"Don't know. She could be in the mix as a suspect. There's also this Ginny Bell person to consider. Mignon told me Claxton had a long-standing affair with her and that it ended badly."

"You're talking about the Ginny Bell who heads the Arts Alliance?" Drayton asked.

Theodosia practically dropped the teacup she was holding. "You know her?"

"Know *of* her. If this is the same Ginny Bell, she's the executive director of the Arts Alliance. It's a small nonprofit organization that offers art classes, awards microgrants to artists, and sponsors free art programs and lectures in schools and in the community."

"It's got to be the same person. Okay, now you've really piqued my interest," Theodosia said. "I think I'd like to meet this Ginny Bell."

"I'm not sure how you'd go about doing that."

"I am. I'll call her up."

"Now?" Drayton said.

"No, Drayton, next Tuesday. Yes, I'm going to call Ginny Bell right now. And when I speak to her I intend to ask her some very probing questions."

11

"Messy," Theodosia said to herself as she walked into her office. She was referring to both her clutter-bug desk and the Claxton murder case. Neither were going to be resolved today, however, so she plunked herself down in her chair, pushed a stack of tea magazines aside, looked up the number for the Arts Alliance, and called.

But when a chirpy voice answered and Theodosia asked to speak to Ginny Bell, she was told the woman was out of the office.

"I'm sorry," the upbeat receptionist said, "Ginny Bell is attending a meeting right now, may I take a message?"

"Doggone, I really need to get hold of her. It's important."

"She should be back real soon because of our fundraiser tonight."

"Fundraiser?" Theodosia said, perking up.

"Oh yes, it's our annual silent auction. Of donated art. Some pieces by well-known local professionals, a lot by amateurs. But it's good because it's been carefully curated." The receptionist giggled. "We've been working on it for almost three months."

"Can anyone come?" Theodosia asked.

"Absolutely everyone is welcome," the receptionist said. "Just be sure to bring your checkbook."

Theodosia hung up, spun around in her chair, and decided she might just pay a visit to the Arts Alliance's silent auction tonight. After all, what could it hurt? Maybe she could even talk Drayton into going along.

But when she walked into the tea shop, it was obvious Drayton had a lot on his mind.

"I've been thinking," Drayton said. "You were the one person who dared chase after that phony beekeeper. Who we keep referring to as a guy . . . a man." He paused. "But could it have been a woman? Could it have been Mignon?"

"Could have been, I guess. Or even this Ginny Bell," Theodosia said. "Who we have yet to meet." She pondered Drayton's question for a few moments. "It's hard to say. I was running after the beekeeper in a kind of blind rage so I wasn't exactly putting together a detailed profile."

"Was the beekeeper tall? Short?"

"I honestly don't remember."

"What does your intuition tell you?" Drayton asked. "Were you able to get any kind of feeling or impression from the assailant?"

"It felt as though he—or she—was radiating tons of anger. As well as a kind of smugness and self-satisfaction about the toxic gas. Like it had worked out well and they were glad for it. But that's about it."

"That, my dear," Drayton said, "is quite enough." He turned at the sound of the front door snicking open. "A late customer?" he murmured, glancing at his watch.

Theodosia glanced over as well. And her heart sank.

Detective Burt Tidwell, shoulders slightly hunched, came

huffing toward them, his heavy cop's shoes making a clopping sound against the wooden floor.

"Detective Tidwell," Theodosia called out. "Are you here for tea?"

Tidwell swerved toward the nearest table and sat down heavily without answering. He glanced around, saw Miss Dimple with a tub of dirty dishes, gave her his trademark glower, and sent her sprinting for the kitchen.

"Not nice," Theodosia said as she slipped into the chair across from him.

"Hmm?" Tidwell projected an air of total innocence.

"Scaring older women. Scaring any women."

"I didn't mean to."

"Of course you did." Theodosia wasn't about to be buffaloed. "Now, what can I do for you?"

"I have a few more questions concerning the Claxton murder."

"I'm sure you do."

"When you made the irrational decision to chase after the perpetrator, did anything catch your eye or stand out? I ask you these questions again with the thought that you've had a couple of days to process the incident." Tidwell lifted a bushy eyebrow. "Perhaps your memory has improved over time?"

"I'm afraid not," Theodosia said. "In fact, Drayton just asked me the same thing."

"And what was your answer to him?"

"That nothing major jumped out at me."

"But you must have had an impression? Or a hunch?"

"That doesn't sound very scientific. Don't police generally operate on facts?"

"Humor me," Tidwell said.

"Believe me, I am."

Tidwell rocked back in his chair and stared at her, beady eyes bright with intensity. "Nothing?"

"Nothing."

"Fine. A request, then."

"Of course."

"Leave this alone."

"I'm not sure I can do that."

Tidwell's lips puckered unhappily. "Of course you can. Please don't try to obfuscate this investigation."

"Meaning?"

"I don't want you getting involved. Searching high and low for suspects. The mayor and the chief of police have taken a keen interest in this case, so I don't need you trying to play savior for your friends at the Imago Gallery."

"It's difficult to stand by and watch Holly and Jeremy lose everything they've worked for."

"I'm sure they'll survive just fine."

"You don't know that. Buyers have canceled commissioned work, several of their artists have abandoned them."

"Yes, yes." Tidwell drummed his fingers against the table, looking bored.

"To top it off, Mignon Merriweather is suing the Imago Gallery."

Tidwell stopped drumming and gave her a sharp look. "Mrs. Claxton is suing them?"

"That's right."

"I'm not aware of any lawsuit."

"Now you are," Theodosia said. Then, "Is Mignon a suspect?"

Tidwell gave no reaction except to say, "That would be confidential police department information."

"Oh come on," Theodosia said, feeling an ooze of frustration.

"I know you're talking to Ben Sweeney, an artist named Booker, probably Lamar Lucket, and maybe even Jeremy Slade."

Tidwell regarded her with an owlish glare. "And how do you know all this?"

She favored him with a crooked grin. "Look around. I run a tea shop. Where people get together and talk."

Tidwell jabbed a finger in her direction. "No, you ask. *Then* they talk. You charm people into giving up juicy little tidbits of information, then you attempt to weave it all together."

"Isn't that what a good investigator does? Puts together bits of critical information, then makes an educated guess?"

Tidwell leaned back in his chair. "Hmmph."

Theodosia smiled. "Hit too close to home, did I?"

Tidwell was quiet for a few moments, then said, "This is not something you want to stick your nose into."

"Why not?" she countered.

"Because you'll end up in harm's way. Our lab analyzed the gas that incapacitated Claxton and several of the other guests and determined it was a kind of juiced-up mustard gas."

"I thought mustard gas went out in World War I."

"Unfortunately, no. However, this particular gas was an interesting amalgam of bleach and ammonia that, when mixed together, produces chloramines."

"So you're telling me the killer is a chemist?" Theodosia said.

"Possibly," Tidwell said. "Or he has access to certain chemicals or even industrial-strength cleaning supplies."

"What about the gun the killer dropped?"

"What about it?"

"Did you find any prints?" Theodosia asked.

Tidwell shook his head.

In her mind's eye Theodosia pictured the killer, running

through the park, trying to elude her, fighting with the dog. "Because the killer was wearing gloves," she said.

"He was dressed in the perfect killing outfit," Tidwell said. "Nylon zip suit, helmet that prevented anyone from seeing his face, booties, and gloves."

"The murder was well-thought-out, that's for sure. Which leads me to believe this is a fairly smart guy."

"Not that smart," Tidwell said. "Criminals are never that smart." He stood up so quickly his knees cracked. "Because sooner or later I catch them."

Unless I catch them first, Theodosia thought.

Once Detective Tidwell had left, Miss Dimple crept out of hiding.

"Is he gone?" she asked, looking around.

"You're safe, dear lady," Drayton assured her.

"Good," Miss Dimple said. "Haley says he's just a blustering gasbag, but he scares me to death."

"Deep down, he really does mean well," Theodosia said. "Tidwell's solved a lot of tough cases in his career."

Miss Dimple looped a pale peach scarf around her neck. "If you say so."

"Will you still be able to help out at our Glam Girl Tea on Thursday?" Theodosia asked.

"Will the chubby police detective be here?" Miss Dimple asked.

Theodosia smiled. "I promise you, Tidwell will not be in attendance."

"Okay then," Miss Dimple said. She shrugged into her sweater coat and headed for the door. "I'll see you dear souls on Thursday."

"Toodles," said Drayton. Then he turned to Theodosia and said, "You haven't told me how your conversation with Ginny Bell went."

"It didn't," Theodosia said. "She wasn't there." She held up a finger. "But there's a good chance we can confront her tonight."

"We? As in you and me? I'm to be your wingman again?"

"It just so happens the Arts Alliance is having their big silent auction this evening. Their annual fundraiser. And the receptionist I spoke with told me that anyone and everyone is welcome."

"And you genuinely see Ginny Bell as a suspect?"

"Drayton, she had a torrid love affair with Claxton. Then he broke it off. If I can believe Mignon, Ginny Bell was both angry and humiliated."

"Angry enough to kill him?" Drayton asked.

"You know the old saying. Hell hath no fury . . ."

"Like a woman scorned," Drayton said, finishing her sentence. He picked up a tin of Japanese green tea, studied the label for a moment or two, then set it down. "Okay, count me in. You can give Ginny Bell the third degree while I peruse the art that's for sale."

"Excellent."

"What's excellent?" Haley asked. She'd just come strolling out of the kitchen and was looking a little pooped.

"You are, my dear," Drayton said. "Compliments on your luncheon menu were piling up so high today I could hardly dare tell you for fear you'd run off and open your own bakery or start a restaurant. Leave us in the lurch."

"I'm leaving," Haley said. "But not in the lurch." She shook her head. "Is that right? The lurch thing?"

"It's all right as long as you continue to turn out such lovely scones, tea breads, and lunches," Theodosia said.

Haley reached back, gathered her fine blond hair into a ponytail, and popped on a scrunchie. "Hey, you know I love it here." She yawned. "Okay then, gotta go. Busy night."

"Is Ben picking you up?" Theodosia asked.

"Naw, we're gonna get together tomorrow night and try out a new recipe for beef braciole. Tonight I have my advanced cake decorating course at the Culinary Institute."

"See," Drayton said to Theodosia. "Haley *is* going to open her own bakery."

"Maybe someday," Haley said. "Just not in the foreseeable future."

"What about that American bistro course you told me about?" Theodosia asked. "Where you learn how to make torched burrata, chimichurri, and Roman-style gnocchi?"

"That's next semester," Haley said.

"Yum," Drayton said. "I can hardly wait."

12

The Arts Alliance was housed in a rehabbed warehouse over on Bay Street near the Cooper River. It was a redbrick monstrosity that had been updated with industrial carpet and track lighting, with most of the overhead beams and patchy brick walls left exposed. It looked, Theodosia thought, like thousands of places all over the country where old buildings had been repurposed and touted as historic landmarks that were perfect for arts organizations.

Theodosia and Drayton walked down a hallway where closed doors had signs that said WRITER'S RESOURCE and THE KINDRED PLAYERS. When they got to the Arts Alliance, a young woman at the front door held out her hand and said, "Tickets?"

"We don't have tickets," Theodosia said.

"Three dollars each, then," the woman said, adding, "It's a donation more than an admission fee."

"No problem." Theodosia handed over six dollars and they stepped inside a large, well-lit room that was already jam-packed with people. They were crowded around easels that held paint-

ings and tables filled with ceramics. More oil and acrylic paintings were hung like a mishmash of colorful postage stamps on
every bit of wall space. There was a bar set up in the far corner,
a DJ with a soundboard, and a few servers circulating with trays
of appetizers.

"Impressive," Drayton said. "A good crowd as well as an
exceptional amount of art to choose from."

"Except," Theodosia said, "we haven't actually *looked* at the
art yet. It could all have been done by amateurs."

But as they elbowed their way through the crowd, the caliber of art for sale turned out to be very nice indeed. Drayton
immediately found a contemporary-looking teapot, a square
blue ceramic piece with a yellow handle, that he simply *had* to
place a bid on. Then Theodosia discovered a moody watercolor
that depicted a sailboat regatta cutting across the choppy waves
of Charleston Harbor, so she also placed a bid.

"This silent bidding is far more civilized than a regular auction," Drayton said. "Where you have to shout out your bid."

"Except somebody can come along after you've written your
bid and put down a higher bid," Theodosia said. "Then you
have to circle back and beat that bid."

"Good point."

They wandered through the room, looking at the art, chatting quietly, keeping a lookout for Ginny Bell.

"Which one is she?" Theodosia asked Drayton. There were
any number of officious-looking young women scurrying about.

"I'm not entirely sure. I only met her the one time."

"Then we'll ask someone," Theodosia said. "Excuse me," she
said to a young man who was walking past her, juggling a large
canvas. "Are you with the Arts Alliance?"

He stopped and nodded. "I'm Duncan Hall, the membership coordinator."

"We're looking for Ginny Bell," Theodosia said. "Could you point her out to us? That's if she's here?"

"Ginny Bell is definitely here tonight," Duncan said as he tried to rebalance the painting he was carrying. "No way she'd miss our major fundraiser." He looked around, nodded, and said, "That's her over there. Ginny Bell's the one in the black velvet blazer and long skirt. Talking to that older couple."

Theodosia spotted Ginny Bell in the crowd. Besides looking a little Goth, she had a cap of short dark hair, arched dark eyebrows, and an angular face. Her complexion was pale and she wore not a speck of makeup except for a slash of red lipstick.

"Thanks," Theodosia said to Duncan. "And do you always call her Ginny Bell?" She was amused that everyone seemed to call the woman by her full name. "Do you ever call her Miss Bell or even Ginny?"

Duncan shook his head. "Everyone always calls her Ginny Bell. I don't know why, they just do."

"Okay, thanks again," Theodosia said. She turned to Drayton. "What do you want to do first? Go talk to Ginny Bell or indulge in some refreshments?"

"Refreshments," Drayton said. "After you pepper her with questions we may not be welcome here anymore."

They made their way to the bar, ordered two glasses of white wine, then found a tiny café table to sit at while they sipped their wine. Theodosia noticed it was mostly a twenty- and thirty-something crowd tonight with a sprinkle of well-heeled older couples added to the mix. Probably, the Arts Alliance was hoping the wealthier, serious art collector types would help run up the bidding.

"Theo?" Drayton was looking at her. "Appetizer?" He'd snagged a server and was wondering if she wanted a cracker with pâté.

"You know what, Drayton? No thanks." Theodosia half stood and peered through the crowd. "I'm going to run over there and try to catch Ginny Bell. Ask her a few questions."

"Good luck with that. I'll hold on to your wine."

Theodosia shouldered her way through a crowd that continued to grow in number. As she rounded a trio of Plexiglas ovals that held tall, graceful metal sculptures, she saw Ginny Bell up ahead. She was saying something to the coordinator, Duncan, who nodded and quickly moved off.

"Miss Bell," Theodosia called out, giving a little wave. "Ginny Bell."

Ginny Bell stopped in her tracks and looked around to see who was calling her name. When she noticed Theodosia heading straight for her, she smiled pleasantly and waited.

"I know you're super busy tonight," Theodosia said, a little breathlessly, but I need to talk to you."

"Busy isn't the word for it," Ginny Bell said. "Can you believe this crowd? It sure pays to get the word out even if it means writing umpteen press releases and hitting the local talk shows until you're blue in the face."

"Whatever marketing you did, it worked like crazy," Theodosia said. Up close she noticed that Ginny Bell was in her late thirties and that her skin appeared even more pale, almost translucent. Also, now that she was face-to-face with the woman, she was starting to lose her nerve.

"I'm not sure we've met before," Ginny Bell said.

"We haven't," Theodosia said. "My name is Theodosia, Theodosia Browning. I own a tea—"

"And you're an art lover," Ginny Bell said, cutting her off. "Lovely."

"I'd like to ask you a few quick questions because I believe our interests align somewhat."

"Of course," Ginny Bell said. "If you'd like to know more about the Arts Alliance, I can kind of quote you our basic mission statement—which is that we're a nonprofit that exists to bring art and art education to humans of all ages who have a thirst for beautiful knowledge and imagery."

"That's wonderful," Theodosia said. "But I'm afraid my questions are more of a personal nature."

"How so?"

"You're aware, of course, that Osgood Claxton was murdered two days ago."

At the mention of Claxton's name, it was as if a dark curtain dropped over Ginny Bell's face.

"No," she said, her tone crisp and almost defiant. "Anything to do with that man is extremely personal and I'm not about to answer any questions. I don't care who you are." She peered at Theodosia. "*Who* are you again?"

But Theodosia was not to be deterred. "Is it because of the heinous nature of Mr. Claxton's murder? Or because the two of you recently broke off your, um, relationship?"

Ginny Bell's red mouth contorted. "How very impertinent of you. What's your interest in this, anyway?"

"Let's just say I'm trying to run interference for my friends at the Imago Gallery."

"And in so doing, you're butting into my private life?"

"Also I've heard rumors," Theodosia said.

Comprehension dawned on Ginny Bell's face. "Let me guess, that awful Mignon Merriweather has been spitting venomous lies about me, hasn't she?"

"I don't know. Are they lies?"

"Of course they are," Ginny Bell cried. "And if you're asking me about Claxton's death—and it seems that you most certainly are—then I'd have to say that if anyone wanted the man dead, it would be Mignon herself."

"You think *she* murdered him?" Theodosia pressed.

Ginny Bell snorted. "Mignon could have because she's nuts enough. Mignon is your basic evil, money-grubbing shrew. She's also canny enough to hire an assassin to do her dirty work."

"Have you talked to the police about Claxton's murder?"

Ginny Bell's mouth dipped downward. "Unfortunately, they've already sought me out."

"Did you suggest Mignon to them as a possible suspect?"

"Yes, I did. I got dragged into this fiasco—reluctantly, of course—so I gave the investigators all the information I could possibly scrape together." She drew a deep breath and lifted her chin. "Now if you don't mind, this conversation is over. I need to focus on my event and tend to my guests." And with that, Ginny Bell turned and walked away.

"How did it go?" Drayton asked when Theodosia joined him back at the table where he was lounging, still sipping his wine.

"It didn't. Ginny Bell clammed up immediately."

"Doesn't surprise me. She was probably embarrassed to have her relationship with Claxton brought up."

"I'd say she was more angry than embarrassed," Theodosia said. "And guess who she pointed her finger at?"

Drayton thought for a few moments. "Let me take a wild guess. Mignon?"

"Bingo."

"If the affair is to be believed, those two women probably hated each other. Still do, for that matter."

"It would be like World War III if they ever faced off against each other." Theodosia sat down and slumped in her chair. "I'm afraid coming here was a big waste of time."

"Not if I get that teapot. Remind me to check the bids on the way out," Drayton said.

"Where's that server?" Theodosia said. "I could use a nosh right about now. Something to rev up my blood sugar." She looked around for the server with the appetizer tray and suddenly found herself gazing across the room at a familiar face. A bushy-haired man who stood almost a head taller than everyone else in the room. Startled, she nudged Drayton and said, "Look who just turned up like a bad penny." She pointed discreetly in the direction of the front door.

"Booker," Drayton said, catching sight of the artist. "I wondered if he might put in an appearance tonight."

Tonight, Booker was slightly more presentable than what Theodosia had seen previously. He wore a red-and-black plaid shirt, blue jeans with a silver chain hanging off his belt, and black, clunky boots that she guessed might be Doc Martens. His frizzle of hair was pulled into a semi-decent ponytail.

"Is he part of this group?" Drayton asked. "Did you see any of his work on display here?"

Theodosia shook her head. "Nothing jumped out at me. Then again, I didn't really look at the paintings."

"You say his work is distinctive?"

"Lots of graffiti and strange faces. Weird animals, too."

They both watched, somewhat fascinated, as Booker waded casually through the crowd. Then, when he caught sight of Ginny Bell, he hurried over to greet her and give her a big bear hug. Which she returned with gusto.

"They know each other," Drayton said.

"Sure looks that way."

"Judging from earlier today, when Booker came storming into our tea room, I had no idea he could be so friendly and affable."

"Neither did I," Theodosia said. She watched carefully as Booker and Ginny Bell chatted with each other. From their smiles and gestures, they clearly knew each other well; maybe they were more than just friends. Which caused a nasty thought to flit through Theodosia's brain: If Ginny Bell and Booker were tight—and they both hated Osgood Claxton with a passion—could Ginny Bell have talked Booker into murdering Claxton? Or maybe it hadn't taken all that much prodding. After all, Booker was still furious at Claxton for pulling his grant.

"What are you thinking?" Drayton asked. He knew Theodosia was ruminating on something.

"I'm wondering if Ginny Bell could have been the mastermind behind Claxton's murder."

"That *she* killed him?"

"Or she talked Mr. Booker into killing him."

Drayton studied the two of them again. Booker whispered something into Ginny Bell's ear and she threw back her head, laughing happily. "They act like bosom buddies."

"Maybe Ginny Bell's the one pulling the puppet strings." Theodosia closed her eyes for a moment, then opened them. "Oh."

"What?"

"I think Booker rides a motorcycle. Remember how the police said there was a motorcycle involved?"

"The one they thought might've been Ben's."

"But it wasn't. After I chased the phony beekeeper, I heard something, a noise. In the back of my mind I was aware of this throaty rumble but I didn't realize what it was at the time. I didn't realize it was a motorcycle until the police started looking at Ben. And I'm pretty sure Booker owns a bike. Now that I think about it, there was a bike parked outside the tea shop this afternoon. You think it was his?"

"Don't know," Drayton said. "Booker looks like a biker, dresses like a biker. The chain on his belt, those heavy boots. I suppose you could ask Riley to search through the DMV records to see if Booker holds a motorcycle license."

"I've got a better idea. Let's go outside and see if his motorcycle is parked on the street."

"Now?"

"Yes. Well, finish your wine first."

Drayton tilted his glass back and swallowed the last inch. He set the glass down and said, "Now you've got me all worked up and curious."

13

Clouds bubbled overhead as glowing orbs atop wrought-iron streetlamps cast faint, yellow-tinged puddles of light. The night air was damp, and just a half block away, the Cooper River flowed turgidly into Charleston Harbor.

"Do you see it?" Drayton asked. They were walking down a cracked sidewalk, trying to avoid the parts that had heaved up from age and summer heat, checking out all the parked vehicles. Most were older cars and SUVs with the occasional new BMW or Mercedes interspersed among them.

"I don't see any motorcycles at all," Theodosia said. She sounded disappointed.

"Maybe you were wrong about Booker riding a bike."

"I don't think so," Theodosia said. "Just because he didn't ride it tonight doesn't mean he doesn't own one."

"Looks like you're going to have to ask Riley after all."

"There's another way to play this," Theodosia said.

Drayton gazed at her, brows pinched, looking more than a little leery. "I'm afraid to ask, but what are you thinking?"

"That we should go check Booker's garage."

Drayton clapped a hand against the side of his head. "I knew it. I knew coming here tonight wasn't going to be the end of it."

"Drayton, if this is going to upset you, I'll be happy to drop you at your place and go on alone."

"Then I'd miss out on one of your exceedingly bizarre adventures," he said.

"You know, Drayton, sometimes I don't know if you're kidding or not."

Drayton pursed his lips. "Sometimes I don't, either."

"How do you know where Booker lives?" Drayton asked as they cruised down East Bay Street, then cut over to Rivers Avenue. They crossed the Memorial Bridge, the one locals still called North Bridge, and headed into the adjacent city of North Charleston. A business and transportation hub, North Charleston was the third-largest city in South Carolina. And tonight, with the warm spring weather, that city was busy. People were out jogging and walking their dogs. Flashy neon signs announced Turtles Gumbo Bar and Porkie's Rib Joint. A line of customers stood outside Club Hyacinth waiting to get in. As they breezed past they caught the thumping strains of a rockabilly band.

"Holly gave me a sheet with all the artists' contact information. I took a snapshot of it so it's on my phone," Theodosia said.

"Smart," Drayton said. "At least I think it is."

Theodosia crossed Aviation Avenue, passing the airport and then the North Charleston Coliseum.

Drayton watched as the neighborhood changed and became a bit more working-class. "I say, his home is certainly off the beaten path."

"Booker told me he was a starving artist."

"He probably is, judging by that greasy-spoon diner we just passed. They had a sign in their window advertising chitlins and dirty rice. Does that sound like a palate pleaser to you?"

"The dirty rice, absolutely. As far as chitlins go, I've never been a fan."

"An acquired taste, I suppose," Drayton said.

They drove for another twenty or so blocks.

"We have to be getting fairly close," Theodosia said. She pulled to the curb, checked her phone and Google Maps. "Booker lives on Drummond Street. Which I'm pretty sure is just up ahead."

"You're the navigator," Drayton said.

Two more blocks brought them to Drummond Street.

"Which way, right or left?" Theodosia mused.

"I think left."

Theodosia hung a left. "Now we're looking for 318. Do you see any numbers on these homes?"

"The streetlights here are so far and few between I can barely make out the homes," Drayton said. "They're mostly smudges of darkness with a few pinpoints of light." He pressed his face up against his side window gazing at duplexes, bungalows, and a few Charleston single houses.

"But do you see 318?" Theodosia asked.

"No, but I think I see 315."

"Other side of the street, then," Theodosia said. She slowed to a crawl and scanned the row of dark houses. One, a narrow, dilapidated Victorian that was snugged up against the street and sporting a side piazza, looked promising. "I think maybe . . ."

"Is that it?" Now Drayton was leaning across the console, studying the old Victorian as well.

"I see numerals that say three and one. I think this might be it. I think the last number, the eight, must have peeled off."

"I'm not surprised, given that every inch of architecture, whether it be good or bad, is at the mercy of our tempestuous hurricanes and industrial-strength humidity."

Theodosia pulled to the curb.

"You're sure this is Booker's house?"

She looked right, then left, and nodded. "Pretty sure."

"So now what?"

"I'm going to circle around the block and cruise down the alley, then we'll take a look-see in Booker's garage."

"What if there isn't a garage?"

Theodosia remained determined. "We'll still take a look-see."

She drove down to the corner, turned left, drove a half block, then coasted down a narrow, dark alley. It was lined with trash bins, several junked cars, and a hulking green dumpster tattooed with the words BIRD'S SANITATION. In a few places fencing materials and discarded furniture had been piled up, including an old lime-green recliner.

"You could scavenge back here and furnish your home," Drayton said. "If you weren't too picky."

"This from a man who eats off Spode china and owns a pair of Louis XIV chairs?"

"Well, you know what I mean."

"Shh," Theodosia cautioned. They were almost at the back of Booker's house now, crunching down an unpaved alley that was a basic mix of gravel and crushed seashells. She slowed behind the old Victorian, saw there was a garage, and stopped. The single garage listed slightly to one side and had faded gray paint that was peeling off in long ribbons.

"This is it."

"Good heavens," Drayton said. He was sitting stiffly, his fingers gripping the dashboard in front of him.

Theodosia glanced over at Drayton and her heart went out

to him. He was tense and clearly uncomfortable. No doubt he'd prefer to stay put in her Jeep.

"You wait here," she said. "I'll just be a minute."

"You're sure? I could come with if you'd like. Serve as a sort of lookout."

"Not necessary," Theodosia said as she climbed out of her Jeep. "I'm just going to tiptoe around front and see if there's a door. Or maybe a window I can peek in."

"Okay," Drayton said as she closed the door softly.

Theodosia walked gingerly around the front of her Jeep, touched a hand to the aluminum garage door, tried to raise it, and found it locked. Okay then, she needed to do a little exploring. With her hand touching the garage to guide her, she slowly walked along its full length, heading in the direction of the old Victorian some twenty feet away. As she drew closer, she could see a light burning in the back of the house—maybe the kitchen?—and thought somebody might be home.

Booker's got a roommate?

Theodosia pushed that thought out of her head as she flattened herself against the garage, trying not to stumble on a tangle of overgrown caladium. She was suddenly feeling hypersensitive, attuned to the noises of the surrounding neighborhood. A dog barking a block away, a car with a bad muffler passing by on Drummond Street, the sound of a door slamming two houses down.

Theodosia froze. Was someone coming this way? No, she didn't think so. Like a ninja in the night, she stole around the corner to the front of the garage that faced the rear of the house. And in the dim light saw the outline of a door.

Yes!

Moving ever so slowly, she edged up to the door. Gripping the doorknob, she gave it a twist. Nothing happened.

Maybe it's stuck?

She tried again using both hands, but it still didn't budge an inch. Feeling frustrated because there was no window to peer in, Theodosia dug in her purse and found a credit card. Then, ever so gently, she slid the card into the crack between the door and the doorjamb. Positioning her card next to the locked door-knob, she moved it back and forth, hoping for the best. She'd worked this little trick a few times before and was usually suc-cessful. But this time the lock was tenacious and wouldn't budge.

Theodosia took a deep breath to calm her nerves and forced herself to try again. This time she tried to be supersensitive to slipping the plastic right into the groove where the tongue of the lock rested. She jiggled it carefully, testing it, then moved the credit card back and forth in a seesaw motion.

And was rewarded with a tiny click.

Did I get it?

She pulled out her card and grabbed the doorknob with a firm grip. The doorknob turned smoothly in her hand just as . . .

"Hey!" a rough voice shouted. Then a yard light flashed on. "Get away from there!"

Theodosia shrank back from the blinding glare. Someone inside the house had seen her!

Not only were they inside the house, but loud bumps and bangs told her the man would soon be *outside* the house.

What do I do? Run? Risk peeping inside?

The decision was made for Theodosia when a shotgun blast exploded directly over her head—BANG—nearly rupturing her eardrums. Then the man inside came flying out the back door. He was a big guy, half-dressed in a wifebeater shirt and saggy khaki pants. "Is that you, Binger?" he cried. "How many times do I gotta warn you to stay away!"

Not willing to stand her ground and try to reason with the

man, Theodosia was already on the run. Flying down the length of the garage, gasping for breath as she rounded her Jeep, she pulled open the door and jumped in.

"What was that horrendous noise?" Drayton asked as Theodosia hastily cranked the engine.

"Trouble," she said as she threw her Jeep into drive and took off, tires spinning momentarily as they spewed a mix of dirt and seashells.

But not before the man with the shotgun bolted out after her and leveled his shotgun at the back of her Jeep.

"Go!" Drayton shouted as he turned and caught sight of the wild-looking man. "Faster!"

Theodosia tromped down hard on the gas pedal. And just as she gained what she hoped was a safe distance from the gunman, another loud BOOM split the air and the back window of her Jeep blew out.

"Duck!" she cried as shards of glass exploded inward, tinkling like silver bells and flying everywhere. "Drayton, head down, cover your eyes!"

Theodosia drove like the devil himself was on her tail. Down six blocks, then a hard right, then six more blocks. Finally, she pulled over in front of a dark church.

"Are you hurt?" she asked Drayton.

"No, no," he stammered as he brushed bits of glass off his shoulders. "I'm fine, unharmed, but what about you?"

"Good, I'm good," Theodosia said.

"You weren't hit by any flying glass?"

"No, I'm . . ." Theodosia's right hand reached back and scrubbed at the back of her head. "I'm okay." Then she felt something warm and wet on her scalp. "Oh wow, something stings. I think I *was* hit." Her hand came away showing flecks of bright red blood.

"Turn on the overhead light and let me look."

Theodosia obliged, parting her hair for Drayton to take a look.

"I can see a few shiny flecks caught in your hair and, I'm afraid, stuck in your scalp as well."

"So I was hit?" she asked in a tremulous voice. This wasn't what she'd bargained for at all.

Now Drayton sounded calm. "You have a few bits of glass embedded in your scalp. We need to get you to an ER."

"Oh man." Shots of adrenaline continued to surge through Theodosia's veins, making her feel shaky and weak in the knees.

At seeing her discomfort, Drayton said, "Get out and switch seats with me. I'm going to drive."

"You sure?"

"Oh yes."

Drayton drove (slowly and cautiously) to the ER at the Charleston Medical School, then helped Theodosia out of her Jeep and into the nurse's station. A few quick words got Theodosia into a curtained area where a nurse took her vitals and assured her that Dr. Samuels would be along shortly.

"I feel so dumb," Theodosia said, perched on a padded table, her legs dangling. "I should have anticipated something weird like this."

Drayton shook his head. "You couldn't have known we'd encounter a person who was armed and dangerous."

"Still, this is my own fault. I went bumbling in without thinking about any consequences." As she was talking her cell phone buzzed. She glanced at it and saw it was Riley. "Oh, crap, it's Riley."

"Don't answer it," Drayton said.

"I don't intend to."

"Knock, knock."

They both looked over to find a young resident, presumably Dr. Samuels, in a white jacket and looking concerned.

"There was a car accident?" Dr. Samuels said.

"Not a car accident per se," Theodosia said.

"But definitely a sort of accident," Drayton said. "This dear girl desperately needs to have some bits of glass removed from her scalp."

"Ouch," Dr. Samuels said. "Better grab my forceps."

When Theodosia finally arrived home, after dropping Drayton off and assuring him she was definitely okay, her phone was ringing off the hook.

Oh dear, she thought as she picked it up. *It's probably Riley again.*

It was Riley again.

"Theo," he said. "I've been trying to get a hold of you. You didn't answer your cell phone."

For a quick, uncomfortable moment she was afraid Riley had found out about her car getting blasted tonight. And about her trip to the ER. But no, he'd just called to talk.

"Where were you?" he asked. But in an interested, casual way.

"Drayton and I decided to go to an art auction at the Arts Alliance over on Bay Street," she said without hesitation. Earl Grey looked up at her, from where he lounged on his kitchen dog bed, as if to say, *That's the only place you went?*

"What kind of art auction?"

"All sorts of different media. Painting, sculpture, pottery . . . it was the Arts Alliance's annual fundraiser."

"Sounds like fun."

"It turned out to be a blast," Theodosia said. *In more ways than one.*

"Great."

"Drayton even put a bid in on a teapot." No way was she going to tell Riley about seeing Booker, going to Booker's home, and getting shot at. "What have you been up to?"

"Mostly work. On the Claxton case and a couple of others. Oh, I have some interesting news. The police lab came up with an analysis of the contents of the fogger can."

"I heard. Tidwell dropped by the tea shop today."

"Doesn't surprise me," Riley said.

"So has the toxicology report led anywhere?"

"Not yet, but we're still hopeful." Riley paused, then yawned. "I was supposed to attend Claxton's funeral tomorrow, but now I've been pulled off that. Got to check out a print shop where the two owners are suspected of forging fifty-dollar bills."

"Isn't the Treasury Department supposed to handle things like that?"

"Only if we find sufficient evidence. Then we turn the whole ball of wax over to them." He yawned again.

"You sound tired."

"I'm beat," Riley said. "Time to ring off and hit the hay. Don't forget, we have a dinner date tomorrow."

"I won't forget."

"Okay, sweetheart, sleep tight."

"You too."

Theodosia took Earl Grey out into the backyard and stared at the sky as her dog snuffled around. The clouds had scudded off somewhere, and now stars glittered brightly in the blue-black sky. Which suddenly reminded her of the glints of glass that had been removed from her scalp. Shuddering, she turned, called to Earl Grey, and they both walked back inside.

Upstairs, as Theodosia got ready for bed, brushing her hair very gingerly, she thought about Osgood Claxton's funeral tomorrow. And wondered where it was being held.

A quick check on her iPhone and she found Claxton's obituary, which listed his service at nine o'clock tomorrow morning at the Unitarian church on Archdale Street.

Theodosia thought about this for a few minutes, then walked into her closet and picked out a nice black skirt suit. With its sedate, tailored jacket and straight skirt, it was perfect camouflage for a mourner who was hoping to unearth a few more bits of information.

14

❦

This was for investigative purposes only, Theodosia told herself as she climbed the steps of the Unitarian church this sunny Wednesday morning. She'd tossed and turned all night, wondering if she had the nerve to show up today. Turned out she did. In fact, it was the first thing that popped into her head when she woke up. Well, that and her Jeep. After a gulped breakfast of Darjeeling tea and an almond croissant, she called the tea shop and told Haley she'd be late because of Claxton's funeral. Then she drove her Jeep to the dealership and got a cheery assurance from Clark, the service manager, that they could have the back window fixed by five that night. Filled with trepidation, she drove one of their loaners—a Jeep Compass with a loosey-goosey transmission—to the church.

So here she was, edging into a magnificent Gothic structure that, in its first iteration, had been used as quarters for the British militia during the Revolutionary War. Then there were a series of renovations that went on until the eighteen fifties when the church was remodeled and Gothified (Theodosia's term) to replicate the Henry VII chapel at Westminster Abbey.

Theodosia slipped into a pew that was third from the back, hoping she wouldn't be recognized.

Turned out she needn't worry about that. Because even though the press was there in full force—newspaper people and TV reporters with their cameramen had crowded in—their undivided attention remained strictly on the dignitaries who were attending the service. Standing on tiptoes, peering over heads, Theodosia recognized the mayor, two aldermen, a couple of city council members, and a judge.

She wondered if they were attending as allies of Claxton, were showing the flag in hopes of protecting their own reputations, or were assuring themselves that a divisive and sometimes feared adversary was really and truly dead. She figured it might be the latter.

A string quartet, seated at the front of the church, began playing a slow, somnolent version of Barber's "Adagio for Strings" as Osgood Claxton's casket was wheeled down the aisle by six pallbearers. It was a showy affair, a large rosewood casket with shiny brass fittings and covered with an enormous spray of white roses, the pallbearers dressed in black tie. Weird but striking.

Walking behind the casket was Mignon Merriweather Claxton. She wore a black dress that was almost but not quite a cocktail dress with a short veil tucked in her upswept hair. Delaine Dish walked with Mignon, also looking somewhat theatrical in a black beaded top and short skirt. Both women teetered along on black high-heeled stilettos, neither looking particularly sad.

As the entire procession made their way down the center aisle, accompanied by a somber-looking funeral director, one of the men in front of Theodosia turned to the man next to him and said in a stage whisper, "What a complete sham. Claxton wasn't one bit religious. If he bowed his head in prayer, how would he get his hand in your pocket?"

The other man, with a crooked, knowing smile, whispered back, "He'd find a way."

As the funeral director seesawed the casket into place at the front of the church, Lamar Lucket slipped into a seat across the aisle from Theodosia. And just as Theodosia wondered what other surprises might be in store, Ginny Bell walked in and quietly took a seat behind Lucket.

When the music concluded, the minister walked to his podium. Bowing his head, he said a few choice words about the hereafter then ceded his place to the mayor.

The mayor glanced around, put on his half-glasses, and pulled a paper out of his jacket pocket. He then proceeded to deliver a five-minute eulogy on Osgood Claxton that was as bland, carefully worded, and circumspect as anything Theodosia had ever heard. Almost as though he were tiptoeing around a slumbering rattlesnake.

Two more people got up to speak, there were a few more prayers, and then the minister gave a final benediction. In concluding his words, the minister invited the mourners to join Mrs. Claxton for a reception at Petit Montrouge, a small French café just down the block.

As Theodosia exited the church with the rest of the mourners, she decided not to go to the reception because she didn't have time. Then she saw Ginny Bell heading that way, wondered what her motive was, and decided it might be interesting to find out.

Theodosia didn't have to wait long. After going through a short buffet line and getting a French crepe loaded with strawberries, she headed for a seat at a nearby table. That's when the fireworks started.

Mignon, hands planted firmly on hips, told Ginny Bell that she wasn't welcome here. Ginny Bell fired back that she was as welcome as anyone else.

"You little guttersnipe," Mignon shouted. "You tried to ruin my life. Get out of here before I throw you out."

"I'll go when I'm good and ready," Ginny Bell said in a haughty voice.

"I said *leave*!" Mignon cried.

Ginny Bell curled her lip and laughed out loud.

"Jackson!" Mignon turned and shouted to one of the pall-bearers who was standing nearby. "A little help would be nice."

Jackson, a red-faced man of about fifty, shuffled toward Mignon. He was clearly reticent about getting involved.

Theodosia looked around to see if anyone else was as shocked as she was by this spectacle. She saw Lamar Lucket watching with glee. His assistant, Clarice, was on her cell phone, completely ignoring the noisy outbursts.

Finally, a silver-haired man in a gray suit walked up to Mignon and Ginny Bell and spoke to them in a soft voice. Everybody leaned forward, trying to hear what was being said, but to no avail.

After a few more snippy back-and-forths between the two women, they finally parted. No hair extensions had been ripped out, no punches were thrown. The man who'd interceded seemed to have cooled down the situation.

"Who is that man who stepped in and calmed things down?" Theodosia asked a woman who was seated at her table.

"That's Buck Baldwin," the woman said. "He's the candidate who's replacing Osgood Claxton."

"Interesting," Theodosia said as she watched Baldwin put an arm around Mignon's shoulders and gently lead her to the buffet table.

"Theo!"

Theodosia turned to see who was calling her name. It was Delaine, looking wild-eyed and nervous.

"Wasn't that absolutely cray-cray?" Delaine asked.

"Shocking," Theodosia said.

"I wanted to come to Mignon's defense in the worst way, but I was terrified to get caught in the cross fire. I mean, what if someone threw a punch at *me*?" Delaine waved a hand around her head. "I just had Botox and . . . well, who needs to ruin nine hundred dollars' worth of filler, right?"

"Heaven forbid," Theodosia said.

"You're still coming to my trunk show this afternoon, aren't you? Pretty please, Theo, say yes, because I'm counting on you."

"I'll be there," Theodosia said, albeit reluctantly.

Back at the tea shop, Theodosia was greeted by an upbeat Drayton.

"There she is," Drayton said. "A trifle late but hopefully none the worse for wear. How do you feel this morning?"

Theodosia reached up and touched the back of her head. "A little sore."

"I would imagine you are. Getting glass picked out of my skull, even by a skilled doctor, wouldn't be my idea of a relaxing evening."

"Thank goodness it was flying glass and not exploding bullets," Theodosia said.

"And your car is being repaired?"

"It's in the shop now," Theodosia said. "Should be ready tonight."

"So . . . when you left a message saying you'd be late because of Claxton's funeral, I have to tell you I was a little surprised."

"So was I. Going there was kind of a last-minute decision on my part."

"And how was the service?"

"Nicely done, rather formal, as expected. But the reception afterward took a sharp turn into crazy town," Theodosia said.

Drayton lifted his teacup in a semi-salute. "After last night nothing would surprise me." He took a sip of his tea. "What happened?"

"Mignon and Ginny Bell got into your basic catfight."

"Screaming and yelling, or did it escalate to hair pulling?"

"Mostly shrieks and hurled accusations," Theodosia said.

"So they ruined the event?"

"It wasn't that much of an event. Only about twenty or twenty-five of the mourners showed up for the post-funeral reception."

"You think most people were trying to distance themselves?"

"Absolutely, especially the politicos," Theodosia said. "They couldn't wait to get out of there. I think they're happy to wipe their hands of Osgood Claxton." She looked around at the half-filled tea shop and said, "We're busy, I better get moving."

"Haley's already working on orders, so you just have to do a dash and grab from the kitchen."

"I'm on it."

"Oh, and I got the teapot," Drayton said.

Theodosia gave him a curious look.

"You know, from last night. I was high bid."

Theodosia stayed busy for the next hour or so as customers finished their morning tea and left, and a few new customers trickled in. By eleven o'clock things were winding down, with only a few tables occupied.

"We just received a delivery," Drayton told her as she set a teapot on the counter.

"What is it? Who's it from?" Theodosia asked. It was always fun to get a package.

Drayton tipped a good-sized box on its side, squinted, and said, "True Renew Cosmetics?"

"That's the delivery I've been waiting for. Stuff for our Glam Girl Tea tomorrow."

"We're giving out cosmetics?"

"Samples, Drayton. Oh, this is exciting. I can't believe we were able to get this many samples as well as having representatives from Donna Britton Cosmetic Studio, Bibelot Nail Salon, and Better Than Natural Wigs show up tomorrow to do demos." Theodosia paused. "Open the box. Let's see what we've got."

Drayton slid a knife under a cardboard flap and ripped it back.

"Loot," he said, tilting the box so Theodosia could see inside. "Looks like bunches of lipsticks, mascara, and something called . . . what is this? Brow gel? Do you know what that is?"

"Do I ever. I wouldn't be without it." Theodosia pulled the box toward her and dug in. "This stuff is great. Now I can put together swag bags for all our customers."

"This is a rather unusual event for us," Drayton said. "Have you thought about decorations?"

"I'm still working on that. But I'm leaning toward using pink dishes and pink tea-rose bouquets as centerpieces."

"That sounds . . ."

WHAM, BAM, THWACK.

Their heads spun in the direction of the front door, where it sounded as if a herd of wild horses were stampeding their way in.

Standing there was Philip Boldt. And he didn't look happy.

15

"Philip," *Theodosia said* as she scurried to greet him. "What's wrong?"

"Everything," Philip said. His normally placid face looked unnaturally pinched and his eyes had deep circles under them. His shoulders slumped and his clothing looked rumpled. This was not the spit-and-polish Philip who Theodosia had always seen.

"Tell me." Theodosia threw a quick backward glance at Drayton and said, "Can you fix us a pot of tea? Maybe something . . ."

"Strong," Drayton said, reaching for a tea tin. "Give me a minute. I have just the thing."

Theodosia led Philip to a table for two, where they both sat down.

"More problems at the Imago Gallery?" Theodosia said. She knew Philip didn't have a financial interest in the gallery, but he certainly had a deep personal interest in Holly's well-being.

"It feels like everything's coming apart at the seams. A

few more artists have unceremoniously departed, looking for representation elsewhere. So sales aren't just flat, they're in the sub-basement. And what breaks my heart is the terrible toll all this is taking on Holly. She's scared and desperate and losing her self-confidence."

"But it's a terrific gallery that's been reasonably successful for, what, three years now?"

"And in three days it's hit rock bottom."

Philip paused as Drayton set a tea tray on their table and said, "Goomtee Garden. Strong and nicely brisk."

"Thank you, Drayton," Theodosia said as she poured two steaming cups of tea. "Here." She slid a teacup across the table to Philip. "Drink this. It'll make you feel better."

"I hope so," Philip said. He didn't sound convinced, but he obligingly took a sip anyway. "Mmm, it is good. And hot." He blew on the surface of his tea, then took a second sip. "I'm wondering—hoping, really—that you're still sniffing around, looking at suspects in the Claxton murder. If the police arrested someone—indicted them, even—it would take an enormous amount of pressure off Holly. Offer up proof that none of this is her fault."

"None of this *is* her fault," Theodosia told him. "And I've definitely been on the hunt."

"Thank goodness."

"Amazingly, there are more than a few people with unsavory ties to Osgood Claxton. And who might have wanted him dead."

"I know you've taken a look at Lamar Lucket," Philip said.

"He's a candidate," Theodosia said. "In more ways than one. There's also Mignon Merriweather, Claxton's soon-to-be-ex-wife; Ginny Bell, a woman Claxton had a long-term affair with; and

Booker, that weird artist you and Holly turned me on to. All of them with good, solid reasons to have wanted Claxton dead. Any one of them could have dressed up in that beekeeper outfit and killed him."

Philip lifted his eyebrows and said in a low voice, "Have you by any chance considered Jeremy Slade as a suspect?"

Theodosia was taken aback. "Holly's silent partner?" She hadn't expected Philip to toss his name into the mix.

"Not so silent," Philip said. "In the last month or so Slade has been pushing Holly awfully hard."

"How so?" Theodosia asked.

"Slade wants Holly to hurry up and sign more artists, stage dozens more gallery receptions, and try to get close to the wealthier people in Charleston." Philip glanced around. "You know, the folks who reside here in the Historic District, the ones who are huge fans of art and antiques and have discretionary dollars to spend."

"That's what Holly's guest list was all about, wasn't it?" Theodosia said. "For last Sunday's Honeybee Tea she'd invited quite a few art collectors and prominent citizens. Some of the same people who are benefactors of the Gibbes Museum of Art."

"That's true," Philip said in a slightly defensive tone. "I mean, Holly was *trying* to made inroads."

"Which isn't an easy thing to do. It takes time and patience to cultivate an audience of that caliber."

"I know, I know." Philip took another sip of tea. "I'm just thankful you're still working on this Claxton thing, nosing around. I appreciate it. Holly and I are both grateful for your efforts."

Theodosia reached over and touched a hand to Philip's arm. "How are *you* doing in all of this?"

Philip's mouth twisted into a wry smile. "Me? I don't like to complain, but things have been kind of rocky. You know I'm still struggling to get my restaurant open."

"The Boldt Hole," Theodosia said. She thought it was a fun name, a memorable name.

"There have been financial issues, long waits for permits." Philip sighed. "The usual hoops a new business has to jump through."

"Tell me about it. I'm still wrestling with the city zoning committee over how many outdoor tables I can legally have."

Philip chuckled. "I don't mean any disrespect, but that's kind of reassuring to hear. It tells me I'm not the only one out there who's been getting the runaround."

Twenty minutes later, the Indigo Tea Shop was once again filled with customers. Lunch was in full swing and Theodosia got busy seating guests and taking orders. Today, Haley's menu included Tuscan soup, chicken salad on pumpkin bread tea sandwiches, roast beef and cheddar cheese on rye tea sandwiches, a chef's salad, and a chanterelle mushroom and Brie cheese quiche. For desert there was hazelnut tea cake with Moscato poached pears.

Theodosia ran orders back to Haley and happily picked up tea orders from Drayton. He'd outdone himself today by brewing pots of cardamom tea, Nilgiri, and vanilla spice tea.

"The vanilla spice seems especially popular," Theodosia told him.

"That's because it reminds everyone of sugar cookies," Drayton said.

"Oh, and table three is wondering if they could get a pot of Japanese green tea."

Drayton reached up and pulled down a tin of tea. "I believe I have a Gyokuro that should be to their liking."

At one fifteen, Theodosia stood behind the counter, munching one of Haley's just-baked lemon scones.

"You're eating the merchandise," Drayton joked.

"If that's the worst thing that happens today I'll be quite content," Theodosia said. Then the front door opened and Riley walked in. "Or maybe not," she added.

"Hey," she said, hurrying to greet him. "What brings you in? Taking a break for lunch?"

"Don't I wish." Riley pulled Theodosia aside. "You remember that Booker guy, the artist?"

"Sure."

"Well, he's disappeared off the radar."

"You're kidding," Theodosia said. And then, without giving it a second thought, added, "But I just saw him last night."

Riley did a slow reaction. His brows puckered, then pulled together, his mouth worked soundlessly for a few moments. Then he said, with more than a tinge of curiosity, "I thought you weren't going to get involved in this case. That you and Drayton attended some arts thing last night."

"Right." Theodosia knew she'd better think fast. "The silent auction at the Arts Alliance. Booker happened to come in just as Drayton and I were leaving." She kept her tone light, hoping Riley wouldn't get suspicious and start asking more questions. But he did.

"How did you know who he was?"

"Um, I guess I must have been introduced to him once upon a time at the Imago Gallery."

"And that's it?"

"If you're asking did I get in a fight with Booker or have words with him because I think he's a prime suspect, the answer is no," Theodosia said. She touched a hand gently to the back of her head in the guise of patting her hair, and told herself, *No, I'm not going to blurt out what happened last night. That's going to remain a deep, dark secret.*

Riley lifted a hand in a gesture of surrender. "Okay, I hear you. Don't shoot the messenger."

Now it was Theodosia's turn to be curious. "Why are you trying to find Booker?"

"Because it turns out he has a record of sorts."

"No kidding. What kind of record?" Theodosia asked.

"He's been arrested for a couple of minor offences. Recreational drugs, driving without a license. That kind of thing."

"That doesn't exactly point to Booker being a murderer." Even though Theodosia had serious doubts about Booker, she wanted to hear Riley's take.

"There's more," Riley said. "It turns out your Mr. Booker once worked at Apple Springs Orchard."

"Which means . . . what?"

"That particular orchard is also an apiary," Riley said. "They raise honeybees there."

Theodosia stared at him, letting his words sink in.

"You know, bees . . . beekeepers, smoke pots?" Riley added.

Theodosia was so thoroughly surprised all she could squeak out was "Wow."

"Don't act so shocked," Riley said. "You're the one who pointed me in Booker's direction in the first place."

"I know, but . . ."

"What? You didn't expect your information to pan out? Well, maybe it did after all. Maybe you're a better investigator than I thought you were."

"Thank you," Theodosia said. "I think."

"But here's the thing. On a more personal note, will you take a rain check for dinner? I have to drive up to this orchard and interview the owner. And I can't leave until after a staff meeting. So two hours up and two more back means I won't hit Charleston city limits until eight or nine o'clock tonight."

"That's okay," Theodosia said. Her mind was spinning with possibilities. "I totally understand. You're working an important case."

Riley pulled her into a hug. "But we'll do Saturday night for sure."

Once Riley left, Theodosia crooked a finger at Drayton. "Did you hear any of that?"

"Enough to rouse my suspicions about Mr. Booker," Drayton said.

"Weird to think that he worked at an apiary."

"More like strangely serendipitous," Drayton said. "On the other hand, you seem to have accumulated an abundance of suspects. With Booker in the lead, followed closely by Lamar Lucket, Mignon Merriweather, and Ginny Bell."

"You're not going to believe this, but Jeremy Slade's been tossed into the mix as well."

"Holly's partner? What are you talking about? I thought Mr. Slade was her knight in shining armor. Her angel investor."

"When Philip was in before, he confided to me that Slade has been exerting tremendous pressure on Holly. To sign more artists, attract a higher caliber of clients, and, I guess, make a whole lot more money."

"Now that her revenues have dropped sharply, do you think Slade wants out of the partnership?"

"Could be," Theodosia said.

"And killing Claxton was the way to do it?" Drayton said. "Somehow that doesn't make any sense to me."

"Who knows? It's possible Slade had bad dealings with Claxton somewhere along the line. Maybe Slade figured if he murdered Claxton he'd be free of him for good, with Holly suffering the consequences. Kill two birds with one stone."

"That's a bizarre thought."

"Drayton, this whole case is weird."

Drayton thought for a moment. "With this many suspects, how are you going to investigate everyone? Or better yet, narrow it down to just one and pinpoint the real killer?"

Theodosia, who hated failure more than anything, who prided herself on her unflagging loyalty to friends, said, "I don't know, I still have to figure that part out."

16

Cotton Duck was one of the trendiest boutiques in Charleston. So it was with a fair amount of trepidation that Theodosia dropped in for Delaine's trunk show this Wednesday afternoon. It wasn't that Theodosia was averse to fashion—no, she loved fashion. It was that Delaine had a habit of cooing and pressuring and pushing anything and everything at you, whether it was your particular taste or not. Of course, Delaine changed clothes four times a day and had a wardrobe that engulfed two large rooms in her house. When Theodosia put her clothes on in the morning, they generally stayed on until she took them off at night.

"Theo! Theo!" Delaine squealed in delight as she hurried to greet Theodosia. Her overfilled lips were pursed in anticipation and her nonexistent hips swayed as she took tiny but hurried steps in her outrageously high (four inches!) Manolo Blahnik heels.

Theodosia glanced around the busy boutique as Delaine clutched her arm and pulled her into an enormous crush of people. Delaine's trunk shows were always major fashion events filled with glitz and glam—lots of well-heeled women, flutes of champagne, and good-looking young male waiters. Today she'd invited three different designers to show their brand-new collections and was hoping to write a slew of orders.

"I had no idea you'd be so busy," Theodosia said as the woman next to her jabbed an elbow into her ribs, grabbing for a silk gown.

"Three designers make it triple exciting," Delaine trilled as she ticked them off on her fingers. "Jules Armand creates the most glamorous evening gowns, Marnie Moon does fabulous country-club-type sportswear, and Vladamir . . . well, he has a to-die-for collection of handwoven scarves, shawls, and ruanas."

"What's a ruana again?" Theodosia asked. She knew she wasn't always up on the latest fashion verbiage. Tea, yes. Fashion, no.

"It's a wrap, silly girl."

"Like a poncho?"

Delaine did a dramatic eye roll. "Ponchos are *so* last decade. You need a ruana for when you're out sailing or hanging at the beach and are in serious need of a stylish cover-up."

Theodosia didn't bother telling Delaine that her idea of a cover-up was an oversized T-shirt.

"Let's find you a glass of champagne," Delaine said, "and get you started shopping." She reached over, grabbed a glass off a server's tray, and thrust it into Theodosia's hands. Then she spun Theodosia around, gave her a slight push, and said, "Go. Enjoy. Spend money."

Which sent Theodosia careening off in the direction of a display of ruanas and scarves. Which, turned out, really were gorgeous. Linens and fine wools in colors of pale peach, cornflower blue, mulberry, and terra-cotta that had been hand-loomed, possibly by French nuns or little ladies high in the Andes Mountains who were probably paid pennies on the dollar. She picked up one of the whisper-soft scarves, looked at the price tag, and set it back down.

No, she told herself. *I'd have to sell a hundred scones to pay for that.*

She turned away from the display and found herself staring directly at Mignon Merriweather.

Mignon recognized Theodosia immediately and said, "Fancy seeing you here." Then she grinned and said in a conspiratorial whisper, "Did Delaine twist your arm, too?"

"She means well," Theodosia said. "But . . ."

"Tell me about it. Delaine is a dear soul, but subtlety isn't exactly her strong suit."

"How's your shop coming along?" Theodosia asked, mostly out of politeness. She searched her memory and said, "Belle de Jour."

Mignon was thrilled by Theodosia's perceived interest. "You remembered! Well, I'm almost ready to launch," she bubbled. "My final shipment of French crockery arrives tomorrow, then I'll have a few days to fine tune the displays before I throw open my doors on Monday."

"You must be thrilled."

"Beyond the moon and scared to death," Mignon said. "I know it's a gamble, but . . . I guess I enjoy playing the odds."

"I ran into Ginny Bell last night," Theodosia said. "At the fundraiser for the Arts Alliance. And then, of course, she was at the funeral this morning . . ."

Mignon's mood changed instantly. "That toxic witch," she spat out. "I can't stand her. The nerve of her attending . . . well . . . at least I'm getting some degree of revenge. I understand the police have questioned Ginny Bell a number of times."

"I think they're questioning a lot of people," Theodosia said. She didn't bother to add, *Including you.*

No matter; Mignon spoke the words for her.

"Yes, I've spoken to the police myself. Tried to impress upon them how Ginny Bell went from adoring my husband to utterly despising him."

"That's a pretty wide range of emotions," Theodosia said.

"Which is why I firmly believe Ginny Bell could have had a hand in Osgood's death." Mignon stared intently at Theodosia, her eyes pinpricks of intensity. "You know?"

No, I don't know, Theodosia thought. *In fact, I have no idea who might have killed Claxton. But it feels as if I might be edging closer to an answer.*

Mignon touched a hand to Theodosia's shoulder. "I'm sorry, dear. I'm getting carried away by my emotions when we both came here to have a nice, relaxing shop."

"It's no problem," Theodosia said, as Mignon smiled and then turned and picked up a sea green scarf.

Theodosia wandered over to a rack of sportswear and started going through it. Wondered if polo shirts and white skorts were her style. *No, probably not. Not unless I dyed my hair blond and changed my name to Topsy or Bunny.*

"Theodosia?"

Theodosia turned when she heard her name called. Then she smiled when she saw it was Bettina, Delaine's niece, who worked at the boutique.

"Bettina," Theodosia said, "you're still here." Bettina was supposed to be doing an internship, but Delaine had convinced her to stay on. Probably for the cheap labor.

"Yup, I'm here," Bettina said. "Me and Janine were the idiots who helped pull all this together." Janine was Delaine's overworked assistant.

"I figured you'd be back in New York, working as a buyer for some fabulous boutique."

Bettina gave a rueful smile. "You know how Delaine is. Once she gets her hooks in you, watch out. She even got her aunt Glorene to pitch in." She turned, saw Delaine heading in their direction, and said, "Oops."

"Theo!" Delaine's hiss was like that of an angry cat. "What are you *doing?*"

Theodosia pulled her hand back from the rack of clothes as if she'd touched a hot iron. "Um . . . shopping?"

"You're supposed to be looking at the *new* merchandise. And Bettina, we need a little more help at the front door," Delaine said. "Welcoming the guests, showing our *appreciation.*"

"I'm on it," Bettina said.

"And for heaven's sake, don't let Aunt Glorene gobble up all the crab puffs." Delaine paused in her diatribe and studied Theodosia from across the top of her flute of champagne. A knowing smile spread slowly across her face. "I wasn't going to tell anyone, but I have *major* news." Her voice dropped to a whisper. "And I'm so excited I can barely hold it in anymore."

"Okay." Theodosia knew that Delaine's big news could be about anything at all—from purchasing a new toaster to getting ready to elope with a new boyfriend.

"It isn't public knowledge yet, but I've been elected to the Charleston Film Board."

"Congratulations," Theodosia said. She knew that being a board member was exactly the kind of high-profile position Delaine craved. And the more flamboyant the organization, the more it massaged her ego.

"Not only that, I've already attended my first meeting. Turns out the Film Board is offering financial incentives to production companies who film their movies here in Charleston. And there are already two or three on the hook."

"That's great," Theodosia said, suddenly noticing that Jeremy Slade had just walked in. With a young, stylish-looking woman clinging to his arm.

"One of the movies is a supernatural thriller called *Dark Fortune*," Delaine said. "There's a good chance they'll film it at the Brittlebank Manor."

Theodosia was taken aback. "That old place? It's been deserted for years and is practically falling down."

Delaine dimpled. "Which is exactly why they love it. This particular film company, a group called Peregrine Pictures, has already scouted it as a location. And because the old mansion is such a monstrosity, the producer thinks it might be spot-on perfect. And Theo . . ." Delaine grabbed Theodosia's arm again and dug in her red enameled nails. "There might even be a role for you."

That caught Theodosia's attention. But not in a good way. "A role? Not on your life," she said. "I'm no kind of actor and I have zero interest in auditioning for something that's completely out of my wheelhouse."

"Come on, silly," Delaine prodded. "I didn't mean *acting*, I meant *catering*. You know what a craft services table is, don't you?"

Theodosia didn't really, but she took a guess. "Something to do with food?"

"Good girl. That's it exactly. A craft services table is a well-stocked smorgasbord of food that's maintained for the cast and crew. So they can nibble all day to their hearts' content."

"So we're talking appetizers?"

"More like crackers and cheese, muffins, scones, cookies, that type of thing."

"Gotcha."

"So do you have any interest?"

Theodosia was keeping one eye on Jeremy Slade and his date

as they stepped toward a showy display of evening gowns. "If the shoot fits into my schedule, why not?"

"Excellent. I'll take that as a yes," Delaine said. Then she turned, frowned, and said, "Oh bother."

"What now?"

"Aunt Glorene is having *another* glass of champagne."

Theodosia grinned. "And how many have you had?"

"Not nearly enough," Delaine said as she scurried away.

Standing there, Theodosia was faced with a dilemma. Go over and bid a friendly hello to Jeremy Slade and act as though nothing has happened? Or pull Slade aside and ask him straight out if his interest in the Imago Gallery had suddenly waned?

Theodosia still hadn't made up her mind when she approached Slade and said, as casually as possible, "Good afternoon, Mr. Slade."

Startled, Slade gazed at her with a confused look on his face, as if one of the shop mannequins had suddenly started speaking to him.

"Theodosia Browning," she said. "From the Indigo Tea Shop?"

Recognition dawned on Slade's face. "Of course, Theodosia." He was polite but his voice carried a strange undertone. "Wonderful to see you again. And this is my friend, Jennifer Collier."

"Nice to meet you," Theodosia said. Jennifer was pretty with medium-length chestnut brown hair and a clingy black tank dress that showed off long, coltish limbs. She was also young and a trifle wide-eyed. Maybe all of twenty-two?

"You own a tea shop?" Jennifer said excitedly. "Here in Charleston?"

"Over on Church Street," Theodosia said. "The Indigo Tea Shop."

"Oh, I *know* that place," Jennifer burbled. "I've been by there. And I've always wanted to stop in because I love tea so much."

"Now that we've met, you have to drop by," Theodosia said, good-naturedly.

Jennifer tugged at Slade's arm. "Let's for sure do that, okay?"

"Theodosia was the one who catered the tea this past Sunday," Slade told her with slightly arched eyebrows.

"Oh. I guess that didn't turn out so well, did it?" Jennifer said. Then she shrugged, as if the incident was of no consequence to her, and said, "Still, we really have to do high tea sometime."

"Of course," Jeremy said. He nodded at Theodosia and said, "Nice to see you again." Then he took Jennifer's arm and steered her away.

Theodosia knew when she was getting the brush-off. "Have fun," she said as Jeremy ignored her, while Jennifer glanced back over her shoulder and gave a little finger wave.

Interesting, Theodosia thought. She wondered if Jeremy Slade was suddenly cool to her because the police had interrogated him again. And that Slade thought she'd asked the police to give him a second look. Then Theodosia wondered—could Slade have killed Claxton? Yes, she and Drayton had talked about the possibility, but it seemed far-fetched at the time. And today she still couldn't think of a motivating factor, didn't know of a single connection between Slade and Claxton—although maybe there was one and she just hadn't found it yet.

Okay, she decided as the party swirled noisily around her, *maybe I need to keep Jeremy Slade on the back burner.*

And on the heels of that thought, *For my own sanity, I need to get out of here.*

17

Back at the Indigo Tea Shop, Drayton was sweeping the floor, poking his broom into cracks and crevices, while he talked to Lois Chamberlain, the owner of Antiquarian Books. Lois was sitting at one of the tables, sipping a cup of tea.

When Lois spotted Theodosia, she jumped up from her chair and said, "I have a copy of that British cookbook you were interested in. The one with recipes for things like cottage pie, Lancashire hotpot, and Eccles cakes."

"You do? That's fabulous," Theodosia said.

"So you're still interested?"

"You bet I am."

"I guess I should have brought it along," Lois said. "Instead I've been sitting here jawing with Drayton."

Lois was fifty-something and a retired librarian with a knack for sourcing most any book you wanted. She was a little chubby, had a warm, open face, and wore her long silver-gray hair in a single braid down her back. A grandmotherly Katniss Everdeen.

"That's okay, I'll walk back with you and pick it up," Theodosia said. "That's if you're going back to your shop."

"I sure am," Lois said.

Theodosia turned her attention to Drayton and said, "Anything for me to do here? Or are we done for the day?"

"*Finito*," Drayton said. "You're officially off the clock." He set his broom aside and made a dusting motion with his hands. "By the by, how was Delaine's trunk show?"

"Trunk *shows*," Theodosia said. "She brought in three different designers, so her boutique was pretty much jam-packed. Then again, Delaine's shop is always a madhouse."

"A fire marshal's bad dream," Drayton said.

"I love shopping at Cotton Duck," Lois said. "But, hoo boy, is her stuff ever expensive." Lois might have lusted for Delaine's haute couture clothing and accessories, but she still subscribed to her tried-and-true grad school outfit of blue jeans, a colorful nubby sweater, and leather clogs.

"Tell me about it," Theodosia said. "My budget prevented me from waltzing back here with a new evening gown or beaded jacket." She glanced over at Drayton. "You'll lock up?"

"Count on it. Are you going to pick up your car?" Drayton said.

"Did the dealership call?" Theodosia asked.

"They did and said it's all done," Drayton said. "Ready to roll."

"Car repairs?" Lois asked as they walked out the door together.

"Something like that," Theodosia said.

Antiquarian Books was down the block from the Indigo Tea Shop in a quaint little building with a yellow-and-white striped awning over a bay window that today had a display of Civil War books. Lois's original shop had been destroyed in a fire, but she'd lucked out and found a smaller, newly available shop on the same block. Now she was moved in, packed to the gills with books, and almost open for business. Theodosia wasn't sure if Lois went looking for used books or if they somehow managed to find her.

Lois stuck her key in the lock and pushed the door open. "Come on in," she said.

That's when Pumpkin, an adorable little long-haired dachshund, came barreling toward them.

"As you can see," Lois said, "Pumpkin has already assumed the role of bookshop dog."

"She's perfect at it." Theodosia knelt down and stroked the little dog's soft dappled fur. "The perfect greeter." Lois had adopted Pumpkin a few months ago, after she'd been rescued from an overcrowded shelter in Jasper County.

"Make yourself at home," Lois said.

Theodosia smiled as she cradled Pumpkin in her arms and stood up. She was always at home around books. She'd grown up with her dad's law books and history books stacked floor to ceiling in his home office. She'd also amassed her own horde of books, which she'd carried with her from school to her first apartment and now to her current home. Some of the books were old favorites like *Pride and Prejudice, Beloved,* and *The Clan of the Cave Bear*; others were newer, such as *The Midnight Library*. At any rate, her collection continued to expand.

Just being here in Antiquarian Books, smelling the leather and bookbinder's glue, Theodosia had an urge to start poking through the floor-to-ceiling shelves that Lois had carefully labeled as HISTORY, FOOD & WINE, LOCAL AUTHORS, RELIGION, FICTION, and SCIENCE. Of course, up a little winding stairway was a loft that contained MYSTERY and CHILDREN'S BOOKS.

Lois walked behind the front counter, grabbed an oversized book, and handed it to Theodosia.

"Here's that cookbook," she said.

"Wonderful," Theodosia said. She set Pumpkin down on the counter and flipped through a few pages. Seeing recipes for Bath buns, quaking pudding, and Naples biscuits, she knew she'd be curled up with this book tonight. "How much do I owe you?"

"Not a penny. It was a donation from someone who was frantic to downsize their home library. Besides, Drayton has already promised me free tea and scones for life."

"You deserve it," Theodosia said, tucking the book under her arm.

Lois placed both hands on the counter and leaned forward. She eyed Theodosia carefully and said, "Drayton tells me you're trying to solve another murder mystery."

"He told you what I was up to?" Theodosia said.

"Some of it," Lois said. "Most of it."

"But you already knew that Osgood Claxton was murdered, right?"

"Only what I read in the newspaper. About your Honeybee Tea, the toxic gas that spurted everywhere, and then the shooting." Concern shone on Lois's face. "Drayton told me you single-handedly chased after the shooter."

"Not one of my smarter moves," Theodosia said. Pumpkin stared up at her with soft eyes, as if she understood. And maybe she did.

"You took an awful risk. But, Theodosia, why on earth are you letting yourself get pulled into something like this? Is it because you catered the tea?"

"Mostly I'm trying to help Holly Burns because it was her tea party to celebrate the Imago Gallery. You know Holly, right? You two have met?"

Lois nodded. "She's a sweet woman. A little scattered, but sweet."

"Her Imago Gallery has taken a nosedive since all this happened."

Surprise registered on Lois's broad face. "No kidding."

"Most of the artists Holly represented have bailed on her, and she's lost more than a few sales."

"That's awful. It's difficult enough to keep a small business afloat these days without that kind of trouble. I guess it is nice of you to try and help."

"'Try' is the operative word because I'm not exactly getting anywhere."

Lois looked interested. "No suspects?"

"There are almost too many," Theodosia said. "All with a motive for killing Osgood Claxton. Unfortunately, there's no specific evidence I can pin on any one of them." She stroked Pumpkin's back. "Needless to say, I'm getting a bit disheartened."

"No." Lois shook her head vehemently. "Don't be. Your intuition is usually spot-on. When my daughter was murdered, you practically single-handedly figured out the whole thing. Even the police with their professional investigators were two steps behind you."

"That was then, this is now."

"The thing is," Lois said, "you not only brought me closure, you brought me a good deal of peace."

"That's kind of you to say."

"So maybe you need to keep that in mind. You can help bring peace to Holly and her lovely little art gallery. And maybe that murdered politician's family, too."

"Maybe," Theodosia said.

"You can do this," Lois urged. "You have the smarts, now

you need to put your mind in the right place. Zen out and engage in a free flow of ideas."

"You mean not focus quite so hard?"

"Exactly. Then maybe the answer will come to you sort of organically."

Theodosia studied Lois's face. And saw only kindness and encouragement. "Okay," she said. "It's worth a try."

Theodosia drove her loaner back to the dealership and picked up her Jeep. Talked to them about the insurance for a few minutes, then drove home, windows down, enjoying the final sparse glow of sun on the horizon and the spring warmth that tinged the air.

Theodosia parked in her back alley, whistled a greeting to Earl Grey as she came in the back door, and ran upstairs. Once she'd changed clothes, she took Earl Grey out for a quick walk. It was dark now, a lovely evening, the sky mottled with purple clouds and an almost full moon peeping down from the heavens. A dove cooed from its leafy hideaway in an azalea bush, and as she ducked down a narrow alley, the air was redolent of something cooking on a backyard grill. Springtime nights were still cool and lush, but soon the heat and humidity of a Charleston summer would come creeping in.

Back home in her kitchen, Theodosia heated up some of Haley's chicken and wild rice soup on the stove and popped a buttermilk scone in the microwave. She was planning to eat dinner, watch a little TV, then curl up with her new cookbook. Maybe dream about the quaint tea shops in Bath or the lush green Salisbury Plain. And definitely select a few recipes (with Haley's input, of course) that would be perfect for the Fox and Hounds Tea they were planning to have later this summer.

Arranging her soup and scone on a wicker tray, Theodosia carried everything into her dining room, Earl Grey at her heels, and sat down. That's when her cell phone let out an unmistakable burp.

Drat. Please don't let this be one of those pesky telemarketers.

She pulled the phone from her pocket and checked the caller ID. It wasn't a telemarketer; it was Haley. "Hello?" she answered. She thought Haley had gone to Ben's tonight. That they planned to cook dinner together.

Words flooded out so fast and furiously that Theodosia could hardly take them all in. Haley sounded absolutely hysterical!

"Haley, slow down."

"Theodosia!" Haley yelped. "I need your help!"

Theodosia stood up so fast her chair almost tipped over backwards.

"What's wrong, Haley? What happened?"

"I'm at Ben's house and—I don't know why—but we're surrounded by police cars and guys in black riot gear. They're shouting at us with bullhorns and yelling for us to come out with our hands up!" Her words ended with a choking cry. "What should I do?"

Theodosia's blood ran cold. "Both of you better go out there with your hands up."

18

❦

Haley continued to sob. "And then what?"

"And then I'll be right there," Theodosia said. "Quick, tell me Ben's address."

"Three sixteen Colonial. It's a duplex with a big blooming magnolia out front."

"Hang in there, kiddo, I'm on my way."

Theodosia grabbed her keys and was out the door in a heartbeat. As she jogged to her Jeep in the back alley, she punched up Drayton's number.

"I knew it," Drayton said as he answered the phone. "You've come up with another harebrained idea, right? You're about to tail one of your many suspects and you want me to ride shotgun."

"Drayton, Haley's in trouble." Theodosia was in her Jeep now, cranking over the engine.

"What!"

"She's at Ben's house and the police have the place surrounded."

"Why?"

"I don't know why," Theodosia said as she sped down the alley, braked sharply, then turned down Church Street. "Maybe because Ben's still a suspect?"

"Where does he live? Where's this happening?"

"Um, the address Haley gave me is on Colonial. Three sixteen Colonial."

"Where are you now?" Drayton asked.

"Heading down Church Street."

"You're going to come within two blocks of me. Swing by and pick me up, will you?"

"You sure?" Theodosia asked as she changed lanes, cut off a small blue car, and hung a right onto Tradd.

"I'll be waiting out front."

Drayton was as good as his word. He was standing on the curb, bouncing nervously on the balls of his feet as Theodosia drove toward him. When he saw Theodosia's Jeep, he raised a hand and waved.

Theodosia skidded to a halt, her right front tire scraping the curb as Drayton jumped into the passenger seat. He was still dressed in good slacks and shirt from the tea shop, but he had traded out his tweed jacket for a rust-colored suede jacket.

"Have you heard from Haley again?" were Drayton's first words.

"Not a thing."

"Do you think she's okay?"

"We can only hope. But . . . she sounded awfully scared."

The street leading to Ben's house was blocked by two black-and-white cruisers parked crosswise and a cobweb of yellow-and-black crime scene tape. A uniformed officer saw Theodosia coming and threw up his hands to wave her off. When she kept on coming, he scowled, shook his head vigorously, and motioned for her to stop.

"Turn around," he barked when Theodosia finally stopped and rolled down her window. "This street's closed for police business."

"I need to get in there," Theodosia said. "Haley, the woman who was in the house you guys just raided—she's my friend. She called me asking for help."

"No." The officer made a twirling motion with his hand. "You need to turn your vehicle around right now. The detectives are still sorting things out."

"There she is!" Drayton yelped suddenly. "I see Haley standing on the front lawn. Theo, you see her over there?"

"That's her!" Theodosia shouted. Haley was standing in the front yard of a small duplex surrounded by a circle of police officers. Headlights from police cruisers and two black Suburban vans illuminated the scene, throwing low shadows and making Haley appear tiny and scared. "That's Haley," Theodosia said to the officer again. "She specifically requested our help."

"Impossible," the officer said. "I've got orders to maintain a hard perimeter." He studied the jam of cars around them. "What I want you to do is pull your vehicle ahead ten feet, then turn around in that driveway over there. The one with the stone lion."

"Okay, sure," Theodosia said. She had no intention of turning around. If Haley needed her, then she would show up come hell or high water.

"What are you going to do?" Drayton asked in a low voice.

"Try to bull my way through, what else?"

"And if they stop us again?"

"Then we'll . . . oh, thank heavens, I see Detective Tidwell up there. Wave to him, Drayton." Theodosia tooted her horn.

Three shorts, three longs, then three shorts. A sort of vehicular SOS.

Tidwell heard the commotion and turned around. Scanned the logjam of cars and saw Theodosia and Drayton waving at him like mad. His expression was dour as he seemed to consider their pleas for a few moments, then he gave the high sign for the officers to wave her vehicle on through.

Theodosia slowly picked her way through a lineup of police cars, then pulled halfway onto a sidewalk and turned off her engine.

"Come on, Drayton, our girl needs us," Theodosia said.

They both hurried toward the circle of police that seemed to break apart as they approached.

Theodosia went to Haley and swept her up in a giant hug while Drayton patted Haley's shoulder.

"You came," Haley said tearfully.

"Of course we did," Theodosia said. Then she turned and said, "Thank you," to Detective Tidwell.

Tidwell held up a hand and said, "That's enough of a reunion. You two will have to wait here while the suspects are being questioned."

Haley was quickly led away; there was no sign of Ben.

"They're *not* suspects," Theodosia argued, getting right up in Tidwell's face. "Especially not Haley. You know Haley, she wouldn't hurt a fly. I doubt Ben would, either."

Tidwell gave a dismissive shake of his head. "We received a tip about Mr. Sweeney."

"Tip?" Drayton said.

"What kind of tip?" Theodosia asked.

Just then, a uniformed officer emerged from the front door of Ben's duplex. He was carrying a folded white bundle with a beekeeper's hat resting on top.

"A tip that just panned out," Tidwell said. "Take a look at that."

Theodosia gave the beekeeper paraphernalia a scornful glance. "It's bogus," she said.

"How can you be so sure?" Tidwell said.

"Let me guess, your tip was anonymous, right?" Theodosia said.

Tidwell inclined his large head slightly.

"Of course it was," Theodosia said. "Which means Ben was set up."

Tidwell rocked back on his heels. He wasn't swayed by Theodosia's argument but did continue to listen to her. "By who?"

"I'd guess by the real killer," Theodosia said.

Drayton nudged her arm. "Theo. Look who else is here."

Theodosia spun around to find Pete Riley striding down the middle of the street toward them.

"Oh, thank goodness," she murmured as she bolted off in his direction.

Then Riley had her in his arms. "I came as soon as I got the call," he whispered into her ear.

"Just in the nick of time," Theodosia said as they walked back to where Tidwell was standing, still looking grouchy. "This thing isn't just a misunderstanding, Haley's been pulled into a sticky mess."

"Are you filing charges?" Riley asked Tidwell immediately.

Tidwell was reluctant to answer the question. "We're still investigating," he said.

"Ben was set up," Theodosia said to Riley.

"Somebody stashed a beekeeper's outfit in his house," Drayton said.

"Actually, it was on his back porch," Tidwell said.

Riley wiped the back of his hand against his chin. "Seriously? That's what this is about?"

"Pretty crafty, huh?" Theodosia said.

"Pretty nasty," Drayton said.

"Excuse me," Tidwell said. "Detective Riley, when you finish here I need a word. We have *business* to tend to."

"Of course, sir," Riley said as Tidwell slid away from them.

Theodosia turned pleading eyes on Riley. "What did you find out about Booker?" she asked.

"Not much. It's been several years since he worked at Apple Springs."

"But from what you know about Booker, do you think he could have done this? Tried to set Ben up?"

Riley nodded. "It's certainly possible. Unless Ben really is guilty as sin."

"He isn't."

"You say that with such assurance. But you really don't know."

"I *do* know," Theodosia said. "Because I know Haley and I trust her judgment."

"What do we do now?" Drayton asked.

"Go home. Let me try to bat cleanup on this," Riley said.

"We want to take Haley with us," Drayton said. "We don't want anybody shining bright lights in her eyes and hammering her with questions." He crossed his arms in front of himself, projecting an air of finality.

"That's not going to happen," Riley said.

"Maybe not the rude interrogation part," Theodosia said. "But can we take Haley home with us anyway?"

Riley hesitated a moment, then said, "Let me see what I can do."

19

Haley was still upset this Thursday morning, even though Theodosia and Drayton had shown up last night, reasoned with the police, and taken great pains to assure Haley that under no circumstances was she a suspect. Haley had nodded agreeably, been allowed to say goodbye to Ben, and then let Theodosia and Drayton drive her back to her apartment above the Indigo Tea Shop. But deep in her heart Haley remained fearful—about Ben, about the intensity of last night's raid, about what might happen next.

"Do you want me to ask Miss Dimple to help out in the kitchen instead of doing tea service with me?" Theodosia asked.

Haley shook her head. "No, you need her more than I do. We've got a lot of people coming in for the Glam Girl Tea so you should be front and center with the guests."

"Which Drayton and I can manage just fine."

"It's not a difficult menu today, so I'll be okay. Eventually." Haley turned to her butcher-block counter and added an extra dollop of mayonnaise to her crab salad. "But I'm still ticked off that the cops thought Ben was a murderer. That totally frosts me."

"I know, and I'm sorry you had to be part of that nasty setup last night."

"Who do you think planted that crap in Ben's house?"

"Your guess is as good as mine," Theodosia said.

Haley's lower lip quivered. "The police should have believed us when we told them we didn't know where that beekeeper stuff came from."

"Yes, they should have. On the other hand, the police have to take every tip seriously. They *are* trying to solve a murder."

Haley studied her carefully. "I thought that's what *you* were doing."

"I was . . . I am . . . but I can't say I've made a whole lot of progress."

"You will, I know you will," Haley said.

Theodosia smiled, thinking, *I'm getting pep talks and encouragement right and left. From Lois, now from Haley. So I should be able to figure things out, right?*

"You're sure you're up to prepping today's luncheon?" Theodosia asked again. "My offer to help still stands."

"I'm going to arrange everything on our big three-tiered trays so I only need help carrying them out." Haley drew a deep breath and added, "So I guess I'll be okay."

"Yes, you will," Theodosia said. She put an arm around Haley and hugged her again. "Because I won't let anything happen to you."

Haley's eyes pooled with tears. "You promise? Pinky-swear?"

"Absolutely." Theodosia stuck out her pinky finger and shook with her. "And if any more police come calling, we'll get in touch with my uncle and let him deal with it."

"The one who's the high test lawyer?"

"That's right."

"I'm starting to feel better," Haley said. "It's nice to know I have people who have my back."

"Remember," Theodosia said gently, "family doesn't always have to mean blood relatives."

Haley wiped at her eyes with the corner of her apron. "Okay," she said in a slightly choked-up voice.

Back out in the tea room, Theodosia checked in with Drayton, who was working behind the front counter.

"Everything okay in the kitchen?" Drayton asked.

"Haley's still a little sniffly, but she'll get through the day."

"You're sure she can manage all the tea sandwiches and goodies?"

"I think she can probably make them with her eyes closed."

"Maybe Miss Dimple can help."

"Haley says no. She wants Miss Dimple working the tables with us."

"Well, if you think we're all set food-wise . . ."

"Haley can handle the kitchen, Drayton. Trust me."

"You know I do." He raised an index finger. "Almost forgot. Another package arrived." He reached around, grabbed a cardboard box, and handed it to Theodosia.

"More cosmetics?" She flipped open the box. "Oh yeah, this is fabulous. Lip gloss and magnetic eyelashes."

Drayton pursed his lips. "Magnetic eyelashes? How would that work? Does one need to have magnetic eyes?"

"Each lash comes in two pieces, an upper and a lower lash. You just stick them over your own eyelashes, kind of like an eyelash sandwich."

"Women actually wear those?"

"Sure. In fact, I'm going to take a couple pairs in to Haley right now. She'll get a big kick out of them."

Drayton looked doubtful. "If you say so."

* * *

At ten o'clock, with the tea shop full of morning customers, Bill Glass came clomping in like an overcaffeinated water buffalo. He was dressed in a shabby green army jacket, khaki pants that were too short and revealed too much of his hairy ankles, and a blue checkered scarf wrapped around his neck. Except for a ruddy complexion that indicated he was still among the living, Theodosia thought he looked like a refugee from *The Walking Dead.*

"Take a look at this," Glass cried. He was brandishing several copies of his magazine, *Shooting Star.* The front page was crinkly and garish, crowded with colored photos, three-inch headlines in red ink, and lots of exclamation points. "I put some really terrific snaps on the cover." He looked at his own handiwork and chortled. "I got the bee guy squirting his crap all over the place, people screaming in terror and jumping up from their tables, and Claxton lying dead on the ground. It's a photo bonanza."

"Oh please," Theodosia said. She snatched one of the newspapers out of his hands and waved it at him. "I hope you realize that your cover story is rude and tasteless. I mean, you've got a dead body . . ."

Standing next to her, Drayton caught a quick look at the photos, then rolled his eyes skyward as if hoping for divine intervention.

"That's what sells papers, cupcake," Glass exclaimed. "And garners tons of advertisers. In journalism, sensationalism is the name of the game."

"Your paper is not technically journalism," Theodosia said. "You publish a scandal rag."

"Or worse," Drayton said under his breath.

Glass was unmoved. "Whatever. Hey . . ." He pointed to the glass pie saver that held a stack of almond-orange and gingerbread scones. "Can I have one of those?"

But Theodosia's attention was suddenly focused on a smaller article she'd noticed on the front page, what newspaper people called a sidebar.

"Don't I deserve a freebie?" Glass wheedled.

Theodosia ignored Glass as she scanned the article. There was a picture of Buck Baldwin. The story detailed how Baldwin had been hastily nominated by his party to step in and take Osgood Claxton's place.

Theodosia thumped the front page of the paper. "Do you know this guy?" she asked Glass. "The politician who's taking Claxton's place as the nominee?"

"'Course I do," Glass said. "I interviewed him myself."

Theodosia only knew Baldwin as the man who'd intervened in the Mignon Merriweather–Ginny Bell fight.

"What can you tell me about him?" Theodosia asked as she lifted the top off the glass pie saver, took out a scone, and handed it to Glass. When he grabbed it immediately, Theodosia had to smile. It was like clicker training a dog.

"Thanks," Glass said, taking a bite. "Mmm, gingerbread. This stuff is like kryptonite to me, can't get enough." He chewed noisily. "Yeah, Baldwin seems like a decent enough guy. Agreed to an interview right away, gave me all the time in the world."

"I imagine since Baldwin's now running for political office it doesn't hurt him to get his name out there."

"There's a good chance Baldwin could *win* that seat in the legislature, considering he was one of Claxton's right-hand men," Glass said.

"Knowing what I do about Claxton's dirty tricks, that doesn't come as a glowing endorsement," Theodosia said. She was suddenly wondering about Buck Baldwin. Could he have had a hand in Claxton's murder? It wouldn't be the first time a nefarious politician had bulldozed a path for himself.

Glass pointed a finger at her. "You know what? You're starting to come across as a very negative person, always looking for the flyspecks in the pepper."

"Flyspecks?" Drayton said, turning toward him. "Not in *this* tea shop."

By eleven o'clock, only two tables of customers remained sipping their tea, while the makeup, manicure, and wig ladies had already arrived to set up their stations. Ten minutes later, Miss Dimple sprinted in, a big smile on her face as she boomed out her morning greeting. Then she stopped dead in her tracks.

"Mercy. It looks like a beauty parlor in here," Miss Dimple said. "Or one of those fancy spas where they wrap your toes in seaweed."

"Welcome to our Glam Girl Tea," Drayton said from behind the front counter.

"Glam and glitz," Miss Dimple said. "I'm amazed at all the great stuff you've got going on here."

Theodosia came over and helped Miss Dimple out of her coat, hung it on the coatrack, and led her to a table that held a display of fancy makeup along with a lighted mirror. "This is Donna, makeup artist extraordinaire, who's going to be doing makeovers for our tea guests today. She's a complete whiz when it comes to eyebrows and contouring cheekbones."

"My bones could use a little contouring," Miss Dimple laughed. "What's left of them anyway."

"And over here, Sammy will be showing our guests the latest in nail lacquers and nail art."

"Wow," Miss Dimple said.

"And at this station we have Camilla, who's brought in a whole bunch of fun wigs to try on."

Camilla, who was sporting a spiky blond wig, pulled it off, then popped on a dark brown bob. "Change your look, change your outlook," she enthused.

"When you said Glam Girl Tea, you really meant glam," Miss Dimple said. She nodded, looked around again, and said, "So how do you want the tables?"

"Pink tablecloths and pink dishes," Theodosia said. "Either the Rose Chintz Pink by Johnson Brothers or the Apple Blossom by Haviland."

"Sounds right to me," Miss Dimple said. "But my vote would be for the Haviland."

"You have my blessing. And when you're done setting tables, there's a bucket of pink tea roses in my office that needs to be arranged in crystal vases."

"Got it."

"And we'll have swag bags filled with makeup and perfume samples for all our guests."

From across the room, Drayton cleared his throat. "Though I don't see the swag actually bagged yet."

"I'm jumping on that right now," Theodosia said. "Oh, and Miss Dimple, Haley told me she didn't need any help in the kitchen. But maybe you could sort of pop in now and then to lend a hand?"

"Will do," Miss Dimple said.

Theodosia rushed into her office, set up a dozen pink bags on her desk, and placed another two dozen on the floor. Then she started filling them with goodies, assembly-line style. It was great to see how many samples they'd been gifted by both local retailers and wholesalers. There were little packets of moisturizer, mini lip glosses and mascaras, tiny vials of perfume, and even eyebrow pencils, false eye lashes, and cleansing tissues. All she'd had to do was make a few phone calls and ask, all pretty-please-like. And her donors had been happy to help out because they knew it was smart product placement.

Once Theodosia had finished, she made a half dozen trips carrying the swag bags out into the tea room and putting one at each place setting. While she did that, Miss Dimple arranged the pink tea roses and set the bouquets on the table.

When everything seemed ready, barely ten minutes before their guests were scheduled to arrive, Theodosia stepped back and took a careful look at the tea room.

It looked fabulous. Warm, inviting, sparkling like a little jewel box. And Miss Dimple was right! The place *did* look like an upscale spa. Theodosia beamed at the idea. With Haley's food, Drayton's special tea blend, and the three makeover stations, this should—knock on wood—turn out to be a fabulous tea luncheon.

Miss Dimple strolled over to Theodosia carrying the last of the tea rose arrangements.

"Tables look okay?" she asked.

"Perfection," Theodosia said. She glanced at Miss Dimple, did a double take, and couldn't help but chuckle. "What did you do? Why do you look so different?"

Miss Dimple grinned from ear to ear. "Haley showed me how to put on a pair of those magnetic eyelashes. Do you like them?" She gazed at Theodosia and then at Drayton, batting her lashes.

"Madame," Drayton said, "you're a regular femme fatale."

20

⚜

When the big hand and the little hand both converged on twelve, the floodgates opened. Theodosia stood at the front door, welcoming her guests, shooing them in to Miss Dimple, who led them to their various tables. And even though the guests arrived in a big rush, it was like herding cats to get them to finally sit down. Everyone (everyone!) wanted to either try on a wig, get a little nail art done, or experiment with a dab of makeup.

Theodosia, who was no slouch in the glam department, decided to join them. She grabbed a short blond wig, pulled it over her mass of auburn hair (no easy feat!), and strolled to the center of the room.

Where she was greeted with oohs, ahs, and a spatter of applause.

"Love the blond hair!" Jill cried out.

"Got another one of those for me?" Kristen asked.

"You look like Sharon Stone," Linda hooted.

Theodosia smiled, patted her new 'do and said, "Welcome, fellow glam girls, to the Indigo Tea Shop."

Which elicited another round of applause.

"Today we're going to be a tiny bit informal," Theodosia said. "Since you'll probably be moving around the tea room, enjoying makeovers and trying out lots of new things, we're going to serve our tea luncheon on lovely three-tiered trays."

That was the cue for Miss Dimple and Haley to emerge from the kitchen, each of them carrying one of the showy, goody-laden trays.

"Top tier here are scones," Theodosia said, pointing. "Gingerbread scones and almond-orange scones along with bowls of Devonshire cream and honey butter. Your middle tier is where you'll find your tea sandwiches. What did you fix for us today, Haley?"

Haley stepped forward and said, "Crab salad tea sandwiches on sourdough bread, turkey and Gouda tea sandwiches on potato bread, and cucumber and cream cheese on rye."

"On the bottom tier," Theodosia said, "you'll find an assortment of sinfully rich deserts. There are brownie bites, lemon bars, and French macarons. Oh, and do you see those glistening pink and yellow flowers sprinkled among the various treats? Those are candied edible flowers. Pansies dipped in egg white and hand-painted with superfine castor sugar."

"This is so much to take in," one of the women sighed. "Those three-tiered trays practically groan with goodness."

"Oh, but there's more," Theodosia said. "Besides complimentary makeovers at our three stations, you'll find swag bags at each place setting that are filled with makeup and perfume samples." She paused. "Then, of course, there's tea. Because we are, after all, a tea shop." She glanced in Drayton's direction. "Drayton, if you will?"

Drayton strode to the center of the room, looking very proper in his starched white shirt, tweed jacket, and bright yellow bow tie.

"For your teatime enjoyment, we'll be serving two distinct brews," Drayton said. "The first is called Glam Girl Ginger and is a blend of Sencha green tea, ginger, lemon, and honey. The second is called Precious Plum and consists of black tea with hints of plum and citrus." Drayton paused, gave a slight bow, and spun on his heels.

After that it was a delicious free-for-all. Some of the women dashed immediately to the makeover stations, while others quickly helped themselves to the delights of the tea trays.

Theodosia and Miss Dimple made the rounds, pouring tea, answering questions, and chatting with their guests.

"Where did the idea for a three-tiered tray come from?" one of the guests asked Theodosia.

"We know that cake stands date back to the early sixteen hundreds in Britain," Theodosia said. "Then, as afternoon tea became more popular, the iconic three-tiered tray evolved."

Another guest asked, "Which type of tea has the least amount of caffeine?"

"That would be a tisane," Theodosia responded, "which is mostly a fruit infusion. White tea, which is minimally processed, offers a small amount of caffeine, green tea is a little higher, while black tea is the highest in caffeine."

Drayton remained busy at the front counter brewing additional pots of tea. When Theodosia scampered to the counter to grab a refill, she said, "It's going well, don't you think?"

"Swimmingly well," Drayton said. "You had a lovely idea. The glam idea sounded a trifle over the top when you first presented it to me, but now that I see how it's unfolding, I'm impressed."

"Thank you, sir, now if we could just . . ."

Theodosia paused as the front door swung open.

A late guest? No, all the seats are taken.

And that's when Lamar Lucket strolled in. Dressed in a sharp black sharkskin suit, a powder blue shirt, and a dark blue tie, he looked more like an unsavory banker than an unsavory politician.

Theodosia immediately ran over to head him off.

Lucket saw her coming, stopped in his tracks, and said, "Miss Browning, I believe you changed your hair." He spoke in a manner that was a little imperious, a little bit presumptuous.

"It's a wig," Theodosia said, patting her head somewhat self-consciously. *Why are you here?* she wondered.

"Cute." Lucket leaned to one side and peered around her, taking in the tea room filled with women. But that didn't slow down his approach. "I've heard such wonderful things about your tea shop, I thought I'd stop by and see for myself."

"Unfortunately, we're closed to accommodate a private party right now. But if you'd care to stop back another time . . ."

Lucket raised a hand. "Yes, I see you're quite busy. But perhaps I could trouble you for some takeout?"

"A scone and a cup of tea?" Drayton asked from behind the counter.

Lucket squinted at Drayton. "Sure, why not?" he said as Drayton immediately grabbed a takeout cup and got busy filling it with tea.

Bless you, Drayton, Theodosia thought as she hastily packaged up three of their almond-orange scones for Lucket.

Lucket watched her carefully, then said, "You know, I'm keeping my eye on you."

Theodosia turned to face him. "Why would that be?" *Please just hurry up and leave.*

"I don't mean that in a threatening way," Lucket said, in a slightly threatening tone of voice. "I was thinking that maybe you could cater one of your fancy teas at my hotel some time."

Theodosia favored Lucket with a bright smile as Drayton slid a takeout cup toward him and said, "No charge." Then Theodosia handed Lucket his bag of scones and said, "I'm sure your own food-service professionals can manage just fine."

"I'll take that as a no," Lucket chuckled.

"It's our busy time," Theodosia said as she followed him to the door and shut it behind him. Then watched as Lucket climbed into a dark green Jaguar and sped away.

An hour later, with Lucket's visit over and forgotten, the mood in the tea shop was even more laid-back. Drayton had switched to a chamomile and white tea blend for their guests (which meant *très* relaxation) and most of them had already enjoyed multiple sessions of trying on wigs, indulging in quickie manicures, and getting touch-ups on their makeup.

Theodosia stood behind the counter, nibbling a scone, ready to cash out those guests who'd been busy shopping and had selected tea accoutrements from her various displays.

The tranquil mood was suddenly broken as Delaine rushed in, threw up her hands in a helpless, hapless gesture, and yelped, "Where's Theo? I need Theo!"

"Right here," Theodosia said, stepping out from behind the counter.

Delaine, who was a trifle nearsighted but abhorred wearing glasses, squinted at her and said, "You don't *look* like Theo."

Theodosia pulled the wig off her head, letting her masses of auburn hair tumble down. "See? It's really me."

Delaine gave a surprised gasp, then grasped her arm and

shook it. "Thank goodness. Because I need your help. *Mignon* needs your help."

"For what? What's going on?"

"Mignon's shop has been vandalized!" Delaine cried. "And is it ever *awful*!"

"Have the police been called?"

"Of course they have." Delaine hopped up and down, barely able to control her emotions. "But you still have to come right this minute, Theo. I know you're the *only one* who can figure this out."

Theodosia looked around. "But I'm in the middle of . . ."

"Now!" Delaine screamed with such volume she caused the overhead chandelier to tinkle and sway. "We need your help *now*!"

"Um . . ."

"Go ahead," Drayton told her in a calm voice. "I'll wrap things up here."

"Theo?" Delaine's eyes were wide and pleading. *"Please?"*

"Okay," Theodosia said. "Give me a minute to grab my purse."

21

⁓✤⁓

Delaine drove way too fast (and rather badly) at the wheel of her BMW as they raced over to Mignon's shop on King Street. From outside the place looked quaint and adorable, a tall, narrow redbrick building with an azure blue door and a wooden sign above the front window that proclaimed BELLE DE JOUR in large embellished gold letters. Underneath, it read, GIFTS, CLOTHING, AND EPHEMERA À LA FRANÇAISE. Two miniature Eiffel towers flanked the doorway, and the distinctive tricolor French flag waved and snapped from a pole above the shop.

Inside was another story.

The place should have been charming and gorgeous but now it was a mess. Black and red loops of spray-painted graffiti stained the walls and the merchandise was in disarray and strewn everywhere. The shop looked positively ransacked, with stacks of T-shirts dumped right along with boxes of French chocolates, trays of jewelry, and crystal goblets. A heavy Directoire table was overturned, French stationery had been tram-

pled, and tubes of pink and red Bourjois lipstick lay scattered
and broken across a Chinese rug.

But the walls were the real horror. They were covered in
hostile scrawls and symbols that included numbers, letters, and
nonsense words.

"Mignon!" Delaine cried as she and Theodosia rushed past
the damage.

"Oh, honey, you came!" Mignon cried, throwing herself into
Delaine's arms, where they both burst into tears and clung to
each other, quaking like aspen leaves in a thunderstorm.

"And I brought Theodosia," Delaine finally managed to
squeak out. "She'll know what to do."

Actually, Theodosia *didn't* know what to do, but after taking a careful look around, she discovered a uniformed officer
standing at the back of the shop, just outside a small office. He
was writing on a pad of paper and talking on his cell phone.

When the officer hung up, Theodosia stepped in his direction and said, "You got the callout?" His nametag read J. BARR
and he was young, early thirties, tall and lanky, with an earnest,
almost boyish, face.

Officer Barr looked up, said, "Yes ma'am," in a pleasant tone
of voice. "Fact is, I was cruising down the alley, investigating
what might have been a dumpster fire last night, when I got
the call." He twiddled his pencil and pointed toward the back
of the store. "Cruiser's parked in back."

"So you were here right away," Theodosia said.

"Mm, about four minutes after the 911 call came in to dispatch."

Mignon turned away from Delaine and said, "It took for-
ever!"

There was a commotion at the front door and then two more

uniformed officers walked in. One of them looked around, took off his hat, and said, "What a mess."

Which prompted Mignon to throw herself into Delaine's arms again and bleat out several more high-pitched sobs.

Theodosia wasn't sure if Mignon was truly upset or caught up in a kind of pervasive hysteria. But she knew that only Mignon could give these officers the critical information they needed.

"Mignon," Theodosia said in a sharp voice.

"What?" With her face buried in Delaine's shoulder Mignon's voice was low and muffled.

"We need your help," Theodosia said.

Mignon turned, wiping tears from her cheeks as her eye makeup streamed down in dark rivulets. "How am *I* supposed to help?"

"These officers need to know exactly what happened," Theodosia said.

Officer Barr said, "We really need you to try and answer a few questions, ma'am."

"Go ahead, honey, tell them your tale of woe," Delaine prompted. She pulled a hankie from her purse and swabbed at Mignon's face, smearing her makeup and only making things worse.

Mignon let Delaine dab some more, then grimaced and gave a reluctant, "I suppose." She sighed deeply, tried to pull herself together, and said, "What happened was—I'd just returned from having lunch with a friend." *Sniffle.* "But when I opened the front door, certainly not expecting anyone to be inside, there he was—this madman! And my beautiful boutique was in shambles!"

"So it was a male intruder that you surprised?" one of the newly arrived officers asked. His nametag said P. BARRON.

Mignon nodded tearfully. "I'm pretty sure it was."

"And he didn't harm you in any way?" Officer Barron asked.

Mignon shook her head and glanced at Delaine for reassurance. "He kind of shoved me aside and ran outside."

"Scary," Delaine said.

"Any idea who it might have been?" Officer Barr asked. "Ever seen him before?"

"I don't think so," Mignon said. She turned to Delaine and said, "At first I thought maybe that awful Ginny Bell might be involved—well, she *still* could be—but I know this wasn't her. Ginny's about the size of an ugly stick bug and this person was larger. Stronger. And he wore a mask."

"What kind of mask?" Theodosia asked. "Like from a Halloween costume?"

"Like a bandanna," Mignon said. "A dark blue one. Over the lower half of his face. And he was also wearing . . ." Mignon touched the top of her head. "A cap. A baseball cap that was pulled way down so you could barely see his eyes." She shuddered. "But I could see them drilling into me and they looked mean."

"What about his clothing?" Officer Barron asked.

Mignon shook her head. "I don't know. I was so stunned, so terrified, that I didn't know *how* to react, least of all take a detailed inventory of his wardrobe." Now she sounded both angry and petulant.

"We're just trying to help, ma'am," Officer Barr said.

"I know, I know. It's just that I was so darned *scared*," Mignon cried.

Delaine put an arm around her. "Of course you were, sweetheart. You went through a terrible ordeal." She glanced at Theodosia. "Theo, what do you think?"

"I don't know about the vandalism to the merchandise," Theodosia said, "but the graffiti on the walls is a little strange."

"You think so?" Delaine said.

All three officers looked at Theodosia.

"I kind of hate to say this, but it's slightly reminiscent of a local artist named Booker," Theodosia said.

"How do you know this, ma'am?" Officer Barr asked.

"Because I've seen Booker's work," Theodosia said. "Booker does murals on local buildings as well as large paintings on canvas. Most of them are done in an aggressive graffiti style."

The three officers exchanged looks, then Officer Barr said, "We're going to bring in an investigator. One of our detectives." He turned to Mignon. "Mrs. Claxton, we'd like you to stick around and speak with him when he gets here."

"Where would I go?" Mignon screeched. "Excuse me, but in case you haven't noticed, this is like a toxic waste dump. I have to start cleaning immediately. Monday was supposed to be my grand opening." She suddenly looked lost and helpless. "Now I don't know what to do."

"First things first," Theodosia said, "you have to change your locks."

"And make sure they're better, stronger locks," Officer Barr said. "That one on your back door was busted clean through."

"We can give you the name of a reputable locksmith," Officer Barron said.

"Do you have anyone who can help you clean up?" Delaine asked Mignon. Clearly she was antsy to get going now that the initial shock had worn off.

"My two employees," Mignon said. "Sasha and Joyce. They're brand-new, but I can give them a call."

"Good thinking, dear," Delaine said. She looked over at Theodosia. "Theo? Any other ideas before we take off?"

"We'd like to know more about this artist Booker," Officer Barr said.

"Last I heard he was being represented by the Imago Gallery," Theodosia said. "I'm sure if you spoke with them . . ."

Barr nodded and said, "Thank you, I know where that gallery is located. We'll for sure follow up on that information."

"Oh, and I know Booker also hangs out at the Arts Alliance over on Bay Street," Theodosia said.

"Theo?" Delaine gave a stiff nod toward the door.

But Theodosia was back to surveying the graffiti-covered walls. Wondering if Booker was responsible for this frenzied vandalism. And if he was, what motivated him to cause such wanton destruction? Was he trying to scare Mignon or warn her? If that was the case, did it mean that Booker *had* killed Claxton? Or, as Mignon had surmised, was Ginny Bell involved? Could Ginny Bell, in her hatred for Mignon and Claxton, have *encouraged* Booker to do this?

Theodosia studied the angry whorls and dripping letters. For some reason they didn't look exactly right to her. Had someone imitated Booker's work? Plagiarized it? Because the more she looked at it, the more it *felt* like a bad copy.

Of course, there was only one way to be sure.

22

Since the Imago Gallery was only a five-block walk from Belle de Jour, Theodosia assured Delaine she didn't need a ride and that she was fine walking back to the tea shop.

"Are you positive?" Delaine asked even though she'd already jumped in her car and was gunning the engine.

"No problem. You go on."

Theodosia wasn't about to tell Delaine that she wasn't going directly back to the Indigo Tea Shop. That she was taking a side trip to the Imago Gallery instead. Because right now she was feeling a strong imperative to look at Booker's work—if some of his pieces were still there—and decide for herself if he might have had a hand in trashing Mignon's shop. She was also curious to see if there'd been any sort of improvement in the gallery's financial picture.

But when she arrived at the Imago Gallery, Holly and Philip were still bemoaning the gallery's ongoing plight.

"Another artist pulled out," Holly told Theodosia. She looked weepy but cute, dressed in a hot pink T-shirt and filmy light pink skirt that looked almost like a ballet skirt. "That's the tenth one. Well, actually, this one was a photographer." Holly gestured to where Philip was busy taking photos down from the wall, wrapping them in bubble wrap, and then placing them in a large crate.

"I need to talk to you," Theodosia said to Holly.

"Sure," Holly said in a distracted tone. "Come on back to my office. I need a cup of java to keep me going."

Holly's jam-packed office smelled of burned coffee, oil paint, and a top note of Chanel No. 5. As Holly poured herself coffee from a funky-looking urn, Theodosia told her about the vandalism at Mignon's shop. And how the graffiti on the walls reminded her of Booker's art.

"Oh no!" Holly set her mug down and clapped a hand over her mouth. Her eyes widened, then she pulled her hand away and said, "Do you think it was actually Booker?"

"The police—and Mignon for that matter—don't know who's responsible."

"And you didn't say anything about Booker?"

"Actually, I did," Theodosia said. "I pretty much had to tell the officers that the graffiti was somewhat similar to Booker's work."

"Which means the police will be contacting me." Holly's mouth turned down. "Again."

"The damage to Mignon's shop was fairly severe. Which is why I wanted to stop here and give you a heads-up. Also, I'd like to take another look at Booker's work." Theodosia hesitated. "Do you still have any of his paintings?"

"I think we might. One or two anyway. They're . . ." Holly seemed beyond frazzled. "They're out in the gallery."

They walked into the gallery just as Philip placed the last of the photos in his crate. He looked up, dusted his hands together, and said, "Well, that does it for Bobby Rousseau. He may be a great landscape photographer but we won't be seeing his work anytime soon."

"Philip, Theodosia needs to take a look at one of Booker's pieces," Holly said. "Can you pull out that really big painting? The blue one with the crazy wolf drawing?"

"Sure," Philip said. He ducked behind a tall bronze sculpture of a sand crane, ran his hand across the edges of four large paintings that were leaning up against a wall, then tapped one and slid it out. "This is . . . um, one of Booker's better, more saleable pieces."

"Can you pull it all the way out?" Holly asked.

Philip pulled the six-by-eight-foot canvas out, manhandled it awkwardly, said, "Oops," then finally got it leaned up against the wall. "There you go," he said. Then he looked at Theodosia and said, "Are you thinking about buying one of Booker's pieces?" He sounded hopeful.

Theodosia quickly explained to Philip about the vandalism that had just taken place at Belle de Jour. And how the boutique was owned by Mignon Merriweather, Claxton's wife.

"Oh my Lord!" Philip cried. "Do you think there's some sort of connection? I mean, first Claxton is killed and now his wife's shop is vandalized."

"I don't know," Theodosia said. "There could be. But the weird thing is—the damaging graffiti on Mignon's walls struck me as having a similar look and feel to Booker's work."

Philip looked completely stricken. "Oh no," he said. "No. Booker wouldn't . . . he couldn't . . . at least I don't *think* he would." He peered at Theodosia, who was studying the painting closely and said, "What do you think? Is the iconography the same?"

Theodosia studied the painting. It was a series of snarling

blue wolves, looking almost like paper dolls strung together. Painted over the wolves were numbers, letters, and symbols. It was a striking piece that would fit beautifully into a supermodern home.

"It's not quite the same," Theodosia said slowly. "This has focus and a rare kind of beauty, while the vandalism at Mignon's boutique was practically mindless, more like a cheap imitation of Booker's style."

"So that's good, right?" Holly said. She looked even more twitchy than she had before.

"I suppose so," Theodosia said. "Unless . . ."

"Unless what?" Holly asked.

"Unless Booker changed up his style for the vandalism. I don't know why he'd do that except to throw the police off his trail."

"Or maybe it was a deliberate provocation?" Philip asked. "Booker was saying, 'Look at me, I can get away with this?'"

"I suppose that's a possibility," Theodosia said. She gazed at the blue wolf painting again and said, "Have either of you talked to Booker lately?" This prompted Holly and Philip to exchange nervous glances.

"What?" Theodosia said. Something was clearly worrying them.

"The weird thing is, Booker seems to have disappeared," Holly said.

Theodosia nodded. This didn't come as news to her. Riley had mentioned the same thing earlier today.

"We've been thinking that Booker might have gone away on a kind of self-imposed retreat," Holly said.

"What makes you think he's on retreat?" Theodosia asked.

"For one thing, he does that now and then," Holly said. "Goes off to think or meditate."

"Contemplate his navel," Philip said.

"The other thing is, I tried to call him because we actually have a check for him," Holly said. "One of his paintings sold. I called him late yesterday and again today and left a message but he hasn't responded."

"Is that unusual?" Theodosia asked.

"Booker basically lives hand to mouth, so yes," Holly said. "When we have a check for Booker he's usually Johnny on the spot, practically beating down the door."

"And there's for sure no sign of him?" Theodosia asked.

"Philip even drove over and checked Booker's place. Knocked on the door but he wasn't there. He talked to a guy who was working out back, another artist, who hinted that Booker might have taken off to parts unknown." Holly wrinkled her nose and threw another quick glance at Philip.

"Holly," Theodosia said. "Do you have any idea where these parts unknown might be?"

Holly gazed at Philip. "Should I tell her?"

"I think you pretty much have to," Philip said.

"What's going on?" Theodosia asked.

"Booker supposedly has a place on Little Clam Island. It's one of those tiny islands off the tip of James Island. Anyway, he talked about having a place there, maybe still does . . . a kind of studio. Well, the way he tells it, it's really more of an old fishing shack. There's no electricity or anything and it's way out in the boonies. There's an overgrown trail that weaves in through the swamp, but it's probably easier to reach by boat." She hunched her shoulders forward and gave a shiver. "I think there are probably creepy-crawlies on that island . . . you know, snakes."

Philip stared at Theodosia. "You did the right thing, telling the police that the vandalism was similar to Booker's work.

Even if he's not responsible for tearing up that shop, maybe they can find him, get him some help."

"Booker needs help?" Theodosia said.

"He's been known to drink a bit," Philip said. He mimed tipping back a glass and drinking it. "Well, more than a bit. Sometimes he goes on these terrible ragers."

Holly was suddenly standing there, arms at her sides, head bent forward as silent tears streamed down her cheeks.

"*Holly*," Philip said. "What, honey?"

"It's one thing piled on top of another," Holly said, her voice quavering. "I feel like the world is collapsing around me. First the shooting at the tea party, then artists started abandoning the gallery—to say nothing of our customers. Now this Booker thing. To cap it all off, I've got Jeremy Slade banging away at me day and night. He put two hundred thousand dollars into this gallery and, with everything spiraling out of control, I have no idea how we're ever going to recover that kind of money, let along pay him back."

"Holly, business *will* turn around," Theodosia said. "You're smart and resourceful and have a unique talent for discovering up and coming artists." Her heart went out to the poor girl. She knew Holly deserved so much more than this. Holly was kind, sweet, and perpetually hopeful. At least she had been up until a few days ago.

"You know what I'm going to do?" Philip said.

Holly shook her head and wiped at her tears, as if to bring herself back to the here and now. She managed a weak smile and said, "What?"

"I'm going to put my chef's hat on tonight and create a superspecial dinner for you." Philip turned his gaze on Theodosia. "And for Theodosia as well. I'd like you and Drayton to be my special guests." He flashed an encouraging smile. "Would you both join Holly and me for dinner tonight at the Boldt Hole? Around five-ish, before my regular dinner orders start coming in?" He reached out, grabbed Holly's hand, and squeezed it. "We'll all sit down together, enjoy some good food and wine. Maybe toast to better times?"

"That sounds wonderful," Theodosia said. "We'd love to come." After all, how could she say no to an invitation like that?

Back at the Indigo Tea Shop, the tables and chairs had been put right, the glam squads had packed up and left, and only two tables remained occupied.

"A slow afternoon?" Theodosia said to Drayton.

"Not all that slow. How did it go at Belle de Jour? Was the disaster as earth shattering as Delaine made it out to be?"

"It was pretty bad." Theodosia quickly filled Drayton in about the masked intruder who'd broken in, graffitied the walls, and basically upset the apple cart.

"And you say the scrawled script and symbols were similar to Booker's work?"

"Similar but not exactly alike," Theodosia said.

"A copycat?"

"Maybe. Except I can't figure out why that would be."

"To make Booker look guilty? To point the police in his direction?"

"They're already pointed in his direction," Theodosia said. "Except now nobody can find him."

"That's weird," Drayton said.

"What's weird?" Haley asked. She'd wandered out of the kitchen and was standing a few feet away, looking tired and giving them a questioning look.

"The fact that Mignon's shop has been vandalized," Theodosia said. She didn't want to give Haley too much information and upset her all over again.

"Oh," Haley said. "Is everything okay now?"

"I'm sure it will be soon," Drayton said. "So . . . a fabulous luncheon today, Haley, thanks to your exceptional skill in the kitchen."

Haley waved a hand. "That was easy-peasy. But I've been thinking about tomorrow . . ."

"And?" Drayton said.

"I hate to bring this up, but we have all sorts of honey left over," Haley said.

"You mean honey from last Sunday's tea?" Theodosia said.

"Yup. Jars and jars of it," Haley said. "So I was thinking about doing a honey-themed luncheon. Nothing super fancy because I know it's too late to advertise. But I thought it would be fun to incorporate honey into a few of my dishes."

"That's a wonderful idea," Theodosia said. "And we could actually still promote it. By word of mouth, anyway. I'll phone a few of the nearby B and Bs and tell them we're doing a special Honey Tea. There's always a good chance they'll send some of their guests our way."

"I love that idea," Haley said. "The neat thing about being in the Historic District is having all sorts of small businesses clustered around us. We can all work together and benefit from a kind of reciprocity."

"A quid pro quo," Drayton agreed.

Then Haley smiled, hunched her shoulders forward, let out a wide yawn, and said, "Tired."

"Then hustle your bustle upstairs," Theodosia said. "Chill out with your little cat Teacake in your apartment and take it easy. Lord knows you deserve it. Especially after last night." She peered at Haley. "Did you talk to Ben today?"

"He called me a little while ago," Haley said.

"And he's doing okay?" Theodosia said.

"No harm done?" Drayton asked.

"He's still angry," Haley said. "But I guess he'll get over it." Then she yawned again, gave a tired wave, and wandered back into the kitchen.

"Can you believe she worked the entire day after last night's chaos?" Drayton asked.

"Yes, I can," Theodosia said. "Because Haley's got moxie."

Drayton smiled. "There's a word you don't hear much anymore."

"I'll tell you someone else who knows how to hang tough—and that's Philip Boldt. He's not only trying to get his restaurant up and running, he's constantly supporting and cheerleading for Holly."

"A fine young man," Drayton said.

"Actually, that fine young man invited us to dinner tonight at his ghost kitchen."

Drayton frowned. "What are you talking about? You mean the place is haunted?"

"No, it's because the Boldt Hole isn't officially open yet. So Philip is making do with a limited takeout menu. People stop by a window in this cute little back alley and pick up their orders—thus a ghost kitchen. Or customers can place their order through delivery services like Grubhub or Uber Eats."

"Ah, like a drive-in," Drayton said. "But we'd be dining at a table?"

"That would be the general idea, yes."

"Sounds good. Count me in."

Theodosia looked at her watch. "We should take off in another ten or fifteen minutes. But first I need to make a phone call."

"Calling Riley? To see how the Claxton investigation is going?" Drayton asked.

"Actually, this is a just-in-case kind of phone call."

"Sounds mysterious."

Theodosia smiled. "It kind of is."

23

Theodosia drove down Broad Street, then over to Queen, her sound system oozing moody jazz as they headed for the Boldt Hole.

"This is nice," Drayton said.

"You mean the music?"

"Really the whole package. Music, fine dining, good company."

"Let me ask you something, Drayton."

"Hmm?"

"Holly told me that Jeremy Slade made a two-hundred-thousand-dollar investment in the Imago Gallery and that they'd run through most of it."

"Goodness, no wonder Mr. Slade is upset."

"But here's the thing, Drayton. Two hundred grand is a whole lot of jack, don't you think?"

"Indeed it is."

"But what did Holly actually *use* all that money for? What

has she got to *show* for it? I mean, from the way she's been talking, it's as if the money's all been spent."

"Maybe it has been," Drayton said.

"Spent on what? Think about this. We charged them three thousand dollars for the catering. Rent for their gallery space must be, what? Maybe four thousand a month?"

"Something like that."

"So where's the rest of the money?" Theodosia asked. "Where'd it go? What was it spent on?"

"Party invitations? Liquor?"

Theodosia looked over at him and raised an eyebrow.

"I see what you mean," Drayton said. "Can't you just come out and ask Holly?"

"Not that it's any of my business, but I'm going to try to do exactly that at dinner tonight. But only if there's a good opening."

Theodosia pulled up in front of the Boldt Hole, where parking wasn't a problem since it was still early and most customers of the soon-to-be-open restaurant came in through the back alley.

"Here we are," she said.

They got out and gazed at the front of the restaurant. It was done in a modified Tudor style with brickwork, stucco walls, and a steeply pitched gable roof. The lower part of the exterior was accented with window boxes that held some kind of prickly greenery. A dark blue awning over rough-hewn double doors proclaimed THE BOLDT HOLE. Underneath were the words FINE DINING, WINE, AND MIRTH.

"Catchy," Drayton said.

"Philip does have a laid-back sense of humor," Theodosia said. "I only wish some of it would rub off on Holly."

"I hear you. She does seem a bit twitchy." Drayton put his hand on the front door and pulled it open for Theodosia to step through. They both walked in and found . . .

Darkness.

The interior of the restaurant was dark as pitch with only a faint bluish light shining at the back of the place. As their eyes grew accustomed to the dimness, they could see chairs stacked on top of tables.

"Hello? Is anybody here?" Theodosia called out.

"Are we even in the right place?" Drayton asked. He peered into the darkness. "This really is a phantom kitchen."

"Ghost kitchen," Theodosia said. "But you're right. It does seem awfully deserted."

Just as they were about to give up, a door flew open in back. Then there was the patter of feet and Holly came running out, waving her arms.

"Apologies," she squealed. "I didn't realize the front door was unlocked. We figured you'd come in through the alley. That's where everyone always comes to grab their orders."

"Of course," Theodosia said. "Because it's a ghost kitchen."

"That's also deserted," Drayton said as he swept an arm to indicate the darkened restaurant.

From what little they could see, the chairs were Bentwood style, the tables a lovely light birch. Underfoot were heart-pine floors covered in a few spots with faded but still gorgeous Oriental rugs. At the far end of the room was a glass-enclosed, faintly illuminated wine cellar stocked floor to ceiling with bottles of wine.

"The restaurant's dark because Philip is still waiting for his liquor license to come through," Holly explained. "Once that happens, probably this week, he'll be able to have a grand opening and this place will be—knock on wood—packed with diners."

"Philip must be thrilled," Theodosia asked.

"He's counting the hours," Holly said, "until he's able to realize his lifelong dream of running his own restaurant."

"I believe that's our chef now," Theodosia said as the door to the kitchen swung open, backlighting and silhouetting Philip in the doorway.

"Greetings," Philip called. "Come on into the kitchen, where our dinner table's all set up." He chuckled. "Where we'll be able to actually see each other."

They pushed their way through the swinging door and emerged into a brightly lit, perfectly designed chef's kitchen. An enormous commercial Vulcan gas range dominated one entire wall, and several stock pots simmered on its burners. A nearby stainless steel counter was staffed by two sous chefs, who were busy prepping ingredients for upcoming orders. Stainless steel racks held all manner of pots, pans, and utensils.

"Wow," Theodosia said. "Professional."

"Like a set for a TV cooking show," Drayton said.

"That's right," Philip said. "All the latest and greatest just like the big boys." He ushered them into a cozy annex where a table for four was set with candles, flowers, flatware, and sparkling wineglasses. "You're going to have to excuse me while I jump up and down to help with the various courses," he added. "My sous chefs have most everything prepped and ready, but I prefer to do the finishing touches myself."

"Please," Drayton said, looking delighted. "Finishing touch away."

The dinner wasn't just divine, it was an eye opener as to Philip's prodigious skills in the kitchen. The starter was a crispy zucchini salad lightly dressed with tomato vinaigrette. Theodosia ate it, loved it, and scraped her plate judiciously, dying for more. But Philip had warned them there was much more deliciousness to come.

"Just wonderful," Drayton proclaimed. Then his eyes widened as Philip brought out their second course of grilled avocado with basil pesto. "Amazing," he said upon tasting his first bite. "So fresh and zingy. Really tickles the taste buds."

"And you say you *didn't* attend culinary school?" Theodosia asked.

"Philip's self-taught," Holly said proudly.

"Well, I did apprentice at the Morning Dove in Savannah, Georgia," Philip said. "Tried to absorb everything I could from Chef Cooper, their chef de cuisine."

"I do believe you were successful," Drayton said, nibbling away.

But it was Philip's main course of grilled steak with roasted peppers and fingerling potatoes that blew them all away.

"What a treat," Theodosia said as she stabbed a tasty morsel of steak with her fork. "Like eating at the chef's table."

"Because it *is* the chef's table," Holly laughed.

"Everything is amazing," Drayton said. "And this wine . . . absolutely superb." He reached for the bottle, scanned the label, and gave a knowing smile. "Of course it is, because we're drinking a Château Latour ninety-six."

"I'm impressed," Theodosia said. "You must have stocked your wine cellar with only the best, Philip."

"Only the best," Philip agreed.

"Where do you . . . how do you source such fresh ingredients?" Drayton asked.

"My two main producers are located just south of here near Osborn," Philip said. "Frog Hollow Farm grows organic vegetables and raises Muscovy ducks that lay the most perfect eggs.

Of course, the ducks are fine eating, too. Muscovy ducks are the only ducks not descended from a mallard. They're closer to a goose, actually, but are ninety-eight percent fat-free."

"All I can say is wow," Theodosia said.

"As for sourcing my beef, the Red Hat Cattle Ranch is right next door. They crossbreed Japanese Wagyu cattle with Black Angus cattle, with the result being an American hybrid called Wangus." He pointed to their plates. "That's what you've been dining on."

"This is fascinating," Theodosia said. "Talking to you is like unraveling all sorts of wonderful foodie mysteries."

Philip gazed at her. "But not half as exciting as what you do. Or should I say doing. I know you've put in a lot of effort on Holly's behalf to try and figure out this Claxton murder." He lifted his wineglass in a salute. "And I want to thank you for it."

"Theodosia's been a real lifesaver," Holly said.

Theodosia shook her head. "No, I must confess I'm feeling somewhat stymied right now. Just too many suspects, but not a whole lot of evidence that would single out one and lead to an arrest."

"You'll find something sooner or later," Philip said. "I know you will." He reached over, grabbed Holly's hand, and squeezed it. "I can feel it, can't you, sweetheart?"

"I can, I really can," Holly said. She finally looked relaxed and almost happy.

Philip stood up. "And on that final note, I'm afraid I must step back into my lair. Besides preparing our regular Thursday night menu, I've been asked to create some light snacks for one of our regular customers over on Archdale Street. They're hosting a small party tonight and asked me to cater what they're calling a light supper buffet."

"What will you be preparing?" Drayton asked.

"Grilled eggplant pizza, squash ravioli, sautéed rock shrimp, and, for the pièce de résistance, chocolate tiramisu."

"Tiramisu? Be still my heart," Drayton said as he stood up from the table, happily sated.

Theodosia, who had a ferocious sweet tooth, simply said, "Yum."

Philip came around the table and pulled out Theodosia's chair for her. "C'mon," he said. "I'll walk the two of you to the door."

As they all strolled through the darkened restaurant, Drayton hung back, talking with Holly.

"She'll talk an arm and a leg when it comes to art," Philip said to Theodosia as he glanced back.

"Then she's met her match in Drayton," Theodosia said. "He's crazy about art *and* antiques."

As they pushed open the front door, light from an overhead streetlamp spilled down, spotlighting the two of them. Ten seconds later, Drayton and Holly emerged.

"Wow," Holly said to Theodosia. "In this light your hair looks like it's burnished with silver."

Theodosia reached up to pat her hair. "Except when the humidity is on the rise, like it is tonight, it seems to have a mind of its own."

"Still, it looks pretty," Holly said.

Theodosia patted her hair again, this time a little self-consciously. "Pretty hard to deal with sometimes."

24

꙰

On the way home, Theodosia rolled down her window and inhaled the sweet scent of magnolia in the air. They were driving down Legare, which was not only lined with mansions, but verdant with palm trees, magnolias, and jessamine. That was the thing about Charleston, so many homes had their own elaborate gardens filled with statuary, shrubs, ponds, flowers, and exotic greenery. Theodosia knew for a fact that the house on the corner, a fanciful Victorian, had a backyard filled with carefully tended Japanese bamboo as well as a small teahouse.

Then her fingers squeezed the steering wheel as her thoughts turned to the break-in at Mignon's shop and the question that still sat heavy on her mind—had Booker been responsible?

"Drayton," Theodosia said. "I have a favor to ask."

"Ask away," Drayton said. "While the night is still young and I'm in a good mood." He'd had two fully topped-off glasses of wine and was feeling ebullient.

"You're not going to like what I'm going to ask."

"Try me."

"Here's the thing. I called my friend Danny Rivera and asked if I could borrow his motorboat."

"I'm guessing this is directly related to the just-in-case phone call you made earlier?"

"Right. I was hoping we'd be done eating at a reasonable hour—which we are—and could take a run over to Little Clam Island, where Booker's place is located."

"In this so-called borrowed boat? You don't even know how to find Booker's place."

"I've explored those islands before in a J/22. They're like little specs just a few feet above the waterline. So I don't think his place will be that difficult to find."

"Still, haven't you had enough of chasing after Mr. Booker? First you got shot at . . ."

"We've agreed those shots were fired by his crazy roommate."

"Does Booker really have a roommate?" Drayton asked.

"Philip told me he did."

"As I was saying . . . then Mignon's brand spanking new shop was trashed."

"We don't know for a fact that Booker was responsible for that. It could have been Ginny Bell hating on Mignon. If you could have seen those two at the funeral luncheon this morning—talk about horrific cat fights."

"Why are you so all-fired anxious to find Booker?" Drayton asked.

"I want to look him in the eye and ask him outright if he killed Osgood Claxton. Ask him if he trashed Mignon's shop."

"You've got guts, I'll give you that," Drayton said.

"Come on, Drayton, it'll be an adventure."

"I'd have to change. I certainly can't slosh through mangroves and pluff mud in my good clothes."

"When we get to your place you can change."

"Nothing I say will dissuade you?"

"If you don't want to go, I'll go by myself. It's no big deal."

Drayton's head spun in Theodosia's direction. "Are you kidding? It *is* a big deal. Let you wander around in the dark and try to locate Booker all by yourself? Not on your life!"

Theodosia smiled to herself. "Is that a yes?"

Drayton sighed. "A reluctant yes."

"Good. Thank you," Theodosia said as she pulled to the curb outside Drayton's house. "I mean that."

"Even though we may be putting ourselves in harm's way?"

"I've been thinking about that. And I kind of wish we had a gun. You know, just for protection purposes."

Drayton was silent for a few moments, then he said, "I hate to admit this, but I have one."

"What!" Theodosia could barely contain her surprise.

"Don't look so shocked."

"But I am. I always thought of you as a natural-born pacifist. Someone who abhors guns. That time we went bird shooting, you didn't even want to handle the shotgun."

"Because I didn't want to kill innocent birds," Drayton said.

"Still, you own a gun." Theodosia couldn't get over this strange revelation. Then again, Drayton continually astounded her.

Drayton shrugged. "It's your basic hand-me-down pistol that I inherited a couple of years ago when my aunt Polly died. Her executor foisted a few cartons of books and hideous knick-knacks on me, and lo and behold, there was the gun, beneath a dog-eared copy of *Great Expectations*. An old Belgian Velo-dog. I don't even know if it works. If push came to shove, I don't know that it would accurately fire a bullet."

"Do you have ammo?"

Drayton looked suddenly uncomfortable. "Yes." He drew out the word slowly. "A box of Remington .22's came with it. But, again, you know how I feel about shooting."

"Maybe you should think of your pistol as a defensive measure."

"Or maybe I should leave it at home," Drayton mumbled as he got out of the car.

Theodosia followed behind Drayton as he hoofed it up the cobblestone path that led to his side door. He unlocked the door, pushed it open, and, in answer to a cacophony of barks, said, "Yes, it's me." At which point Honey Bee, Drayton's King Charles spaniel, launched herself into his arms.

"Yes, yes, I love you, too," he told her as he snuggled her close, kissed the top of her furry little head, then gently set her back down. "Did Pepe stop by and give you your dinner?" He looked over, noted her clean stainless steel food bowl and a water bowl filled with fresh water, and said, "I see that he did." Pepe was the sixteen-year-old boy who lived two houses down from Drayton. He walked and fed Honey Bee when needed and sometimes lent a hand with pruning and trimming in Drayton's backyard bonsai garden.

Theodosia plunked her purse down on Drayton's kitchen counter and said, "Where's this gun?"

"I keep it under the sink." Drayton bent down, opened a cupboard door, and fumbled around inside looking for it.

"That's a good place for a gun. Easy to get at in case of an emergency."

"Don't make fun," Drayton said as he finally pulled out the pistol and set it on the counter along with a box of shells. He took a step back and added, "I really don't want to touch it."

"Then don't," Theodosia said. "You go get changed and I'll figure this out."

"Be careful," he warned as Honey Bee followed him out of the room.

No stranger to guns, Theodosia flipped the pistol open and checked to make sure that it was empty. It was your basic easy-to-load, point-and-shoot pistol. She hefted it in her right hand—it had some weight to it—then dug six shells out of the box and popped them into the chamber. Haley's words from this afternoon came floating back to her—easy-peasy. And that's what this gun was, too. Basically, anyone could load, point, and shoot a gun. The real trick was knowing when you were in genuine physical danger and could make the right split-second judgment call.

Theodosia stuck the pistol in her jacket pocket and looked around the kitchen. Drayton lived in a historic house that had originally been built by a Civil War–era doctor. Over a century and a half of owners, updates, additions, and changes had been made. And when Drayton had moved here some fifteen years ago, he'd turned it into a showpiece. His kitchen stove was a six-burner Wolf range, the sink was custom-hammered copper, and the cupboards were faced with glass, the better to show off his collection of teapots and Chinese blue and white vases. A small indoor herb garden sat on a windowsill. His living room had silk wallpaper and elegant furniture slipcovered in French linen. A Chippendale table sat in his dining room with a French chandelier dangling overhead.

Five minutes later, Drayton came tromping into the kitchen. He'd changed into khaki slacks and a dark green Barbour jacket, the same brand that England's royal family favored for riding horseback and stalking the moors. On his feet was a pair of Wellington boots.

"You look like you just stepped out of a fancy British outdoor clothing catalog," Theodosia said.

"Thank you," Drayton said. "That was the exact look I was going for."

"Really?"

"No, not really. I'm so nervous I have no idea what I threw on. In fact, I'm getting more and more upset because I still think your idea of going to that island borders on unhinged."

"Like I said, you don't have to . . ."

"But I do. If only to humor you. And try to keep you safe." He glanced at Honey Bee. "Do you think we should bring Honey Bee along? As a kind of guard dog?"

Theodosia gazed at the little dog as she danced around the kitchen. She was the essence of a girly-girl pup, petite with adorable liquid brown eyes, a professionally groomed coat, and a pink suede collar complete with sparkles.

"Probably not," she said.

They located the boat at slip twenty-nine on pier three of the Charleston Yacht Club just south of the U.S. Coast Guard station.

"It's chained," Drayton said, throwing up his hands. "How on earth are we going to . . ." He stopped. "Oh."

Theodosia had already climbed aboard the boat and was standing there holding a shiny brass key. It gleamed in the faint light cast by a lantern on the dock.

"Danny always stows his extra key under the aft seat," she said.

"Lucky us," Drayton said as he scrambled into the boat, looking unsteady as well as uneasy.

But Theodosia was far from being deterred. "Come on, cast off and let's get going."

Drayton unhooked the lines and tossed them back onto the dock. "You know how to work a powerboat?"

"Sure," Theodosia said. "Only us seasoned sailors generally refer to these vessels as stink boats."

The engine sputtered to life under her practiced hand, then caught and gave off a throaty roar along with a few noxious puffs of smoke.

"I understand how they earned that moniker," Drayton sniffed as he sat down.

Theodosia took them out, slowly putt-putting past the docks, then into Charleston Harbor. Off to their left they could see other boats, port lights glowing red, starboard lights green, crisscrossing the harbor. There were larger vessels as well. One was an enormous freighter that was probably on its way up the Cooper River, where it would dock close to where the big cruise ships came in.

A stiff breeze off the Atlantic whipped up a chop on the dark water as they crossed the mouth of the Ashley River, taking their time, being cautious. A full moon, iced in silver, rode low in the inky sky.

"Like a ripe wheel of Camembert," Drayton observed.

Some fifteen minutes later they were nearing James Island. As they drew closer to shore, Theodosia saw the dark outline of the Plum Island Wastewater Treatment Plant and made a course correction. Then they were motoring up a small waterway that wove in and out among a scatter of small islands.

"Are we even in the vicinity?" Drayton asked. He sounded nervous as he sat stiffly on his seat.

"Getting close," Theodosia said. She was thankful for the moonlight that dappled the water and helped guide her way.

"How do you know which one is Little Clam Island?"

"I looked it up on a maritime map. Also, Holly told me it was the only one that had a dock. So we need to keep a sharp lookout."

They motored past bald cypress and tupelo gum trees, listening to night sounds. Low chirps from insects, the croak of tree frogs, rustling in the grass on nearby islands as the shiny eyes of foxes and nutria peered out at them.

"This is a trifle unnerving," Drayton said. "Like a jungle cruise through uncharted territory. There's an end-of-the-world quality that . . ."

"Shh," Theodosia cautioned. "We're getting close. In fact . . ." She powered down and steered the boat in the direction of a small rickety dock that stuck out into the water. "We're here. Welcome to Little Clam Island."

"How awful." Drayton wrinkled his nose as the front of the boat bumped against the dock. "Ah, and there's that telltale smell."

"Pluff mud. Anybody who lives in the low country should be used to it by now."

"I try not to be."

Theodosia scrambled out onto the dock and wound a line around a half-rotted post. "I hope this dock is sturdier than this post."

"It's not going to collapse on us, is it?"

"Just . . . walk carefully," she advised.

They tiptoed down the dock, then stepped off into . . . what else? Pluff mud. Not quite solid, not exactly bog, pluff mud was decaying spartina moss that was oozy, viscous, and rich with nutrients. In fact, it used to be spread on cotton fields to help bolster depleted soil.

Drayton lifted a boot, tried to scrape off a greasy hunk of mud, then gave up. "Definitely not dry land," he huffed.

"C'mon," Theodosia said. She'd spotted a faint path that led through stands of broom grass, pumpkin ash, and pond pine. "Let's go."

They crept along, swatting at bugs, pushing through nettles and cinnamon ferns that were overgrown and running rampant.

A few *plink*s and *plunk*s sounded from nearby standing water. There were soft rustles at ground level from bushes they passed. And an occasional sound like air being released from a tire.

"Please tell me that's not a hissing seven-foot alligator ready to pounce," Drayton said.

"That's not an alligator," Theodosia said.

"You're sure?"

"I don't know, maybe a turtle."

"A snapper?"

"Don't knock snapping turtles, they make for good cooter soup." Theodosia reached back, grabbed Drayton's sleeve, and tugged him forward. "Come on, we can't chicken out now."

"Are you kidding? I'm so chicken I've got cornbread stuffing oozing out of my jacket sleeves."

They continued down the path, the full moon so silver bright it felt like it was about to burst through the trees at any moment. Another sixty paces in and they came upon the shack. It was small, maybe twelve by fifteen feet, with a silvered wood exterior, a canted roof, and a gravel path that led to a single door.

"Is that it?" Drayton asked in a low whisper.

"I think so," Theodosia said. "It matches the description Holly gave me."

"But it appears uninhabited. And completely dark. Perhaps Booker's not hiding out here after all."

Theodosia studied the cracks around a tar-paper window. "I think there's a light on inside."

"It would have to be from a kerosene lamp, then," Drayton said. "Because I don't see any power lines."

Theodosia tiptoed up to the cabin, drew a deep breath, and knocked on the rough wooden door. When nothing happened, when Booker didn't fling open the door and appear, she knocked again. When there was still no answer, not even a faint stir from inside, she turned to Drayton and said, "Any ideas?"

"We could leave."

"Other than that."

"Then I think maybe you should shout out Booker's name," Drayton urged. "There's a chance he's asleep or . . ." He glanced with trepidation into the swampy woods. "Or he's wandering around out there?"

Drayton's twitchiness and apprehension was beginning to wear off on Theodosia. Fact was, she was starting to get cold feet. What had seemed like a dandy idea two hours ago now felt like a wild goose chase. Or even worse, an encounter tinged with danger.

"If I call out Booker's name and he answers me, what should I say?" she asked. "Something like, 'Hello, we've been worried about you?' Or 'We were in the neighborhood and decided to drop in?' Whatever I say is going to sound kind of silly."

"Well," Drayton said. "This isn't exactly a social call because we *are* out here on this godforsaken island. So . . . better just shout his name and take your chances?"

"Booker?" Theodosia called out. "Booker?" This second time her voice was louder and more demanding.

"Still nothing," Drayton said. "He must not be here."

Theodosia squared her shoulders, stepped up to the door again, and gave it a shove. Unexpectedly, the door swung inward on hinges that creaked like a rusty coffin.

"Booker?" Theodosia said. "It's Theodosia. And Drayton."

Drayton made a sound in the back of his throat. "The man doesn't know me from Adam."

A shiver ran down Theodosia's spine. What was going on? Had Booker heard them coming? Was he lying in wait for them?

She pulled Drayton's pistol out of her pocket, pressed the tip of it against the door, and pushed the door open a few more inches. Which yielded more creaking noises and a partial reveal of the dark interior of Booker's cabin. She peered in and saw the edge of an old iron bed frame along with a battered wooden dresser.

"Booker?" Theodosia said again.

Drayton crept up behind Theodosia and said, "Are you in there?" in a tremulous voice.

Still no response.

Drayton's shoulders relaxed. "No answer *is* an answer. Booker's clearly not in residence."

"Weird," Theodosia said. "Because I still see a tiny sliver of light." She drew a shaky breath and took a step inside. The air that assaulted her smelled of dampness and mildew and kerosene oil. Still feeling apprehensive, not sure what she might find, Theodosia took another step inside. The interior of the cabin was shrouded in darkness except for a dancing flame in an old-fashioned lantern. Now the scent of oil paint filled her nostrils. And something else, too.

But what?

25

Fresh blood.

Booker lay sprawled on the floor of his cabin like a giant that had been felled. He'd landed on his back with his arms splayed out wide as if he'd been making some kind of final grand gesture. He didn't seem to be breathing; there wasn't a single twitch.

"Holy cats," Theodosia breathed as the dancing light from the lantern's flame suddenly revealed a small black hole in the center of Booker's forehead. Feeling panicked, her heart practically beating out of her chest, she backpedaled out of the cabin so fast her heels crunched down hard on Drayton's toes.

"Ouch. What?" Drayton said. He hadn't yet caught a glimpse of Booker lying there.

Theodosia stepped to one side and made a broad, sweeping gesture. "Go ahead and take a look. But I warn you, it's not a pretty sight."

"Oh no," Drayton said as he peered into the gloom and saw Booker lying there. "He's . . ."

"Dead?" Theodosia said. "I think that's the case, yes." She wrinkled her nose. "But I suppose we have to make sure. Because otherwise . . . he might need medical help."

They both tiptoed in, mindful of the spooky shadows, terrible smell, and distressed, almost neglected interior of the cabin. Booker's body still lay on the floor, dark blood pooling around it.

"He's definitely been shot?" Drayton said.

"I don't think that hole in his forehead is religious stigmata," Theodosia said.

"Please don't joke."

"I'll try not to," Theodosia said. She knelt down, touched Booker's ice cold hand, tried to take his pulse, and felt nary a beat. Booker had left the building. Then, upon making a more detailed inspection, she said, "Drayton, take a look at what's resting in his right hand."

"Lord have mercy," Drayton said.

The fingers of Booker's right hand were curled around the handle of a gray snub-nose pistol.

"So it's a suicide?" Drayton asked. "I mean, it must be. There's blood all over the place."

"I don't . . ." Theodosia's eyes searched the darkness, hoping for some kind of clue, some shred of evidence that might explain what had happened here. Then her eyes landed on a half-finished painting that was propped on a wooden easel. "Oh no."

"What?"

"Look at the painting on his easel."

Fascinated as well as repelled, they both stepped closer to study the angry slashes of red and orange paint on canvas with the words I'M SORRY scrawled across it.

"Is that what I think it is?" Drayton asked.

"A signed confession?" Theodosia said. "I think it might be."

*   *   *

"Now what do we do?" Drayton asked.

"I've got two bars on my phone, so I'm going to call Riley and . . ." Theodosia stopped abruptly. Off in the distance she'd heard something. A sound. Or maybe a vibration. Low and rumbling.

"So you can call Riley and tell him what?" Drayton asked.

"Hush." Theodosia held up a hand. "Do you hear that?"

Drayton cocked his head and listened. The vibration increased until there was the sudden high-pitched whine of a motor off to their left!

"You don't think . . ." Drayton began.

Alarm bells were clanging in Theodosia's head. "What? That maybe Booker *didn't* kill himself? That maybe someone murdered him and staged all this? And that his killer has been watching us and is making a getaway right now? Drayton, I think it's a possibility," Theodosia shouted. "Come on, we gotta get back to the boat!"

They tore down the narrow path, branches swatting them in the face as they dodged and ducked their way through nettles and swamp grass. When they got to the rickety pier Theodosia untied the boat and jumped in. Drayton made a flying leap into the boat just as she started the motor. She took the boat out some fifty feet, throttled back, and scouted the area. Searched the darkness for a sign of the boat they'd just heard.

"Do you see anything?" Drayton asked.

"Not yet." Theodosia guided the boat between two islands.

"Think that boat's still out there? Somewhere?"

"Yes, I do," Theodosia said.

They drifted with the current for a minute or two, listening, glancing toward shore just in case the killer had hidden his boat among the reeds and bushes. Then, as they slowly rounded the far tip of another small island, Theodosia caught shadowy movement and heard the sound of a small boat puttering away.

"There they are!" she cried, gesturing for Drayton to hurry up and change places with her. "Drayton, you steer the boat while I call Riley."

"Steer a boat? I've never . . ." But he cut his argument short as he obligingly took her place at the rear of the boat and grabbed the tiller.

"You see those tiny red and green lights? They're about to disappear if we don't kick it into high gear."

"Yes, yes." He fumbled with the motor.

"I'm fairly sure that's the boat with Booker's killer on board." Theodosia gestured in the direction of the elusive craft, and added, "Better punch it, he's probably spotted us, so he'll start pouring it on."

"I'll do my best," Drayton said gamely as he hastily increased their speed.

Theodosia sat down, grabbed her phone, and quickly hit speed dial. When Riley answered she had to shout to be heard above the roar of the motor. "You're not going to believe this!"

"Believe what?" Riley asked. He sounded calm, relaxed. Like maybe he'd even enjoyed a nice refreshing beverage or two.

"Drayton and I dropped by Little Clam Island where Booker has a studio."

"*Where* are you?"

"It's one of those teeny islands off the tip of James Island," Theodosia said.

"What are you doing there?" Now Riley was confused.

"Looking for Booker, the artist."

"Whoa. And you *found* him?"

"I not only found Booker, he's *dead*," Theodosia shouted. "It looks like he was murdered. That some weasel snuck in and shot him. Then tried to make it look like a suicide."

"What!"

"I said some weasel shot him and . . ."

"No, I got that part just fine. What I'm asking is . . . wait, never mind. You said Little Clam Island?"

"Well, we *were* there. Now we're chasing after the killer in a boat."

"No!" Riley cried. "Don't do that. *Please* don't do that. Oh man, I've got to call the boss."

"You mean Tidwell?"

"Of course. And notify the Coast Guard, too," Riley said.

"Now there's a good idea, I'm sure they could be very helpful."

"To be clear, Booker's at Little Clam Island?" Riley said. "Because I've also got to dispatch a team of . . ."

Theodosia cut in. "You might also want to . . ."

"What?" Riley said.

"Send a coroner."

Theodosia hung up and crawled to the back of the boat.

"You want to take over?" Drayton asked. "Please?"

She moved into Drayton's spot while he edged away.

"I've been following best I can," Drayton said. "He hasn't outrun us, but I don't seem to be getting any closer either."

The killer was weaving in and out, pulling close to shore, then heading out again. Zigzagging his way around several of the small islands.

Seconds later, they lost sight of him.

"Where'd he disappear to?" Drayton cried.

"Doggone it," Theodosia said. "I think he somehow out-foxed us."

"Maybe he pulled into shore and is hiding among some of those big mangroves."

"I don't know, Drayton."

Theodosia cut the motor and let the boat drift soundlessly for a few minutes.

"You hear anything?" she asked.

"Nothing," Drayton said. "Just nighttime chirps and trills."

"That boat's got to be around here somewhere."

"He's gone. Like a haunt in the night."

"I don't believe in haunts," Theodosia said.

"Even out here where there's all sorts of fluorescent apparitions that can't be explained?"

"Swamp gas," Theodosia said. She pushed her hair—which seemed to have expanded to twice its size due to the high humidity—out of her face and looked around. "What we need is . . ."

Like a buzz saw starting up, a boat came zooming around the corner of a nearby island, heading straight for them.

"Sweet Fanny Adams!" Drayton yelped.

There was a loud BANG and then a ZING as a bullet flew past!

"Get down!" Theodosia cried. "He's shooting at us!"

Drayton dove under the front hull of the boat while Theodosia crouched down behind the gunwale. One more shot banged off the prow of their boat, then the shooter corrected his course and bore down on them with all the power he could muster from his engine.

"Hang on!" Theodosia yelped as the offending boat sped toward them. "He's going to hit us!"

A cataclysmic clash rent the night as they were rammed broadside. Earsplitting, high-pitched squeals of metal against metal rose up as their boat rocked violently and began to tip sideways.

"We're going to capsize!" Drayton shouted in panic.

"Not if I can help it," Theodosia cried, hastily shifting her weight to counterbalance the unnatural upending of the boat. "Help me, Drayton. We've got to heave our boat back over."

"We're taking on water," he shouted as the offending boat buzzed away from them.

"Doesn't matter, we can *do* this," Theodosia grunted. "Grab the gunwale and lean into the high side with me."

Scrambling, hanging on for dear life, Theodosia and Drayton put all their weight on the upended side of the boat and slowly, painfully, eased it back over until there was a loud plop and they were righted again.

"We did it," Drayton said panting hard, touching a hand to his fluttering heart.

"That jackhole almost killed us," Theodosia cried. She looked around, didn't see a thing.

"Well, he didn't. We survived." Drayton gulped a mouthful of air, then said, "But can we please get out of here?"

Theodosia tried the motor. There was a grunt and a strangled cough, but the motor didn't want to catch. After five minutes of struggling, of coaxing the motor, of trying again and again, she said, "That does it, the motor's either broken or flooded."

"Oars?" Drayton said.

Theodosia shook her head. "Cell phone."

She called Riley's line, found it was busy, and left a voice mail. "No luck," she said to Drayton. "We'll have to sit tight for a while."

But as they sat there, Drayton cast a horrified look into the bottom of the boat, where water was starting to stream in. Within minutes, they were up to their ankles; in a few more minutes, water would be up to their knees.

"We're sinking," Drayton said.

"I think it's too shallow for us to actually sink," Theodosia said, trying to sound reassuring. "But we could sort of rescue ourselves if we jumped in the water and pulled the boat to shore. The bank is only, like, five or six feet away."

"Okay, okay," Drayton cried as he swung one leg over the edge of the boat. There was a *splash* and a *ker-plop* and he went into water up to his waist. Where he immediately started to struggle.

"What's wrong?"

"I think there's quicksand here. I can't pull my feet up. I . . . I think I'm getting sucked down into this muck!" His arms thrashed the water as he fought to pull himself up from the soft bottom.

"Stop pedaling your feet," Theodosia told him. She knew that pluff mud was notoriously similar to quicksand: the more you struggled, the faster you sank. And with pluff mud, the suction could be almost unbearable.

"What I'm going to do is . . ." She crept to the bow of the boat, hunted around, and came up with a white life ring. "Here. I'm going to toss this to you." She held the life ring up, then flung it in Drayton's direction. "Grab on to this and pull it down around your waist."

Drayton reached out, managed to snag the life ring, then struggled to pull it over his head.

"Help!" He'd hit the panic button.

"No, you're okay, you've got this. Get your shoulders through and then just shimmy it down to your hips." She watched as

Drayton struggled with the life ring. But he was following her instructions, moving it down around his body. "You okay now? Feeling more secure?"

The expression on his face said no, but he responded positively with, "I think so."

"Now I'm going to toss you a rope. You hang on tight to your end while I take the other end."

"What are you going to do?" Drayton asked.

"Make a shallow dive and swim to dry land. Then I'll reel you in, okay?"

"Don't touch the bottom or your feet will get stuck, too."

"Not to worry, I'm going to swim over."

"Okay, but . . ." The rest of Drayton's words were completely drowned out by the loud bellow of a horn. Then a bright searchlight lit up the night. It flashed along the shore, searching the reed-covered bank, then readjusted its aim and settled on them.

"Ahoy," someone called from the large boat that was slowly approaching them.

"Who's there?" Theodosia called back.

"Coast Guard. You need help?"

"We need rescuing," Drayton cried.

"Help would be good," Theodosia called out, thanking her lucky stars that Riley had called the Coast Guard and they had immediately dispatched a cutter.

A few seconds later, a rubber raft splashed down into the water, then two coastguardsmen jumped into it. They quickly paddled to Drayton, rescued him, then came back and pulled Theodosia into their rubber boat.

"Your boat sprang a leak?" the first coastie asked her.

"We were shot at," Theodosia said. "But I'm pretty sure our boat is salvageable."

"We can pump it out, slap on some temporary sealant, and tow it back with us," the second coastie said.

"Bless you," Theodosia breathed.

When they drew alongside the Coast Guard cutter, Theodosia immediately recognized Tidwell's bulk leaning over the railing.

"I'm not sure I should give you permission to come aboard," Tidwell said. He sounded supremely annoyed.

"I don't think I can swim home," Theodosia replied. She was feeling tired, bedraggled, and in no mood to trade verbal barbs with Tidwell. "So I'd appreciate a lift."

Tidwell disappeared as the coastguardsmen hauled Drayton and her on board.

"Thank you," Theodosia told them. "Thank you all so much."

As they watched their boat being pumped out, Drayton nudged Theodosia and said in a low voice, "Where's the gun?"

Theodosia patted her cross-body bag. "Tucked away safely in here."

"For goodness' sake, don't let anybody know you've got it or they'll think *we* shot Booker."

"Mum's the word."

Eventually, Tidwell strolled out of the wheelhouse to speak with Theodosia.

"You had no reason to come out here looking for Mr. Booker," Tidwell told her in a crabby voice. Dressed in baggy jeans and a sweatshirt that said FBI, he wore a bright orange life vest on top of all that, which gave him an odd appearance of the Michelin Man. "Booker was a suspect in a murder investigation."

"Not anymore," Theodosia said. "Now *he's* been murdered. A strange twist of events, don't you think?"

"Which we shall deal with. So you no longer need to meddle in what is an ongoing police investigation."

"Meddle," Theodosia said. "Such a quaint term. And if I hadn't come out here and found Booker shot to death, you might still be looking for him. Heading down the wrong path."

But Tidwell didn't want to hear it.

"Do not—I repeat—do *not* insinuate yourself into this investigation." And with that, Tidwell spun sharply on his heels and didn't speak to her for the rest of the trip.

Back at the dock, Theodosia thanked the coastguardsmen for their help, then spoke to the night manager at the yacht club about getting the boat repaired. Finally (finally!), she grabbed Drayton and drove him home.

"I'm sorry the evening turned out so badly," she said as they pulled up to his house.

"Are you kidding?" Drayton said. "It was the most excitement I've had in years. Discovering a dead body, getting shot at, and then being mired in quicksand. It was like being conscripted by Captain Bligh."

They sat in the dim interior of her Jeep.

"Are you really okay?"

"Aside from the noxious odor still clinging to my clothing, I believe I'll eventually dry out."

"Okay then," Theodosia said. "See you tomorrow."

Drayton climbed wearily out of her Jeep, hesitated, then turned around and said, "The one positive outcome is that we now know for sure that Claxton's killer is still out there."

"The problem being," Theodosia replied, "we don't know who that is."

* * *

Or maybe we do, Theodosia thought as she drove home through the dark, almost deserted streets.

What if Booker had murdered Claxton on account of his arts grant being pulled? And then Mignon killed Booker? Could it have played out that way?

Theodosia considered this. What if Mignon knew that her husband had pulled Booker's grant? And what if Mignon still had a few shreds of love left for her husband and figured that Booker had to be his killer? So she decided to take matters into her own hands? That would mean that Mignon had been the one shooting at them tonight. Would she do that? Did Mignon own a boat? Or a gun? Had Mignon trashed her own shop to make it look as if Booker did it? Then tried to stage Booker's death as a suicide? Was she that crazy?

Maybe, just maybe, she was.

Oh man, did I just stumble into an even bigger, twistier mess?

26

⁓⁂⁓

Theodosia and Drayton were not exactly in tip-top shape this Friday morning.

"I'm black-and-blue from jouncing around in that boat," Drayton complained, rubbing a shoulder.

"From the trip over to Little Clam or afterward?" Theodosia asked.

"Both."

"On the plus side, we did eliminate one of our suspects."

Drayton gave a thoughtful look. "In the clear, cold light of day, I'm not sure that can be counted as a plus."

Theodosia set a tray stacked with teacups down on one of the tables and walked over to the counter. "Really? Have you changed your mind? What are you thinking?"

Drayton poured a stream of fresh-brewed Assam silver needle into a teacup and pushed it across the counter to Theodosia. "And then there were none," he said in an ominous tone.

"You're referring to Agatha Christie's *Ten Little Indians?*"

"Where all the suspects get bumped off, one by one. Yes. That's exactly what I meant."

"You think all our suspects are going to be killed?" Theodosia asked.

Drayton gave a weary look. "I don't know. I hope not."

Theodosia took a sip of tea. It was delicious. Delicate with a buttery silk texture. Normally it would perk her up, but today she had too many other things on her mind.

"Drayton, what would you say if I told you Mignon could have killed Booker?"

"I'd say you're thinking way outside the box." Then Drayton leaned forward and said, in a hushed tone, "Do you really think Mignon could kill her own husband as well as Booker?"

"Hear me out. What if it was Booker who killed Mignon's husband? Over the arts grant that got pulled. What if Mignon *knew* the details of the grant and immediately suspected Booker, and then, after some consideration, decided to kill him?"

"In retaliation for killing her husband. But I thought she hated her husband."

"Maybe Mignon didn't hate-hate him in the way we think she did, maybe she just wanted to exit their marriage. She could have still had a few shreds of respect left for Claxton."

Drayton considered this. "Or love?"

"Maybe." Theodosia took another sip of tea. "If not Mignon, then who's left?" she said quietly. Then answered her own question. "Lamar Lucket, though he doesn't feel exactly right. And Ginny Bell."

Drayton raised an index finger. "My vote is on her."

"How so?"

"When we saw Miss Bell at the silent auction, she struck me as a fairly tough cookie. One of those sociopath types who could shoot you dead and then walk away with an unblemished conscience."

"And escape in a boat? Then circle back and take a few shots at us?" Theodosia asked. "You think Ginny Bell was the one who shot at us last night? Then rammed her boat into ours and tried to sink us?"

"Like I said, it feels to me as if she might have a crazy streak."

"Huh," Theodosia said as the front door opened and a half dozen customers streamed in. "Something to think about."

Then Theodosia and Drayton got busy. Because it was Friday, lots of tourists were in town for the weekend. Folks who'd come to gaze at Charleston Harbor, take in the historic sights, snuggle up in gracious B and Bs, and explore Gateway Walk. Which inevitably led them to the Indigo Tea Shop on Church Street.

Theodosia served eggnog scones and blueberry muffins. Drayton worked his tea alchemy by brewing pots of Earl Grey, Pu-erh, and Grand Keemun.

At ten o'clock, Pete Riley came strolling in. Theodosia, feeling more than a little sheepish about last night, ran to greet him.

"You're looking none the worse for wear," Riley said. He bent forward, gave her a kiss on the tip of her nose.

"I'm sorry about last night," Theodosia said. "Hitting the panic button like that."

"But you're not sorry you snuck over to Little Clam Island and discovered a dead body?"

"We didn't sneak, we simply went."

"And caused a ton of trouble. Tidwell told me you were shot at, that your boat was rammed and practically sunk."

"Only partially," Theodosia said, brushing off the shooting part. "The Coast Guard was kind enough to engineer a temporary patch and tow it back to the marina. I've already talked to the owner of the boat and he was fairly cool about it. Said his insurance should cover the incident."

"Incident." Riley tried to sound gruff but his mouth twitched at the corners. "That's what you call it?"

She looked up at him, hoping for a sign of understanding. "Unfortunate incident?"

"That's my Theodosia," Riley said. "Always downplaying the danger. But sweetheart, you've got to start keeping your distance. Tidwell almost gave himself a stroke this morning just talking about the Booker murder. And about you, of course."

"Did the vein in his forehead turn pink?"

"More like purple."

"He *was* upset."

"So in the interest of Tidwell's well-being and my job security, let's not torment him any more than we have to, okay?"

"Sure," Theodosia said. "Works for me."

Riley studied her. "You *sound* contrite, you almost *look* penitent, but why do I have a feeling it's all a big act?"

"It's not," Theodosia said.

"Riiiight," Riley said. "So." He glanced over at the front counter. "I'm off to a meeting so whatcha got in the way of takeout?"

"Trade you an eggnog scone and a cup of Earl Grey for a fast answer to a couple of questions."

"And those would be what?"

"Does Mignon Merriweather own a boat? And do you have a ballistics report yet? Was the gun used on Booker the same one used on Claxton?"

Riley smiled and shook his head. "Nope. Sorry. There's a lockdown on any and all further information."

Theodosia gave Riley his scone and tea anyway. Because she

had another way to get at least one of her questions answered. A better way. After he left, she simply went into her office and called the Charleston Yacht Club. When she had Bud Claskey, the club's manager, on the line, she popped the boat question to him.

"What was the name again?" Bud asked. "Conklin?"

"Claxton. The membership would be in either Osgood Claxton or Mignon Merriweather's name."

"Let me check the directory," Bud said. Paper rattled as pages in a book were turned. "Yeah, we got an Osgood Claxton. Pier one, slip number seventeen."

"Do you know what kind of boat?"

"Um . . . yup. A Sea Ray."

"Thank you. Oh, do you by any chance know what shape it's in? Like, if it's been in an accident or anything?"

"Sorry, no."

On the way out into the tea room, Theodosia looked in the mirror, said "Eek!" and smoothed her hair.

In between a pot of rooibos and a pot of black jasmine, Theodosia pulled Drayton aside and said, "Claxton owned a boat."

Drayton peered at her. "A boat?"

"You know, vroom vroom, putt putt?"

"Oh! You mean Mignon could have been driving that boat last night?" He let the full impact of the news settle in, then said, "Goodness."

"Not so good. Because if it really was Mignon, then she tried to kill us, too."

"You make a good point," Drayton said. "Are you going to tell Riley about this?"

"I'm not sure. He's probably looked into it already."

"He seemed awfully upset when he dropped by earlier."

"That's because he hadn't had his morning dose of caffeine or sugar yet."

"You have an answer for everything, don't you?"

"Usually." Theodosia smiled. Then her expression turned serious. "But not for whoever's been running around Charleston killing people."

"Got to show you something," Haley said.

Theodosia looked up from her desk, where she was busy paying bills. Tea vendors, food suppliers, Dominion Energy, everyone wanted money. "What's that, Haley?"

Haley handed her a small three-by-eight-inch card. "I printed out menus. You know, for our Honeybee Tea 2.0 today."

Theodosia grinned as she scanned the tiny menu. "These are adorable, Haley." Haley had printed out her luncheon menu on cream-colored cardstock, rubbed the edges of the cards with gold paint, then punched holes at the top and affixed pieces of gold gossamer ribbon. "All this work for a simple luncheon."

Haley flipped back her blonde hair in a move that was pure theatrics and said, "Not so simple. Have you read my offerings?"

"Sorry, Haley, let me take a look."

Theodosia read the card.

"This is wonderful. Honeybee scones, honey chicken, mixed fruit salad with honey dressing, and, for dessert, ricotta cookies and honey brownies. Our guests are going to adore this."

Haley plucked the card out of Theodosia's hand. "They already are. In fact, the tea shop's half full and it's only eleven thirty."

"It's that late? Then I'd better finish up my paperwork posthaste."

But Theodosia continued working on invoices, writing checks, and telling herself, "Just one more," and then, "Gotta do one more," until Drayton suddenly loomed in the doorway.

"Oops," Theodosia said. "I'll be right out." Then she noticed the serious look on his face and said, "What?"

"There's a problem."

"In the kitchen?"

Drayton shook his head. "In the tea room."

"What is it?"

Drayton fidgeted with his cuff links. "A guest."

"A disruptive guest?" Theodosia stood up from her chair and came around the desk. But Drayton had barred the way into the tea room.

"She's not disruptive yet," he said. "But I imagine she will be fairly soon."

"Drayton, you're talking in riddles. Just give it to me straight. What's the problem? Who's out there?"

"Ginny Bell."

Theodosia clapped a hand to her cheek. "Oh no. Did she come in and specifically ask to see me?"

"I don't think she's even aware that you own this place. Somebody brought her as a guest. Innocently, I presume."

"But I have to go out there. I can't hide in my office all through lunch. Our customers need to be served and . . ." She glanced at her watch. "I'm late already."

Drayton stood aside. "Venture out at your own peril."

Which is exactly what Theodosia did. She greeted two tables of guests, took orders, and ran them into the kitchen. Then she came back out and approached the table where Ginny Bell was seated.

"Good day," Theodosia said. "Have you had a chance to look at our menu? As you may have noticed, we're doing a full complement of honey-flavored entrées and baked goods today."

At hearing Theodosia's voice, Ginny Bell looked up abruptly from her menu.

"You!" she cried as recognition dawned on her face. "What are *you* doing here?" Her eyes blazed with anger; two pink circles insinuated themselves high on her cheeks.

"I own this tea shop," Theodosia said. She kept her tone low-key and unapologetic.

"If I'd known that, I would have never come here!" Ginny Bell bellowed while the woman she was with cringed in her chair.

Drayton came over to the table immediately.

"Is there a problem?" he asked.

"Yes," Ginny Bell snapped. "Under no circumstances do I want this woman to wait on me." She flipped a hand to indicate Theodosia.

"I'll be happy to take your order," Drayton said.

"Fine," Ginny Bell said as Theodosia shrugged and walked away. "But I'd like to get our food as fast as possible so I can eat and leave."

"That," Drayton said, eyebrows raised, a touch of chill in his voice, "won't be a problem."

27

Aside from Ginny Bell's snippiness—and quick departure—
Friday's lunch was a cinch. Everyone loved the honey-inspired
menu, a few customers lingered and shopped for tins of tea, and
a group that came in late ordered a pot of toasty Japanese Bancha
tea, much to Drayton's delight.

"While this tea must be brewed with hot water, the tem-
perature should be considerably less than boiling water," Drayton said.

"And less steeping time, too?" Theodosia said.

"About two minutes." He pulled a jade green teapot out and
rinsed it. "I wonder if this recent spat with Ginny Bell means
I won't get my teapot."

"I guess you'll just have to sneak over and pick it up when
she's not there," Theodosia said. She got busy pouring refills,
chatting with the remaining guests, and feeling decidedly better about things—much more upbeat than she'd felt last night
or even this morning. But all that came to a screeching halt
when Bill Glass sauntered into her tea shop.

"Glass," Theodosia murmured under her breath.

Glass saw her standing there, teapot in hand, and shot her another of his military-style salutes.

"Hi-yo," he said. Today he wore an ill-fitting corduroy blazer in a hideous mustard color.

"What?" Theodosia said, practically sighing as Glass walked up to her with a smarmy grin on his face. It was getting to the point where she could barely tolerate the man.

"I've got news," Glass said. He puckered his lips and emitted several high-pitched tweets. "Something a little bird told me." His hands made a fluttering motion.

"What now?" Theodosia asked, wishing she could somehow stop him from pushing her buttons as much as he did.

"You know I've got contacts on the police force." Glass grinned wide, showing a row of capped teeth.

"I know you try to weasel information out of a few informants, paid, unpaid, or otherwise."

"No, this is really something," Glass said. "That hotel guy . . . Lamar Lucket? The one who's running for office?"

"Yes?" Much to her dismay, Theodosia realized she *was* interested in what Glass had to say.

"One of my contacts told me the police are still looking hard at Lucket. Even asked him to come in for questioning again."

"Because of the Claxton murder," she said, wondering if the police had uncovered some sort of hard evidence against Lucket.

"Righto," Glass said. "But you know what?"

Theodosia waited for Glass to spit out his news.

"I heard that Lucket just laughed in their faces when they asked if he was in any way connected to Osgood Claxton's murder. Showed complete contempt for them."

"That sounds like the Lamar Lucket we all know and love," Theodosia said.

"He also had his PR chick along with him," Glass said. "A real looker who kept interrupting every time the detectives asked Lucket a question. Some gal named Bernice or Candice who could probably chew gristle and whistle Dixie at the same time."

"Was her name Clarice?"

Glass snapped his fingers and pointed at her. "That's it. You know her?"

"Met her once."

"The scuttlebutt is she's hell on wheels." Glass paused as an evil grin stole across his face. "I wonder if she's single and willing to mingle?"

"Why don't you give Clarice a call and find out," Theodosia suggested. She felt slightly guilty about making the suggestion because Bill Glass was nobody's idea of a dream date. Then again, maybe their personalities would mesh perfectly. Maybe the two of them deserved each other.

Glass wiggled his eyebrows comically. "That's the best idea I've heard in weeks. Oh, by the way, I gave the police the rest of those photos I took. Hope that's okay."

It was okay with Theodosia because she'd studied the photos several times and still been unable to find anything sinister.

"What did *he* want?" Drayton asked Theodosia once Glass had left the tea shop.

"He wanted to torment me," Theodosia said.

"No, really."

"Glass told me that the police talked to Lamar Lucket again."

Drayton waggled his fingers, indicating he needed more details. "And?"

"And nothing. According to Glass's informant, which may or may not be credible, Lucket laughed at them."

"Lucket certainly doesn't act like a guilty man."

"I don't know," Theodosia said. "What does a guilty man act like?"

"As if he doesn't have a care in the world?" Drayton scratched his chin thoughtfully. "Or perhaps a guilty woman would act the same way."

"Funny you should bring that up, because I've been thinking about Mignon all morning. Still wondering how and if she's involved." Theodosia glanced at the ornate Gustavian gilt clock that hung next to the stone fireplace. "I've been thinking about paying her a visit. Like, maybe even today."

"There's no time like the present," Drayton said. "So why don't you? Haley and I have things well under control here. And it might be interesting if you applied some pressure to Mignon, gave her your version of the third degree."

Theodosia nodded slowly. "Exactly what I've been thinking."

The front door stood open wide, and inside, Mignon's shop bustled with activity. As Theodosia walked in, she saw three people in aprons and headscarves pushing brooms around, doing their best to put things right.

"Hello?" Theodosia called out.

All three heads shot up. Then Mignon recognized Theodosia and said, "Hey, come on in. That's if you can find a clean place to stand."

Theodosia looked around. There were half a dozen black plastic garbage bags filled with trash and a large gray plastic garbage bin heaped with dirty T-shirts, scuffed note cards, and broken teacups. And there was still a lot more work to be done.

"It looks like you're making some progress," Theodosia said.

Mignon stopped sweeping and walked over to where Theodosia was standing. She looked ten years younger in her denim shirt, jeans, and sneakers. "We're getting there," she said. "Thanks to my assistants, Sasha and Joyce, for their hard work and elbow grease. Ladies, say hi to Theodosia. She owns that lovely tea room over on Church Street."

Sasha and Joyce managed weak hellos, then returned to their cleaning.

"Have you talked to your insurance agent?" Theodosia asked.

"He stopped by this morning. It's . . . it should be okay." Mignon swept an arm at the garbage bags. "Most of this is covered."

"How about the damage to your walls?" Theodosia glanced at walls that still bore obnoxious slashes of paint and graffiti.

Mignon blew a tuft of hair off her forehead. "That's covered as well. In fact, the painters are scheduled for Monday morning."

Theodosia decided not to beat around the bush. "You know Booker was killed last night?"

Mignon's eyes were hard as marbles as she met Theodosia's gaze, while her two employees suddenly looked fearful and seemed to shrink into themselves.

"If Booker was the one who savaged my beautiful boutique, then I'm glad he's dead," Mignon spat out.

"You realize it was cold-blooded murder?"

"I don't much care." Mignon took a step back and her heel crunched down hard on a piece of broken china. "But I can see *you're* fascinated. Still trying to help Holly, or . . ." Mignon stopped abruptly. Then a cagey expression slowly stole across her face. "Ah, I think I know why you turned up here. You think maybe *I* shot Mr. Booker, don't you?" She barked out a harsh laugh. "If I knew for sure that Booker was the one responsible for this mess, then believe me, I would have gladly pulled the trigger." Her mouth twisted into a sneer. "But in case you're asking, I didn't kill him. *Is* that what you're asking?"

"I suppose in a way it is," Theodosia said. She wasn't surprised or even rattled by Mignon's response. Just curious as to what Mignon would do next.

Mignon shook her head, bent forward, and vigorously pushed her broom around, scraping together the remnants of a glass figurine. Finally, she looked up at Theodosia and said, "Maybe you should leave."

Theodosia left.

Sitting in her car, fingers tapping the steering wheel, Theodosia tried to sort through Mignon's rambling words.

Is Mignon lying? Maybe. She's goofy enough. But if she didn't go out there last night and kill Booker, then who did?

Theodosia was fresh out of ideas. And didn't know where she could turn for more information.

Unless . . .

She searched her phone's directory, found what she was looking for, and headed down Meeting Street on her way to North Charleston.

When Theodosia got to Booker's house, the one he shared with his trigger-happy roommate, she hesitated. Should she or shouldn't she go to the door? She'd been shot at by a man she figured must be Booker's roommate. But that was at night, when the roommate thought there was a break-in going on. And this was the middle of the afternoon. And she was already here, so . . . what did she have to lose?

Except my life? No, that isn't quite right.

Theodosia marched up the front walk, avoiding a jagged hunk of concrete that a slow-growing tree root had upended, then knocked on the front door. When nobody answered, she knocked again, this time putting more muscle behind it.

Seconds later, a voice shouted out, "That better not be you, Binger!"

Theodosia remembered that was the name Booker's roommate had yelled out Tuesday night when he spotted her slinking around the garage.

"I'm not Binger," she shouted back. When there was no answer, she said, "My name is Theodosia Browning. And I'm very sorry for what happened to your friend Booker."

Ten seconds went by, then the door opened and a man's shaggy face peered out at her.

"You knew Booker?"

"I only met him a few times, but I admired his work very much."

Those were the magic words, the "open sesame" that got her inside.

"Come in," the roommate said. "I guess."

Theodosia was admitted to the bottom half of a duplex that was surprisingly neat and tidy. From where she stood in the entry, there was a living room with a Goodwill-type sofa and recliner, an enormous bookcase jammed with art history and design books, a threadbare Oriental rug on the floor, and a brick fireplace with a cat sitting in front of it. The cat was black with a white chest and four white paws. A tuxedo cat.

"You wanna sit down?" the roommate asked. He was late twenties, a good six feet tall, and well over two hundred and fifty pounds. His plaid shirt was pulled tight across his chest and he wore dark jeans and motorcycle boots. Long reddish hair and a beard surrounded a curiously chubby and boyish face.

"Thank you," Theodosia said as she seated herself on the sofa.

"Theodosia," the roommate said. "Interesting name. Historical, right?"

"There was a Theodosia who was married to the governor of South Carolina back in the late seventeen hundreds. She was also the niece of Aaron Burr."

"Aaron Burr, huh. Interesting. You a descendent? You ever shoot anybody?"

"No. And, excuse me, but you have me at a disadvantage. I don't know your name."

"Hooper. Just Hooper. Now you wanna tell me why you're really here?"

"I've been looking into the Osgood Claxton murder," Theodosia said.

Hooper's eyes were lasered on her. "Because you're a cop?"

"No, I'm not in law enforcement. I actually own a tea shop."

"Interesting. That's even kinda cool."

"Thank you. And the reason I'm here is because my friend Holly Burns has suffered a tremendous amount of fallout to her gallery following Claxton's murder. You see, Claxton was murdered at the tea party I helped arrange."

"And you feel guilty." Hooper reached into his shirt pocket and pulled out a pack of Marlboro Lights and a Bic lighter. "Got it."

"The police had Booker on their suspect list until . . ."

"Until last night." Hooper lit his cigarette, inhaled, and blew the smoke out slowly.

"Exactly," Theodosia said. "And now that Booker is out of the picture, the police are kind of grasping at straws."

"And so are you."

"Which is why I'm here," Theodosia said. "To see if you could give me something—anything—that might help resolve this case."

"I'm not sure I can help," Hooper said. "Booker and I were roommates, sure, but he was a quiet guy, kind of closed in. He was mostly focused on his work, on making a name for himself."

"Not a lot of friends?"

"More like acquaintances. But I can tell you this. Booker was no killer. He was big, he looked kind of mean sometimes, but he was a good guy. The kind of guy who'd help out a neighbor or donate to a food bank."

"Really," Theodosia said. She hadn't expected this.

"Booker taught the occasional class at the Arts Alliance, too. Mostly to kids. He tried to help them express their feelings and emotions through painting."

"That's very admirable. But I have to ask. Did Booker have a temper?"

"Not so much. He might get a little huffy when he downed a few too many cans of Holy City Pilsner, but nothing too crazy. Now me? I'm the one with the bad temper. Get me riled up and watch out!"

"Did Booker have any enemies that you know of?"

Hooper shook his head. "The cops asked me that same question and I couldn't come up with a soul."

"Not even somebody who was jealous that he'd gained some prominence in the art world?"

"Nobody I can think of."

Theodosia wondered what else she could ask.

"Do you know if there's, um, going to be a service? A funeral?"

"That will be up to Booker's folks. I gave the cops his parent's names and address when they came by last night." Hooper let loose a snort. "Had to give them my alibi, too."

Theodosia stood up. "Booker's folks, are they from around here?"

"Little town called Long Creek up in the Blue Ridge." Hooper looked mournful as he shook his head. "This is gonna crush those poor people."

They walked to the door, both of them lost in thought.

Stepping outside, Theodosia turned and said, "What's with Binger, anyway?"

Hooper made a face. "That miserable little shit? He's always trying to siphon fuel out of our gas tanks. Drives me crazy."

"It would me, too," Theodosia said.

On the way home Theodosia took a short detour to the Early Bird Diner on the Savannah Highway. The Early Bird Diner was a Charleston mainstay that had once been profiled on the TV show *Diners, Drive-Ins and Dives,* and their fried chicken was the best in the state. Maybe in the country.

Waiting in line, Theodosia decided on fried chicken with spicy honey sauce, but was still scanning the list of sides. She was allowed two and it was a tricky decision because their offerings included French fries, fried okra, mac and cheese, butter beans, collards, mashed taters, and corn cakes—and each one was home-cooking good. Finally, she chose fried okra and corn cakes.

Not exactly a heart-healthy dinner, but Theodosia was a diligent runner and could afford to be indulgent once in a while. Plus, she didn't feel like cooking tonight. She'd feed Earl Grey, enjoy her takeout dinner, and flake out with a good book. Maybe reading a mystery by Susan Wittig Albert or Terrie Farley Moran would spark some ideas and help her solve her own murder mystery.

She was still looking forward to a leisurely evening as she parked her car in the alley and grabbed her bag of takeout. Moonlight shone down, frosting the leafy trees, while a soft wind whispered through sweet magnolias.

Even with that bucolic picture, Theodosia knew something was wrong the minute she stepped through her back gate.

28

~❦~

What's wrong? Theodosia asked herself. *What's got me so jumpy?*

Every fiber in Theodosia's being strummed with apprehension. She could hear Earl Grey grumbling in the kitchen while the atmosphere in her back yard felt dangerous—as if the whole area had been charged with electricity.

A few more steps in and Theodosia saw what had caused her spider sense to kick in.

The goldfish from her little pond—almost a dozen of them—lay dead on the lawn. Lined up as if someone had done his killing in a deliberately cold and calculating manner.

As her stomach dropped so did her takeout. Chicken and sauce splattered against the flagstone patio, corn cakes bounced onto the grass.

"Who would do this?" Theodosia's words rose in a mournful cry as she fell to her knees and gazed at the sad, lifeless fish that had been swimming around an hour earlier. She touched a finger to one, hoping it was still alive, hoping she could slide it gently back into the pond. But the little fish was stiff as a board. So were all the others.

Please, not every one of them!

But they were dead, their eyes and mouths wide open as if they'd watched their killer even as they gasped a final breath.

"Who would . . . ?" She started to cry again. Then the answer floated back to her, slamming into her heart like a sledgehammer.

The killer.

Whoever had murdered Osgood Claxton, and probably shot Booker, was sending her a direct warning. A warning that said, *Back off or the same thing will happen to you.*

Dismay turned to white-hot anger as Theodosia sprang to her feet and looked around. Turned 360 degrees, arms out, hands pulled into claws as if she was ready to attack whoever— or whatever—might still be lurking in her backyard.

But there was nothing. Except a lingering sense of danger.

Had the killer been right here in her backyard? Of course he had. Just steps from the cottage she called home, steps from where her precious Earl Grey had been sleeping. Theodosia felt a frisson of fear trickle down her spine.

Yes, the killer had been here. Maybe an hour ago, or maybe a few minutes ago. The idea rattled the hell out of her.

Theodosia flew inside, locked the back door behind her, then double-checked it.

Earl Grey was standing in the kitchen next to his bed, mouth open, panting, confusion in his eyes. He'd been barking out his warning to anybody who would listen. But no one had come to help. He saw Theodosia, bounded over to her, and thrust his muzzle into her hands. He let loose a mournful sound, almost like a cry of regret.

"I know," Theodosia said. "And I'm so sorry." She knelt down, gathered her dog in her arms, and hugged him tight. "But you did the best job you could under the circumstances and I'm here now. The important thing is—are you okay?"

Earl Grey snuggled closer to Theodosia as she kissed the top of his head, then gently kneaded his muzzle. This was where dogs held most of their tension, and she figured Earl Grey must have been plenty tense if he'd known a stranger was creeping around outside and destroying her goldfish.

Now the question was—what to do about the rest of the evening? Stay here? Call the police? Call Riley? But as Theodosia pulled her phone out of her bag, she knew in her heart who she would call.

"Is your guest room made up?" she asked when Drayton answered.

"Always," Drayton said. "My cleaning lady, Mrs. Drew, was just here yesterday and, if she's up to her usual standards, has rendered it spotless, poufed up the coverlets, and put out fresh towels. What's the problem? What poor unfortunate in need of a bed are you sending my way?"

"Me."

"Excuse me?"

"And Earl Grey if you'll have him."

"You're both welcome, absolutely. But why? Has something happened?"

So Theodosia told him about the dead goldfish and her theory that the killer had snuck into her backyard, possibly looking to harm her. And then, not finding her, had taken out his anger and frustration on her poor goldfish.

"You're quite sure all the fish are dead?"

"There's no doubt. If you could have seen those poor little things . . ."

"You're sure you want to come here instead of going to Riley's place?"

"If I go to Riley's, he'll lock me in the coat closet and throw away the key."

"We can't have that," Drayton said. "You'd better come over."

When Theodosia arrived, Drayton's first words were "Are you unharmed?"

"I'm okay," Theodosia said. Physically, she felt fine. But the death of her fish, and the knowledge of the intrusion, had definitely shaken her up. Theodosia was first and foremost a homebody. And when the sanctity of her home was invaded, she lapsed into a cold fury. And while she knew this wasn't a particularly genteel attitude for a lady of the Southern persuasion, that's what it was, plain and simple.

Drayton's next question was "Have you had dinner yet?"

"Unfortunately, I lost my dinner."

He lifted an eyebrow. "Pardon?"

"No," she laughed. "Not like that. When I walked into my yard and saw the poor fish, my bag of takeout from the Early Bird Diner sort of tumbled out of my hands and hit the pavement."

"Understandable. But, oh my, their chicken is tasty. Sounds as if I'd better fix you something to eat. My larder is empty of actual poultry at the moment, but I do have eggs. Would an omelet work?"

"I'll accept anything at this point."

"We can do better than anything," Drayton said as he pulled

an onion and a bunch of chives from his vegetable bin, then eggs, cream, and a half wheel of sharp cheddar from his refrigerator. "Let me get this going and you'll be dining in splendor, or a reasonable facsimile, in no time at all."

Actually, Theodosia did dine in splendor. Because Drayton didn't just break out the melamine dishes and everyday flatware. He slid her omelet onto a Limoges plate, grabbed a pot of Formosa oolong tea, then led Theodosia to his dining room, where they sat down at his Chippendale table.

The thing about Drayton was . . . he loved antiques. Not the fussy, faux stuff, the real-deal classic pieces. And he'd furnished his home accordingly with French provincial chairs, a Georgian mahogany coffee table, and a tufted leather sofa. His white marble fireplace was imported from France and his floors were heart-pine covered with fine Persian carpets. Silk curtains swagged his beveled glass lattice windows and his library was accented with antique barrister bookcases. So fabulous was his home that it had once been showcased in *Southern Interiors Magazine*.

As Theodosia enjoyed her poufier-than-air omelet, she looked up at one of the paintings on the wall and said, "Don't you feel intimidated by that portrait?" Drayton had an oil painting of Charles Grey, the second Earl Grey and a former British Prime Minister, hanging over his table.

"Not in the least," Drayton said as he sipped his tea. "But if I were you, I'd be intimidated by whoever murdered your little goldies. Correct me if I'm wrong, but I'm assuming it's probably the same psychopath who murdered Osgood Claxton and Booker."

"I think you're right," Theodosia said.

"So you should be afraid, very afraid."

"I'm a lot more angry than I am afraid."

"Not good. Not smart." Drayton took another sip of his tea and leaned back in his chair. "I worry about you."

Theodosia smiled at him. "I worry about me. And you were right when you said, 'And then there were none.' I feel like we're scraping the bottom of the barrel on suspects."

"Are you still mulling over the possibility of Mignon Merriweather or Ginny Bell being the killer?"

"I see possibilities, but not probabilities."

"Interesting. Then perhaps we're completely off base," Drayton said. "Perhaps the killer is someone who's not even on our radar."

"I'm starting to wonder if that might be the problem."

"In which case we're nowhere."

"Please don't say that. Because I hate to let Holly down. She's in crisis and her gallery is losing money."

"*Is* her gallery losing money?" Drayton asked. "Did you ever ask Holly about the two hundred thousand dollars that her silent partner put into the business?"

"I never did. But now that you bring it up, I'm going to ask Holly the details of her so-called cash infusion first thing tomorrow."

"Good," Drayton said. "You can settle that once and for all." He glanced at his watch and said, "Gracious, it's gotten late. Shall we take a quick walk in the garden with the dogs?"

"Love to," Theodosia said.

They cleared the table, left everything sitting on the kitchen counter, and walked outside. The moon was just rising, and gazing at it over a stand of bamboo, Theodosia felt as if she'd been magically transported to a garden in Kyoto, Japan. She'd visited Kyoto once and been transfixed by its temples, gardens, and abundant parkland. In fact, with the city's tiny restaurants, shops selling tea wares, incense, and yukatas, and grand vistas of the Higashiyama mountains, the whole city cast a Zen-like spell.

She remembered in particular a walk she'd taken up Kiyomizu-Zaka, a picturesque, narrow lane that led to the wondrous Kiyomizu-dera Temple. Built in the early sixteen hundreds, Kiyomizu was an enormous wooden structure constructed without a single nail. Surrounded by forests and mountains, it was a UNESCO World Heritage Site. And when Theodosia had visited in late autumn, the surrounding woods had been aglow with fire red maples.

A scuff of stones at her feet and a gentle bump told Theodosia that Honey Bee and Earl Grey were having a great time bounding about and playing their little doggy games. Over on the patio Drayton had picked up a clipper and was snipping errant fronds from one of his bonsai trees. Up in the sky the moon seemed smaller but brighter, a harbinger, hopefully, of better things to come.

Which all made Theodosia finally relax and heave a sigh of contentment.

29

On Saturday mornings the Indigo Tea Shop generally offered a prix fixe cream tea. Today, there were two options. The first was a maple scone with Devonshire cream, a citrus salad with fresh strawberries, and a chicken salad tea sandwich. The second option was a Parmesan scone with honey butter, a slice of mushroom quiche, and a ham salad tea sandwich.

And even though Theodosia never formally advertised their prix fixe tea—which was actually a kind of brunch—they were generally mobbed.

Today was one of those days.

"Holy catfish," Drayton exclaimed as he worked furiously behind the counter brewing multiple pots of tea, "I can't believe how busy we are this morning."

"We're busy every Saturday morning," Theodosia reminded him as she gathered up a stack of clean teacups. "It means it's good to be in business. You remember, good-old fashioned capitalism?"

"Thank you for the economics lesson. Now can you please pass me that tin of Irish breakfast tea?"

Theodosia passed him the tea. "Take heart," she said. "You only have to hold out until one thirty. Then we close."

"Unless we're blessed with late arriving guests. You tend to be awfully lenient when it comes to Saturday hours."

"Today I'm sticking to my guns," Theodosia promised.

"Speaking of guns. What did you ever do with my pistol?"

Theodosia looked up and pushed her hair back. "Oh man, I forgot all about that. I stuck it in my tailgate storage bag."

"At some point I should probably get it back."

"Because you're a one-man militia," Theodosia laughed. "Armed and dangerous."

"No, the gun simply has sentimental value."

Theodosia grabbed a teapot of Darjeeling. "Why do I have trouble believing that?" She was feeling upbeat today. She'd gone home this morning to take a shower and change clothes, feed Earl Grey, walk him, and dispose of the fish. Earl Grey's dog nanny, Mrs. Barry, would be dropping by this afternoon to walk him.

As Theodosia was pouring tea for Brooke Carter Crocket, a jewelry shop owner from down the street, Haley came up behind her and tapped her on the shoulder.

"We just ran out of maple scones," Haley said, looking worried. "I—I don't know what happened. I must have underestimated or something."

Theodosia blinked as she thought for a few moments. "Oh, shoot, Haley, it's *my* fault. The Lady Goodwood Inn called in a humongous takeout order and I packaged up the scones and then forgot to tell you. But could we . . . I mean, do we have an alternative?"

"How about strawberry scones?" Haley asked. "I just whipped up a triple batch and stuck them in the oven. But I thought I'd better check with you first." She shrugged. "Sorry."

"Come on, Haley, you know we don't play the blame game around here. Stuff happens—to all of us. And the strawberry scones are perfect. I just have to remember to tell customers there's been a change."

"A switcheroo," Haley said, relieved now. "Hope they don't mind."

"They won't," Theodosia said as the front door opened and a group of four women came fluttering in. They looked around with such anticipation on their faces that Drayton hastily slid out from behind the counter, greeted them, and shepherded them to a newly cleared table. Then the front door popped open once again and Holly Burns walked in.

With one eye on Holly, Theodosia continued pouring refills. Then, when her pot was empty, she dropped it off for Drayton to refill.

Holly grinned when she saw Theodosia crook a finger at her.

"Your shop is so busy." Holly sounded surprised as she hurried over to the front counter.

"Ever since Haley came up with this idea for a prix fixe cream tea, we've had to beat customers off with a stick," Theodosia said.

"Wish *I* could say that," Holly said with a wistful tone. Then her mood darkened. "We haven't talked in a couple of days . . . but isn't it awful about Booker?"

"The police contacted you, huh?"

"Came by the gallery first thing yesterday and asked about a million questions. How well did I know Booker? Did he have any enemies? Where was I that night? That sort of thing. Like you see detectives doing on TV."

"One detective?"

Holly shook her head. "They were out in full force. Two uniformed officers and a big guy, kind of a no-nonsense type, who I assumed was in charge."

"Detective Tidwell?"

"I guess that was his name."

"Did the police tell you anything about the circumstances?" Theodosia asked.

"They explained to me that Booker had been shot at his cabin on Little Clam Island." Holly coughed to clear the slight catch in her voice and added, "And that you and Drayton found him."

"I wish we hadn't."

"Why did you go out there?" Holly grabbed Theodosia's hand and squeezed it tight. "Was it for my benefit?"

"I wanted to tie everything up nice and neat," Theodosia admitted. "Ask Booker straight out if he'd murdered Claxton. Look him in the eye and see if he was telling the truth."

"Then Booker must not have been the killer," Holly said in a tight voice. "Booker couldn't have murdered Claxton if he's dead now, too. There's somebody else out there. But . . . who?"

"I don't know," Theodosia said.

"Now I'm worried about you," Holly said with some insistence. "There are two dead people and I don't want you to be the third. I don't think you should mess around with this investigation anymore, it's too dangerous."

Drayton leaned in. "Exactly what I've been telling Theodosia."

"You see?" Holly's eyes implored Theodosia. "The police were very firm about me keeping my distance from their investigation. So you should, too."

"I think you're probably right," Theodosia said.

"I'm glad someone's come to their senses," Drayton murmured. Then added, in a louder voice, "Would you like a cup of tea, Holly?"

"Yes, thank you," Holly said. "But could you make it to go?"

"Irish breakfast work for you?" Drayton asked.

"Perfect," Holly said.

Drayton poured tea into an indigo blue cup, snapped on a lid, and handed it to Holly. "I do hope your business starts to pick up again," he said. He smiled at Holly, then flashed a knowing look at Theodosia.

"Fingers crossed," Holly said as she accepted her cup of tea.

Theodosia knew this was her chance to talk to Holly and ask her about the money, the investment she'd received from her silent partner. So she walked Holly to the door and went outside with her so they could have a conversation in private.

"How *is* business at the gallery?" Theodosia asked.

"Not great. We've had a few nibbles here and there but no major sales."

Theodosia put her arms around a sad looking Holly and gave her a gentle hug. "You're going to bounce back, I know you will. Your gallery's divine and there are plenty of great artists out there who are probably dying to be represented by you."

"You think?"

"Yes, I do." Theodosia took a step back. "But Holly, there's something troubling me, something I've been meaning to ask you about."

"Uh-huh?"

"You received a good-sized sum of cash not too long ago. From your silent partner, Jeremy Slade. It was an investment of, I believe, two hundred thousand dollars."

Holly looked suddenly panicked. "Oh jeez, I had a feeling you were going to ask me about that eventually."

"And that's a problem?" Theodosia said.

Holly looked like she was ready to cry. "Actually, it's turned into an enormous problem."

"What's wrong? Something to do with the gallery?"

"If you really want to know, and I guess you do, I used some of Jeremy Slade's investment money to pay for Philip's lawyer."

Theodosia knew this was fairly unethical but decided to hold her criticism for now. Instead, she said, "Does Philip know about this?"

Holly flinched. "Philip just figured the guy charged super reasonable rates."

"Oh my. And what did this lawyer do for Philip?"

"Worked to get Philip's liquor license. You know my life's dream has always been to own a successful gallery and have lots of art openings. Well, the Boldt Hole is Philip's ultimate dream."

"I get that, I really do," Theodosia said. "But a lawyer's fee couldn't have been more than, what, two or three thousand dollars?"

Holly shifted from one foot to the other looking uncomfortable. "I guess."

"But you've been lamenting how broke you are. So I have to ask, what did you do with the rest of the money?"

Holly's chin quivered. "I gave some to Philip."

Theodosia was stunned. "What? Holly, how much of Jeremy's investment money did you give to Philip?"

Holly hunched her shoulders forward in a protective gesture. "One hundred and sixty thousand dollars?"

"Is that a question or an answer?"

"An answer. And I knew all along I was wrong to do it," Holly wailed. "But you don't know how desperate Philip was! And now that his liquor license has come through . . . well, he needs everything in place so he can open quick. It's kind of do-or-die at this point."

"Dear Lord." Theodosia said. "Are you telling me the money's all gone?"

Holly squirmed. "Pretty much."

"What on earth did Philip use all that money for?" Theodosia demanded.

Now Holly hung her head. "He bought tables and chairs, kitchen equipment, and a wine collection."

"So *you* furnished his restaurant? Wow. Does your investor know about this? Does Jeremy Slade know that you handed over the bulk of his investment to Philip?"

"No!" Holly blinked back tears. "And please don't tell him, because I'm going to try and work something out. Unfortunately, I haven't figured out exactly what to do, short of throwing in the towel and declaring bankruptcy."

"Please don't do that," Theodosia said. "Bankruptcy would be a point of no return. You've been able to build your business thus far, now you have to rebuild it. What you need to do is buckle down. Bulk up on inventory—find some hot new artists to represent—and work on finding some qualified buyers. Start building a database—I can help you with that—and do some advertising, even if it's just sending out postcards. One hundred and sixty thousand dollars is a huge sum, but I know you can recoup it. Take it from me—just like life, business can turn on a dime."

"I get that. And I know Philip will be making some serious money real soon. In fact, that's why . . ."

Holly's cell phone suddenly tinkled inside her purse.

Theodosia reached out and took Holly's cup of tea as she scrambled to find her phone.

"Imago Gallery," Holly said. "How may I help you?" Holly

listened for a few minutes, said, "Yes, that piece is still available along with some others by him." She shifted on her feet, said, "What time were you thinking?" She listened for a while longer, nodded to herself, and said, "I look forward to seeing you both." When Holly clicked off, she wore a faint smile on her face. "Theodosia," she said, "I think you're my lucky charm!"

"I'm guessing that phone call was good news?"

Holly bobbed her head. "That was a potential new client, a couple who wants to come by the gallery today and look at some paintings by an artist named Gordon Rafael."

"He's the one who does those pointillism landscapes?"

"Of the swamps and old rice fields, yeah." Holly rocked back on her heels, suddenly in good humor now. "Which is great. Except . . ." She glanced at her watch.

"Except?" Theodosia said. She expected Holly to say something more about the money.

"Except for the fact that I promised Philip I'd run out to Frog Hollow Farm this afternoon and pick up six baskets of produce. He's already got, like, fifty takeout orders for tonight." Holly nodded. "You see, word is starting to spread about how terrific Philip's food is, so I know we can make the money back that way."

"When are your art clients supposed to show up?"

Holly glanced at her watch again. "In an hour. I mean, I'm thrilled they want to look at Rafael's paintings, but selecting art for your home tends to be a very personal decision. One not easily made." She managed a wry smile. "Yipes, first I was at odds and ends, now I'm pressed for time."

"Tell you what," Theodosia said. "Haley has been searching high and low for fresh ramps and spinach. Do you think Frog Hollow Farm will have that?"

Holly looked suddenly hopeful. "I know they will."

"Then your short-term problem is solved. You go schmooze your new clients while I drive out there and pick up your produce. That way I can grab a bunch of veggies for Haley as well."

"You'd do that for me? Wow." Holly looked beyond thrilled. "Thank you, Theodosia. You're not only good luck, I couldn't ask for a better friend!"

Theodosia handed Holly's cup of tea back to her and said, "Now I want you to go be charming and make that sale! And we'll talk about this money angle again later."

Back in the tea shop, the prix fixe tea was winding down.

"It's almost one thirty," Drayton reminded Theodosia. He tapped his watch. "Remember what you said?"

"And there are only two tables left, so we should be in great shape," Theodosia replied as her cell phone beeped.

She dug it out of her apron pocket, saw it was Riley, and said, "Hey, cowboy."

"We're still on for tonight, right?" Riley said.

"Looking forward to it."

"Good, because we have an eight o'clock reservation at High Cotton."

Theodosia grinned. "Wow. That's a jumpin'-hot place."

"We deserve it, don't you think?"

"If you say so," Theodosia said.

"I do. So. Are you closing early today?"

"I'm just about to lock the front door. Then I'm heading out to pick up some fresh produce."

"For real? You're not off on some wild chase to investigate a potential suspect?"

"Not today."

"Okay, good girl. Just don't forget 'twas curiosity that killed the cat."

"Or maybe that cat has nine lives."

"You're incorrigible." Riley was still chuckling as he hung up.

Theodosia pointed at Drayton as she walked past the counter and said, "One thirty. That's our official closing time." Then she went into the kitchen to ask Haley about produce.

Haley was ecstatic. "Frog Hollow Farm? Holy guacamole, they're, like, a famous purveyor of vegetables and poultry. Totally farm to table. The chef at Husk Restaurant uses them and he's super picky. Jeepers. I'd better do a little preplanning for next week's menu, so I know what to put on my list."

"Take your time," Theodosia said. She wandered back into a now empty tea room and saw Drayton bent over the counter, glasses perched on his nose, cup of tea at hand, reading the *Post & Courier*.

"Are you checking the help wanted ads? Looking for a better job?"

Drayton straightened up. "What? No, of course not."

"Kidding, just kidding. I was wondering if you're in a mood to take a drive with me."

He closed the paper. "Depends on where you're going."

"Still worried about getting roped into a wild goose chase?"

"The thought had occurred to me."

"Well, you can relax. I'm heading out to Frog Hollow Farm to pick up produce for Philip's restaurant and get an order for Haley as well."

"Sounds lovely," Drayton said. He glanced out the window and gave an affirmative nod. "With plenty of sun and a robin's-egg blue sky, it should be a perfect day for a drive."

30

It was indeed a perfect day for a drive.

Theodosia headed down East Bay Street, hooked a right, and crossed the Ravenel Bridge. They'd rolled the windows down to let in copious amounts of warm sun and cool air, Rascal Flatts played on the radio, and Drayton rode shotgun.

He glanced down at the Cooper River as they spun across the bridge. "Even the river is a brilliant blue today," he said. "Must be a lucky sign."

They drove through Mount Pleasant on Highway 17, cut down Long Point Road, and, after a few turns, ended up in a decidedly rural area.

"You know where we're going?" Drayton asked.

"Got a good idea."

They swept around a tight S-curve, saw sunlight glinting off brackish water and tupelo gum trees standing like lone sentinels.

"Pretty out here," Drayton observed. "How close are we to this wondrous farm?"

"Another few miles," Theodosia said.

They passed an old church—what the locals called a praise house—and then a cluster of roadside stands.

"Look at that," Drayton said. "They're selling fresh blue crabs."

"Nothin' better," Theodosia said.

A few minutes later Theodosia saw the beginnings of a rustic ranch fence set against a forest of shaggy willow oaks. Beyond were lush, green fields and a big sign that said FROG HOLLOW FARM—FRESH PRODUCE AND POULTRY. And under that, in smaller type, it said PICK YOUR OWN.

There was one car and two pickup trucks as they pulled into the parking lot.

"Not too busy today," Drayton said.

"But such a pretty place," Theodosia said as they rolled to a stop.

Nearby was a large white barn, a smaller red barn, and a good-sized open-air stand with displays of vegetables. There was also a large fenced yard that contained a flock of ducks and, just past that, what looked like acres of rolling green fields. Beyond that was a tall fence that must have been some type of large animal enclosure. It was all very rural and Norman Rockwell in its charm.

"Are we going to buy our produce at the stand over there or pick our own?" Drayton asked.

"Pick our own," Theodosia said as she stood in dappled sunlight while a cool breeze stirred the trees overhead. "It'll be fun."

But just as she walked around to the back of her car, a green Jaguar came bumping into the parking lot.

"No, it can't be," Theodosia said as her heart skipped a beat.

"Hmm?" Drayton said. He wasn't paying much attention as the Jaguar pulled in and parked some twenty feet away.

"Drayton, the green Jaguar—that's Lamar Lucket's car."

Drayton turned to look. "An older model, at that. A classic."

But Theodosia had more on her mind than classic cars. "What he's doing here? Did he follow us?"

Drayton frowned as he jingled the change in his pocket. "Perhaps you should go over and ask him."

Theodosia was already striding toward the Jaguar. And when the door opened and Lucket popped out, she said, "What are *you* doing here?"

When he recognized her, Lucket did a kind of double take. "I could ask you the same thing."

"Did you follow me?"

His eyes fluttered. "Follow you?"

"It's a straightforward question."

"Then my answer is no," Lucket said. Now he looked flustered. "Look, I'm picking up produce for my chef. We're hosting a private dinner tonight at Nusa Dua and he needed a few extra things."

"Like what, cilantro?"

"I don't know. I haven't looked at the list yet."

"Right," Theodosia said. "Sure." When Lucket failed to respond, she turned and walked away. "C'mon, Drayton."

But Theodosia was in for another surprise. Because as they drew closer to the produce stand, she suddenly noticed another familiar figure standing near the red barn. "Philip's here," she said to Drayton. "That's weird."

"I thought we drove out here precisely to grab his produce and ferry it to his restaurant," Drayton said.

"So did I. Something must have changed."

They walked toward Philip as he smiled and waved at them.

"I came out here to pick up my produce," Philip told them with a friendly smile. He was wearing jeans, a beige western shirt, and boots. He looked casual and relaxed, as if he'd been hanging around the old corral all day.

"I thought that's what *we* were supposed to do," Theodosia said. "I think we got our wires crossed somewhere along the line."

Philip held up a hand. "No, no, it wasn't you. I just talked to Holly and she said you were driving out here, as a favor to her, to grab my order. But she hung up before I could get your cell phone number so I could tell you the trip wasn't necessary." He spread his arms wide. "I didn't want to call Holly back because she was all excited about some clients coming in."

"I know," Theodosia said. "Holly's terribly worried about money."

Philip breezed past Theodosia's money comment.

"Anyway," Philip said, "my meeting got canceled, so all of a sudden I had some free time. I'm sorry you drove all the way out here for nothing."

"It's not a problem. We're going to grab some produce for the tea shop as well," Theodosia explained. She stepped closer to Philip, deciding this might be the perfect time to confront him about the money. "And just so you know, Holly pretty much told me the whole story about the money she loaned you." She tilted her head to one side and cast a questioning glance at him. "I believe you have some serious explaining to do."

"So Holly spilled the beans, did she?" Philip looked almost relieved.

"She told me that she basically financed your restaurant," Theodosia said.

"Holly is . . . beyond generous," Philip said. "We both knew it wasn't the smartest move in the book to use the money like that, but we rolled the dice and took a chance."

Drayton gazed at Theodosia. "Did I miss something here?"

"Remember when we talked about the money Holly received from her silent partner?" Theodosia said to him.

"Indeed I do," Drayton said.

"Well, Holly gave Philip a good portion of that investment," Theodosia said. "Most of it actually. So he could get his restaurant up and running."

"Oh my," Drayton said. He touched a hand to his bow tie. "That could prove to be problematic."

"It already is," Theodosia said.

"No," Philip said. He reached his hands out and patted the air in a calming gesture. "Believe me, it's all going to work out. We'll be opening the Boldt Hole in less than a week. Not just takeout, but the whole shebang. Sit-down dining, catering, and private parties. Everything under the sun. I'm talking one hundred, maybe even a hundred and fifty covers every night."

"So you're really all set? Your liquor license is squared away?" Theodosia asked.

"Absolutely everything's in place. The situation couldn't be rosier," Philip said.

"And of course you have that world-class wine cellar," Theodosia said in a somewhat chiding tone.

"Putting that collection together was a labor of love," Philip said.

"Even though you used someone else's money?" Drayton asked.

"Look," Philip said to both of them, "The Boldt Hole *is* going to pay off. Probably sooner than later. This isn't my first rodeo. I know what I'm doing. The takeout has already been going gangbusters and my customers have all been begging for full-service dining. Like I said, Holly and I took a chance using that money, but in six months or so, I firmly expect to pay it all back. With interest, if need be."

Theodosia wasn't completely convinced, she didn't like the underhandedness of the deal, but she had to admit that Philip was a go-getter. Charleston had turned into a major foodie town, so there was an excellent chance Philip would turn a fairly decent profit even as he turned his dreams into reality.

"Okay," Theodosia said, knowing she was conceding. "What's done is done, all you can do now is give it your best shot."

"I promise you," Philip said. "It's going to be okay. Better than okay. I'm not some crazy gambler or wild-cat risk taker. This is me, mild-mannered Philip. You look in Webster's dictionary under mild-mannered and you see a teensy little picture of me, right?" He held up his hands to frame his face.

At which point Theodosia couldn't help but laugh.

"And you guys . . ." Philip gestured at Theodosia and Drayton. "I want you to be my guests of honor on opening night. Okay?"

"Okay," Theodosia agreed.

Philip looked at Drayton. "That sound righteous to you, Mr. Conneley? I know you're a wine connoisseur, so I'm sensing you probably have a discerning palate as well. Am I right?"

"You're not half wrong," Drayton said.

"Great," Philip said. "Then it's settled."

Theodosia looked back toward the car park but didn't see Lucket anywhere. A nugget of worry bubbled up inside her, then she gazed out over acres of rolling green fields and decided she'd be safe enough. "So," she said to Philip, "what do we do? How does this work?"

"You can buy produce at the stand—they'll even pack it for you and carry it to your car. But I prefer to pick everything fresh myself," Philip said. "That way I know I'm getting the best selection and that it's really farm to table."

"Like when you pick your own apples or fresh strawberries up in the Piedmont," Drayton said.

"Exactly," Philip said.

"Then let's do it," Drayton said.

"Give me a minute," Theodosia said. "I want to grab a market basket out of my Jeep." Philip's words had left her feeling somewhat reassured. And while she didn't fully approve of what Holly and Philip had done, Philip impressed her as serious and hardworking. His plan to repay the money in six months actually sounded plausible.

"Then you walk with me, Drayton," Philip said. "I want to show you the most amazing crop of butter beans. And you for sure have to take a look at the cattle ranch next door."

Theodosia walked back to her Jeep slowly, deciding this might be a good time to spy on Lucket, but he was nowhere in sight. His car was there, but he wasn't.

Doggone it. Where did he go?

On the way to grab her market basket, Theodosia caught a quick glance at a fluffy red hen sprinting across the grass. Then, as if the hen was being pursued by a hungry fox, it darted inside the red barn.

Curious, wondering if it was a Derbyshire Redcap, similar to the Hamburg chickens her aunt Libby raised, Theodosia detoured over to the barn and peered in. And saw . . . not a single chicken.

Where did that little cutie run off to?

Theodosia took a step inside the barn and looked around. Dust motes twirled in the air and the place felt cool and dim, smelling of fresh hay and chicken feed. The interior wood, the struts, and the crossbeams were pleasantly weathered, and some leather horse tack hung on the walls.

She continued to look around but didn't see the chicken. Could it have fluttered up into the hayloft? She peered upward but saw only a shaggy overhang of hay and small birds—finches?—roosting in the rafters high above.

But there was something. A low, scuttling noise. Maybe chickens, maybe . . . Lucket?

Theodosia was momentarily gripped with fear. Her head pounded as she wondered if Lucket was hiding somewhere inside this barn. Was that where he'd disappeared to?

Doggone, seeing him here just feels too weird to be a coincidence.

Just as Theodosia was about to step back outside to find Drayton and Philip, she heard a gentle clucking sound. And as she looked around, her eyes caught a quick flash of red over in the corner.

The little chicken?

She hesitated a split second, then stepped over to investigate.

But no. The thing that had caught her eye was bright red, but it wasn't any kind of chicken. Rather, it was something shiny and hard, covered with a beige canvas tarp. Maybe a farm implement?

No, it looks too small for that. Then what?

Feeling a blip of nervous energy, Theodosia reached a hand out and pulled back the tarp. And stared at a shiny red-and-black Triumph motorcycle.

Her mouth went dry, her head started to pound again.

It was a Tiger Sport 660, a motorcycle not unlike the one that had been seen speeding away from the scene of Claxton's murder.

What were the partial plate numbers on the motorcycle that the eyewitness had seen?

Theodosia racked her brain even as she felt sick to her stomach. Then she remembered the numbers and suddenly saw them in her mind's eye, like a white neon sign outlined against a brilliant blue background. The numbers were nine five three.

Bells clanged in her head, her heart beat a timpani solo. The last three numerals on this license plate were nine five eight. Could an eight have been misread or misremembered as a three? Of course it could have been.

What to do? And just whose motorcycle was this? Did Lamar Lucket have some strange connection to this farm? And if Lucket was the one who'd murdered Claxton, if he *was* the killer in the beekeeper's suit, then they were in big trouble.

Distraught, terrified at jumping to conclusions, but faced with possible evidence, Theodosia suddenly remembered Drayton! And Philip!

Could Drayton and Philip be in grave danger this very minute?

31

Philip had walked Drayton the entire length of the butterbean field, when, off in the distance, he noticed Theodosia suddenly disappear into the red barn. He thought for a moment, decided she was smart, maybe too smart for her own good. So he turned back to Drayton and said, "Now that you've seen these amazing fields full of produce, how would you like to tour the farm where they raise the Wangus beef?"

"I'd enjoy that," Drayton said.

They walked another fifty feet, then Philip waved a hand and pointed to a wooden corral with high, spiky posts. "We can take an easy shortcut through here to the barns. I think you'll be impressed by the workings of the Red Hat Cattle Ranch."

"I'm sure I will," Drayton said. "Although I'm not exactly dressed for this kind of adventure." Drayton was still wearing a linen jacket and summer-weight slacks, and now his shoes were covered with a fine film of reddish-brown dust.

Philip unlatched a tall gate that opened into the corral. He made a friendly *go ahead* gesture to Drayton and said, "After you." Once Drayton was inside the corral, he added, "It won't matter to the bull how well-dressed you are once he gets a hold of you."

"The bull?" Drayton said, just as Philip shoved a hand into the middle of Drayton's back, gave him a hard push, and sent him flying to his knees. Then he slammed the gate and latched it tight.

Stunned by Philip's sudden aggression, it took Drayton a few minutes to recover, to pick himself up and dust off. Completely shaken by this bizarre turn of events, Drayton spun toward Philip and cried, "Why did you do that? What's going on?"

"Your too-smart-for-her-own-good tea lady just walked into that barn over there."

Confused, Drayton looked over at the barn, but he didn't see Theodosia anywhere. "What are you talking about?" he asked as he put both hands on the gate and peered through the bars at Philip, who was safely on the other side.

"If and when she sees my motorcycle, she's going to put two and two together mighty fast."

"I'm still not following you," Drayton said.

"You see, there was one city official who was holding things up for me."

Drayton stared at Philip. "One city official?" Then the meaning of Philip's words finally sank in. "You mean Claxton?" he asked, surprise lighting his eyes. "*You* killed Claxton? You're the one who escaped on a motorcycle?"

Philip executed a deep bow. "At your service."

"Because . . . why? Because you wouldn't pay a bribe?"

Philip's face darkened with rage. "Claxton was holding me hostage for every penny I had. Promising results but always holding out for more money. Something had to be done—I was desperate to get that liquor license approved. And I needed every cent I could scrape together. Still do. My restaurant is the *only thing* that matters to me."

"Dear Lord," Drayton cried as all the pieces clicked into place for him. "Did you kill Booker as well?"

"That creep Booker overheard me in the gallery talking about my motorcycle, trying to sell it. He was always sneaking in and out, snooping around. I didn't even know he was there half the time. He overheard me and I worried that sooner or later that dimwit brain of his would crank on a forty-watt bulb and figure things out. Anyway, I knew where his hidey-hole was. The rest was easy."

Drayton stared at him incredulously. "You're going to kill me, too."

"No, I'm going to let the bull take care of that."

Drayton spun around. "What bull? I don't see any bull."

Claxton held up an index finger and grinned wickedly. "Give me a minute."

32

The first things Theodosia heard were cries of desperation. Then, rising above that, laughter, high-pitched and almost maniacal.

Someone's in trouble?

Even though she didn't know the how or the why, Theodosia knew the circumstances probably weren't good. Sprinting to her Jeep, her body slammed against the back hatch with full force, almost knocking herself breathless. Then, struggling to catch her breath, she stepped back and jerked the hatch open. Drayton's pistol was where she'd left it. In the tailgate storage bag and still loaded.

She grabbed the pistol without hesitation.

Theodosia ran in the direction of the screams. Past the red barn, veering right at the white barn, ducking past a small orchard, then heading down a well-worn path that led to a high wooden corral.

Something seemed to be going on inside that corral, something dreadful from the sound of all the shouts and cries.

Dear Lord, would she make it in time? Was Lamar Lucket tormenting Drayton and Philip in some way? If so, what was he doing to them?

Theodosia picked up the pace, sucking in air as she ran down the trail. Her hair flew out behind her, her feet kicked up puffs of dirt. When she reached the wood fence where all the shouting was happening, she threw herself against it without hesitation and clawed her way up.

And there was Drayton in the middle of a corral. Frantic. Spinning in circles, slipping in the dirt, then springing to his feet again. He was covered in dust from head to toe, but Theodosia could see the fear etched on his face as he tried to elude the gigantic animal that was slowly stalking him.

The bull itself was an enormous bruiser, black with a shiny coat that glistened in the sun. At least a ton and a half of pure muscle and sinew, each horn curling out at least three feet where it came to a sharp point. A killing point.

"Run for the fence!" Theodosia yelled to Drayton. "Do it now!" Out of the corner of her eye she suddenly saw Philip hanging on the gate, laughing at Drayton's dire predicament, actually *enjoying* himself.

Philip? What's going on? Where's Lucket?

Drayton spun around fast, saw Theodosia waving to him, and almost tripped.

"The fence!" Theodosia screamed again. "Run to the fence and climb up."

The bull, meanwhile, lowered its head and pawed the dirt. It was getting ready to charge.

"Do it now, Drayton!" Theodosia shouted.

Finally heeding Theodosia's shouts, Drayton half ran, half limped for the fence. His long legs stretched out, his hands clawed for purchase. He hit the fence so hard the boards rattled and groaned. And just as he pulled himself up, achingly slow, just as his foot lifted off the lowest rail, the bull charged the fence with all the force it could muster.

WHAM!

The boards shuddered from such a cataclysmic collision.

Theodosia's heart was in her throat as she worried and prayed. But, thanks be to heaven, Drayton had made it! He'd scrambled to safety! Now he cowered on the top two rails of the fence, looking anguished, hanging on for dear life.

Philip, on the other hand, looked furious. He shook a fist at Drayton, shouting a string of unintelligible words. For some reason, he was ignoring Theodosia and focusing all his rage on Drayton.

"Philip!" Theodosia cried. "What are you *doing?*"

"You may have escaped the bull," Philip shrieked at Drayton, "but you can't escape me." Then Philip, a crazed half smile on his face, climbed up onto the very top of the gate, pulled out a gun, and pointed it directly at Drayton.

Theodosia stared in amazement, not knowing what to do. Was Philip stark raving mad? He must be. He had to be. Would he really shoot Drayton?

But there he was. Leveling his gun in Drayton's direction!

Theodosia knew she had to act fast, had to stop this cold-blooded killing. She was Drayton's only hope at this point. But could she hit Philip from this distance? Would her antique gun even fire?

Philip's grin stretched across his face like a malevolent Halloween jack-o'-lantern as he leveled his gun, rested his index finger on the trigger and . . .

BANG!

The explosion was deafening.

*   *   *

Drayton squeezed his eyes shut at the very last moment, tensing every muscle, every fiber of his being, hoping for the best. Praying that Philip was a lousy shot and would only wing him in the shoulder, causing a painful, but hopefully fixable, flesh wound.

As that horrible, cringe-inducing thought settled over Drayton, the world seemed to explode around him. Seconds later, his eyes flew open and he looked down at himself, fully expecting to see blood spurting from a terrible bullet wound.

But no.

Philip Boldt was the one with the shocked expression on his face. He was hanging on to the gate where he'd half fallen, twisting in agony. A gush of bright crimson blood poured from his left shoulder and his gun dropped from his hand. Then he lost his grip completely and slipped slowly down the gate, landing flat on his back in the dirt.

Realizing his fate, knowing he'd sustained a terrible wound, Philip let out an ungodly scream that rose up to the heavens. Then his feet beat hard against the earth as he struggled to sit up. He made it halfway, then uttered a strangled gasp and flopped back down.

"What happened?" Drayton blurted as he jumped down from the fence, landing outside the corral. He ran in Philip's direction, fearful, practically tripping over himself in the process. When he got there, Theodosia was standing over Philip. Her mouth was set in a grim line, her face was white as snow, and her mane of auburn hair billowed about her face. Hands shaking, she was still pointing a gun at Philip.

"I didn't want to shoot him," Theodosia said when she saw Drayton. Her voice was a dry croak, she wore a look of absolute distress. "But he was going to kill you."

"I believe that was his intent," Drayton said in a raspy whisper. Then he looked at the pistol in her hand and said, "Sweet Fanny Adams, that's my pistol."

"Yes." Theodosia lowered the gun. "I'm sorry. I know you're against . . . but I couldn't just . . ." Words seemed to elude her.

"Shush," Drayton said, his voice filling with gentleness and compassion. His mind was starting to function again, his body responding to sensory cues. Finally, he said, "Theodosia, you saved my life!"

They both looked down at Philip, who was now swearing a blue streak as he continued to writhe in the dirt. The front of his shirt was soaked with bright red blood.

"You hit him in the shoulder," Drayton said.

I was aiming for center mass," Theodosia said. "You know, kind of like the police do on TV."

"Doesn't matter where you hit him, you got him. You *stopped* him."

Philip looked up at Theodosia and blinked in astonishment. "You! You tried to kill me!" he bellowed. Then his eyes went round as he suddenly noticed flecks of blood all over his shirt and hands. "You did, you *shot* me, you crazy witch. I'm going to come after you—gonna sue you for everything you've got. When I'm done you'll be lucky to get a job scraping plates in a greasy diner!"

There was a sudden pounding of feet, and when Theodosia glanced over her shoulder, she saw Lamar Lucket standing there, mouth open, breathless from his run, but staring at her in amazement. Then he turned his gaze on Philip and saw his bloody shirt.

"You *shot* him?" Lucket sounded horrified.

"He was trying to kill Drayton," Theodosia said tiredly. "First with the bull in the pen, then with his pistol."

Lucket lifted a single eyebrow and turned to Drayton. "That so?" he asked. Then he took in Drayton's torn jacket, his dust-covered face, and said, "Jeez, I guess she's right."

"Of course, I'm right," Theodosia said. "Philip Boldt is the one who shot Osgood Claxton and murdered Booker as well. And I can prove it."

"You lie!" Philip shouted.

"You're a cowardly, murdering thug," Theodosia said slowly and deliberately. "The police are going to run a ballistics test on your gun and then you'll be convicted of two murders and sent to prison for a very long time."

"Don't threaten me, girly," Philip screamed back. His eyes were shiny and dark, like a pit viper.

"That wasn't an idle threat, Philip," Theodosia said, her voice shaking with anger. "That was a promise."

Then she crept a few paces away so she could call Riley.

33

Calling was easy; explaining the situation to Riley was the hard part.

"You *shot* a man?" Riley sounded incredulous. "Just like that?"

"Not just like that," Theodosia said. The neurons in her brain were starting to fire and she was feeling more like her old self again. "Philip Boldt was about to shoot Drayton. Aiming to *kill* him."

"You're talking about Philip Boldt, the *restaurant* guy?"

"The very same. First Philip let this enormous bull loose to terrorize Drayton and gore him to death. When that didn't work, Philip aimed his gun at Drayton, meaning to kill him. So, you see, I *had* to shoot. Fact of the matter is, Boldt drew *first.*"

"Theodosia, this isn't the O.K. Corral and you're not Annie Oakley." Riley sounded a tiny bit hysterical. Then again, his girlfriend had just shot someone.

"Wyatt Earp," she said. "Wyatt Earp was at the O.K. Corral. And Doc Holliday."

"Whatever."

"We need someone from law enforcement to sort this all out," Theodosia said. "Can you come out here?"

"Where's here?"

"Red Hat Cattle Ranch, just down from Frog Hollow Farm. It's, um, out Highway 17, not too far past Boone Hall Plantation."

"I . . . I still can't believe this."

"The other thing is, we did wring a kind of confession out of Boldt."

"You interrogated the man?"

"Nothing that official," Theodosia said. "Apparently, Boldt shot Osgood Claxton because Claxton was extorting him over a licensing matter. Then Booker got suspicious about Philip's motorcycle, so Philip shot him too."

"Philip was the one on the motorcycle?" Riley was fumbling for words. "Good grief. I need to, um, get a Crime Scene team out there ASAP."

"Sure," Theodosia said, nodding even though she knew he couldn't see her. "That'd be good."

"This is going to take some time."

"I suppose that means we have to cancel our dinner tonight?" Theodosia asked.

"Um . . . probably," Riley said.

"Too bad. I was looking forward to it."

"Theo, dinner is the absolute last thing on my mind right now. I could kiss you for solving this case, but not until I get done screaming at you for about fifty thousand hours."

"Riley," Theodosia said. "I had no idea I'd be pulled in this deep . . ."

"But . . ."

"And, believe me, you would have reacted the same way if

you'd seen Philip tormenting Drayton—and then trying to *kill* him. This guy Philip is some kind of monster."

"Okay, Theo, I'm coming. I'm on my way."

Theodosia wandered back to where Philip was sprawled in the dirt, still clutching his shoulder and moaning like a sick banshee. Drayton was holding the gun on him now, guarding him carefully. Lamar Lucket danced around on the periphery, feeding off the excitement.

"You okay?" Theodosia asked Drayton. He was covered in a fine film of dust from head to toe and his eyes still looked a trifle googly.

"Still feeling light-headed, but none the worse for wear," Drayton said. He seemed to have warmed up to the idea of holding the pistol. Go figure.

"Hey, buddy," said Lucket, trying to insert himself in their exchange. "You look a little whacked and your Harris Tweed is for sure shot."

"It's a Donegal tweed, you nitwit," Drayton snapped back.

Lucket looked shocked. "Hey, just 'cause you got messed with, don't take it out on me," he said in a whiny tone.

Theodosia stood over Philip and nudged his leg with the tip of her toe. "Did you kill my goldfish?"

"He killed your goldfish?" Lucket asked.

"Yes, he did," Theodosia said.

Philip let loose a wet gurgle that was half laugh, half snort.

"I'll take that as a yes," Theodosia said. "Now an even more important question—does Holly know that you shot Claxton? That you were the one who ruined her party?"

Philip's lips curled back from his mouth and he exhaled slowly, like air escaping a balloon. Then he shook his head. "She didn't know jack about any of that." He clicked his teeth and ground them together as if trying to bite back the pain. "Listen, you gotta help me here. Put a tourniquet on my shoulder, administer a little first aid. I'm hurt real bad and losing blood like a stuck pig."

Theodosia peered at Philip. "You don't look so bad to me," she said in a tone that was just this side of indifferent. "What about Booker? Was Holly in on that? Did she help you kill him?"

"No," Philip groaned. "If you want to know the truth, Holly's a not-very-smart little twit. On the plus side, she's also innocent." He lifted his head an inch, groaned again from the effort, and then managed a half smirk. "Without me around to prop Holly up, who knows what the future holds for her."

"I know what it holds for you," Theodosia said, gazing down at him.

Philip squinted at her. "Huh?"

"What's she talking about?" Lucket asked Drayton.

"Shush," said Drayton.

Theodosia ignored Lucket as she handed her phone to Philip. "You're going to make a phone call."

Philip's tongue flicked out like a snake. "What for? Who am I going to call?"

Theodosia gave a self-satisfied smile. "You're going to call your restaurant and inform everyone that it's been closed. Permanently."

"Holy buckets," said Lucket. "Just like that?"

Theodosia dusted her hands together. "Just like that."

FAVORITE RECIPES FROM

The Indigo Tea Shop

Italian Ricotta Cookies

½ lb. butter (2 sticks)

3 eggs

2 cups sugar

4 cups flour

2 tsp. vanilla

1 tsp. salt

1 tsp. baking soda

1 lb. ricotta cheese (16 oz.)

1 chocolate bar for shavings

PREHEAT oven to 350 degrees. Melt butter and pour in large bowl. Add in eggs, sugar, flour, vanilla, salt, and baking soda. Mix all ingredients together gently, using your hands. Then gradually work in ricotta cheese. Using a spoon, place 1 tablespoon of mixture for each cookie onto an ungreased cookie sheet. Bake for 15 minutes or until light brown on bottom of cookie. Shave bits of chocolate onto top of each cookie while still warm. Yields about 30 cookies.

Haley's Honey Chicken

Whole chicken, cut into pieces
2 cups flour
½ cup bread crumbs
4 tsp. salt
½ tsp. pepper
¼ tsp. paprika
1½ cups butter, divided (3 sticks)
½ cup honey
½ cup lemon juice

PREHEAT oven to 400 degrees. Mix together flour, bread crumbs, salt, pepper, and paprika in a large flat dish. Roll chicken pieces in crumb mixture, coating evenly. Put 1 cup (2 sticks) of the butter in a 9-by-13-inch baking dish, then place dish in oven for a few minutes to melt butter. Do not let it brown. Remove pan from oven and arrange chicken in pan, turning to coat the pieces with the melted butter. Bake chicken for 30 minutes, skin side down. Remove from oven. Mix remaining ½ cup (1 stick) of butter with melted honey and lemon juice. Pour honey mixture over chicken and bake for an additional 30 minutes, basting occasionally with the honey sauce. Yields 4 servings.

Honey Bee Cookies

½ cup butter, softened (1 stick)
½ cup packed brown sugar

½ cup honey
1 egg
1½ cups flour
½ tsp. baking soda
½ tsp. salt
½ tsp. ground cinnamon

PREHEAT oven to 375 degrees. Beat together butter, brown sugar, honey, and egg in a medium bowl on medium speed. Stir in flour, baking soda, salt, and cinnamon. Using a spoon, drop cookie dough onto an ungreased cookie sheet. Bake for 7 to 9 minutes until cookies are set and light brown around the edges. Let stand for 3 or 4 minutes before removing cookies from sheet. Yields 36 cookies.

Glory Bee Honey Scones

2 cups flour
1 Tbsp. baking powder
¼ tsp. salt
8 Tbsp. butter (1 stick), cut into small squares
¾ cup heavy cream
1 tsp. vanilla
¼ cup honey

PREHEAT oven to 375 degrees. Mix together flour, baking powder, and salt in a large bowl. Cut in the butter until you have pea-sized chunks of dough. In a measuring cup, combine cream, vanilla, and honey, then pour into flour mixture. Stir with a large spoon until the mixture comes together in a loose ball. Transfer dough to a lightly floured surface and knead briefly, then form mixture into an 8-by-8-inch square. Cut dough into 8 squares, then cut those squares into halves to form triangles. Transfer the 16 pieces to an ungreased baking sheet. Bake for 10 to 12 minutes until cooked through with light golden edges. Remove from oven and let rest on the pan for 10 minutes. Serve warm with jam and Devonshire cream. Yields 16 small scones.

Cheddar and Sausage Scotch Eggs

8 hard-boiled eggs
2 lb. ground sausage
2 eggs, beaten
1 cup bread crumbs
½ cup grated cheddar cheese

PREHEAT oven to 350 degrees. Remove shells from hard-boiled eggs. Divide ground sausage into 8 mounds and press each mound into a square. Wrap each egg in the sausage, making sure each egg is completely encased and sealed without any cracks. Generously brush the sausage with the beaten eggs, then roll each egg in the bread crumbs. Place eggs in a lightly greased baking dish and sprinkle the cheddar cheese on top. Bake for approximately 20 to 25 minutes. Yields 8 Scotch eggs. (Hint: Serve with your favorite potato, vegetable, or side salad.)

Moscato Poached Pears

8 Bosc pears
1½ cups Moscato or other sweet wine
Fresh ginger (1-inch piece)
Lemon
½ cup sugar
6 star anise
Water

PEEL the pears, leaving stalks attached and cutting a slice off the bottom so they stand up in a frying pan. Peel and mince ginger, then zest and juice the lemon. Add wine, ginger, sugar, lemon juice and zest, and star anise to a medium to large frying pan. Heat and stir until sugar is dissolved. Place the pears in the pan and add just enough water to cover them. Bring to a simmer and cook on low heat, partially covered, for about 50 minutes. Remove the pears with a slotted spoon and let liquid continue to cook, about 10 minutes. When reduced to a syrup, pour over pears and serve. Makes 8 servings.

Tuscan Soup

1 lb. ground sweet Italian sausage
1½ tsp. crushed red peppers
2 slices bacon, cut into bits
1 large onion, diced
2 tsp. garlic puree
5 cubes chicken bouillon

10 cups water

3 large russet potatoes, sliced

1 cup heavy cream

SAUTÉ and brown Italian sausage and crushed red peppers in a large pot. Drain fat, then refrigerate while you prepare the other ingredients. In the same pan, sauté bacon, onions, and garlic for 15 minutes or until onions soften. Mix together chicken bouillon cubes and water, then add to pan. Cook until boiling. Add potato slices and cook until soft, about 30 minutes. Stir in heavy cream and sausage and cook until heated. Yields 4 to 6 servings.

Smoked Trout Tea Sandwiches

¼ cup sour cream

¼ cup mayonnaise

1 Tbsp. chopped fresh chives

1 tsp. capers, drained and chopped

½ tsp. lemon zest

¼ tsp. ground pepper

1 cup smoked trout, skin off and flaked

Butter

12 slices white bread, crusts removed

Watercress leaves (about 1½ cups)

IN a medium bowl, stir together sour cream, mayonnaise, chives, capers, lemon zest, and pepper. Gently fold in flaked trout and stir. Lightly butter your 12 slices of bread. Spread smoked trout mixture on 6 bread slices, then top each slice with a bit of watercress. Top with remaining bread slices, then cut sandwiches diagonally into quarters. Yields 24 tea sandwiches.

English Tea Biscuits

2 cups flour
4 tsp. baking powder
1 tsp. salt
5 Tbsp. butter, softened
¾ cup milk
4 Tbsp. orange marmalade
2 Tbsp. sugar

PREHEAT oven to 400 degrees. In a bowl, stir together flour, baking powder, and salt. Work butter into flour mixture with a fork. Make a well in the center and pour in milk. Stir well for 20 seconds until all the flour is moistened. Place dough on a floured surface and knead for 20 seconds. Pat or roll dough until it's about ½-inch thick. Cut into rounds and place on greased baking pan. Combine orange marmalade and sugar together and scoop a bit onto each biscuit. Bake in oven for 10 to 14 minutes. Yields 10 to 12 biscuits.

GET CREATIVE WITH SCONES

Theodosia and the Indigo Tea Shop gang aren't afraid to break the rules and get creative with scones and neither should you be. Here are a few of Laura Childs's favorite scone toppers to get you started.

- **Strawberry Jam and Devonshire Cream**—You can't go wrong with this classic version.

- **Blue Cheese and Honey**—For the diehard blue cheese lovers out there.

- **Fruit Parfait**—Split your scone, top with ice cream, and add sliced strawberries.

- **Smoked Salmon with Cream Cheese**—Turn a basic scone into an updated bagel.

- **Brie Cheese and Chutney**—Spread on softened Brie and top with your favorite chutney sauce.

- **Herbed Butter**—A butter seasoned with tarragon or your favorite herbs is delicious on scones.

- **Avocado and Diced Tomatoes**—Create an elevated version of avocado toast.

- **Melted Gruyère**—Spread on Gruyère cheese and toast under the broiler.

- **Fried Egg and Bacon**—This takes your scone into the realm of hearty breakfast sandwich.

- **Cream Cheese and Maple Syrup**—Turn your scone into a nouveau version of French toast. Add a pouf of whipped cream.

- **Banana Split**—Top a cream scone with banana slices and drizzle on some chocolate sauce. Ice cream is optional.

- **Fig and Cheese**—Spread fig jam on your split scone and top with cheese crumbles.

TEA TIME TIPS FROM
Laura Childs

Honeybee Tea

You don't need to contend with a murder in the park to stage your very own Honeybee Tea. Simply decorate your tea table with a white linen tablecloth, add yellow streamers and white or yellow flowers (sunflowers would be exquisite), and set your table with yellow-and-white china. Display several jars or bottles of honey so your guests can sweeten their tea to their heart's content. Begin with honey scones served with honey butter. Your tea sandwiches might be honeyed ham and cheddar cheese on honey nut bread. If you want to serve a more substantial entrée, think honey-garlic chicken. For dessert there's always honey ice cream or honey cake. Harney & Sons blends a delightful Bee's Knees tea.

Great Gatsby Tea

Bring the Jazz Age to your tea table with a Great Gatsby Tea. Decorate your table in classy black and white, add shiny black vases filled with white flowers and feathers and drape strands of faux flapper pearls on the table. You could even add a few top hats and spin some mood music from the twenties. Cream scones with raspberry jam is your first course, followed by classy cucumber and cream cheese sandwiches. For your entrée, consider curried lobster salad or sliced terrine loaf with cheddar cheese on Italian bread. An upscale dessert might be raspberry-topped tartlets. What tea to pour? Vanilla tea from Republic of Tea is delicious, and Darjeeling is considered the champagne of teas.

Blend Your Own Tea

Blending your own tea and then sampling it is one of life's little delights. So why not build an entire tea party around it? Buy a half dozen tins of various teas, then give your guests empty tea bags made of paper or muslin so they can take a spoonful of one tea, add a pinch of another, maybe even a pinch of a third. While your guests are enjoying their house-blended tea, serve chocolate chip scones along with turkey and Gouda cheese tea sandwiches. You might even want to brew a pot of Stash Tea's Creme Brulee Black Tea just in case.

Angel Tea

Blessed be, an angel tea is perfect for church friends, dear relatives, or even children. Cloak your tea table in angelic white, add as many angel figurines as you can round up, and add some lovely floral bouquets well. White or pink tea ware would be perfect, as would Fitz & Floyd's Cherubini plates. If you have a favorite Bible verse (such as Hebrews 13:2, "Do not forget to show hospitality to strangers, for by so doing some people have shown hospitality to angels without knowing it"), print it out on sheets of paper and use them as place mats or as favors with small keepsake bouquets. Begin your angel tea with white chocolate chip scones and Devonshire cream. For an entrée, angel eggs or angel hair pasta is perfect. Dessert could be divinity fudge or even angel food cake. Your tea should be a white tea such as Harney & Sons White Peony or Upton Tea's Yao Bao White Tea.

Butterfly Tea

There's nothing more relaxing than a summer afternoon in the garden. It's also the perfect venue for a Butterfly Tea. Move your patio furniture onto the lawn, string some twinkle lights in the trees, and add bouquets of fresh flowers. Paper butterflies from the craft store should also help set the mood. Keep it light and start with cinnamon scones with clotted cream, segue to a zesty fruit salad, and then serve apple and Brie cheese tea sandwiches. A berry-citrus tea or sweet lavender tea would be delicious. As would Adagio's Summer Rose tea.

Glam Girl Tea

Glam it up by inviting a local beauty representative (with samples) to your tea. Or collect perfume and makeup samples to give as favors to your guests. Now glam up your tea table with candelabras, the good china, and floral bouquets. Start your tea with cinnamon apple scones and Devonshire cream. Serve shrimp salad tea sandwiches and goat cheese and fig jam sandwiches. Dessert could be a cookie or brownie bite sampler. Keep everyone sipping happily by serving Plum Deluxe's Lavender Daydream White Tea with notes of mango, peach, and floral.

TEA RESOURCES

TEA MAGAZINES AND PUBLICATIONS

TeaTime—A luscious magazine profiling tea and tea lore. Filled with glossy photos and wonderful recipes. (teatimemagazine.com)

Southern Lady—From the publishers of *Tea Time* with a focus on people and places in the South as well as wonderful teatime recipes. (southernladymagazine.com)

The Tea House Times—Go to theteahousetimes.com for subscription information and dozens of links to tea shops, purveyors of tea, gift shops, and tea events.

Victoria—Articles and pictorials on homes, home design, gardens, and tea. (victoriamag.com)

Fresh Cup Magazine—For tea and coffee professionals. (freshcup.com)

Tea & Coffee—Trade journal for the tea and coffee industry. (teaandcoffee.net)

Jane Pettigrew—This author has written seventeen books on the varied aspects of tea and its history and culture. (janepettigrew.com/books)

A Tea Reader—By Katrina Avila Munichiello, an anthology of tea stories and reflections. (kamreads.wordpress.com/about/)

AMERICAN TEA PLANTATIONS

Charleston Tea Plantation—The oldest and largest tea plantation in the United States. Order their fine black tea or schedule a visit at bigelowtea.com.

Table Rock Tea Company—This Pickens, South Carolina, plantation grows premium whole-leaf tea. (tablerocktea.com)

The Great Mississippi Tea Company—Up-and-coming Mississippi tea farm now in production. (greatmsteacompany.com)

Sakuma Brothers Farm—This tea garden just outside Burlington, Washington, has been growing white and green tea for over twenty years. (sakumabros.com)

Big Island Tea—Organic artisan tea from Hawaii. (bigislandtea.com)

Mauna Kea Tea—Organic green and oolong tea from Hawaii's Big Island. (maunakeatea.com)

Onomea Tea—Nine-acre tea estate near Hilo, Hawaii. (onotea.com)

Minto Island Growers—Handpicked, small-batch crafted teas grown in Oregon. (mintoislandtea.com)

Finger Lakes Tea Company—Tea producer located in Waterloo, New York. (fingerlakestea.com)

Camellia Forest Tea Gardens—This North Carolina company collects, grows, and sells tea plants. Also produces their own tea. (teaflower gardens.com)

TEA WEBSITES AND INTERESTING BLOGS

Destinationtea.com—State-by-state directory of afternoon tea venues.

Teamap.com—Directory of hundreds of tea shops in the United States and Canada.

Afternoontea.co.uk—Guide to tea rooms in the United Kingdom.

Cookingwithideas.typepad.com—Recipes and book reviews for the Bibliochef.

Seedrack.com—Order *Camellia sinensis* seeds and grow your own tea!

Jennybakes.com—Fabulous recipes from a real make-it-from-scratch baker.

Cozyupwithkathy.blogspot.com—Cozy mystery reviews.

Thedailytea.com—Formerly *Tea Magazine,* this online publication is filled with tea news, recipes, inspiration, and tea travel.

Allteapots.com—Teapots from around the world.

Relevanttealeaf.blogspot.com—All about tea.

Teawithfriends.blogspot.com—Lovely blog on tea, friendship, and tea accoutrements.

Napkinfoldingguide.com—Photo illustrations of twenty-seven different (and sometimes elaborate) napkin folds.

Worldteaexpo.com—This premier business-to-business trade show features more than three hundred tea suppliers, vendors, and tea innovators.

Fatcatscones.com—Frozen ready-to-bake scones.

Kingarthurflour.com—One of the best flours for baking. This is what many professional pastry chefs use.

Californiateahouse.com—Order Machu's Blend, a special herbal tea for dogs that promotes healthy skin, lowers stress, and aids digestion.

Vintageteaworks.com—This company offers six unique wine-flavored tea blends that celebrate wine and respect the tea.

Downtonabbeycooks.com—A *Downton Abbey* blog with news and recipes.

Auntannie.com—Crafting site that will teach you how to make your own petal envelopes, pillow boxes, gift bags, etc.

Victorianhousescones.com—Scone, biscuit, and cookie mixes for both retail and wholesale orders. Plus baking and scone-making tips.

Englishteastore.com—Buy a jar of English Double Devon Cream here as well as British foods and candies.

Stickyfingersbakeries.com—Delicious just-add-water scone mixes.

Teasipperssociety.com—Join this international tea community of tea sippers, growers, and educators. A terrific newsletter!

Melhadtea.com—Adventures of a traveling tea sommelier.

Bullsbaysaltworks.com—Local South Carolina sea salt crafted by hand.

Thebeeconservancy.org—Learn how to plant a bee garden, build bee homes, and more.

Savethebees.com—Learn about bee colony decline and how it threatens food security.

PURVEYORS OF FINE TEA

Plumdeluxe.com

Adagio.com

Elmwoodinn.com

Capitalteas.com

Newbyteas.com/us

Harney.com

Stashtea.com

Serendipitea.com

Marktwendell.com

Globalteamart.com

Republicoftea.com

Teazaanti.com

Bigelowtea.com

Celestialseasonings.com
Goldenmoontea.com
Uptontea.com
Svtea.com (Simpson & Vail)
Gracetea.com
Davidstea.com

VISITING CHARLESTON

Charleston.com—Travel and hotel guide.

Charlestoncvb.com—The official Charleston convention and visitor bureau.

Charlestontour.wordpress.com—Private tours of homes and gardens, some including lunch or tea.

Charlestonplace.com—Charleston Place Hotel serves an excellent afternoon tea, Thursday through Saturday, one to three o'clock.

Poogansporch.com—This restored Victorian house serves traditional low-country cuisine. Be sure to ask about Poogan!

Preservationsociety.org—Hosts Charleston's annual Fall Candlelight Tour.

Palmettocarriage.com—Horse-drawn carriage rides.

Charlestonharbortours.com—Boat tours and harbor cruises.

Ghostwalk.net—Stroll into Charleston's haunted history. Ask them about the "original" Theodosia!

Charlestontours.net—Ghost tours plus tours of plantations and historic homes.

Follybeach.com—Official guide to Folly Beach activities, hotels, rentals, restaurants, and events.

Gibbesmuseum.org—Art exhibits, programs, and events.

Boonehallplantation.com—Visit one of America's oldest working plantations.

Charlestonlibrarysociety.org—A rich collection of books, historic manuscripts, maps, and correspondence. Music and guest-speaker events.

Earlybirddiner.com—Visit this local gem at 1644 Savannah Highway for zesty fried chicken, corn cakes, waffles, and more.

Highcottoncharleston.com—Low-country cuisine that includes she-crab soup, buttermilk-fried oysters, Geechie Boy grits, and much more.

ACKNOWLEDGMENTS

An abundance of thank-yous to Sam, Tom, Elisha, Yazmine, Stephanie, Sareer, Dru, Terrie, Lori, M.J., Bob, Jennie, Dan, and all the wonderful people at Berkley Prime Crime and Penguin Random House who handle editing, design (such fabulous covers!), publicity (amazing!), copywriting, social media, bookstore sales, gift sales, production, and shipping. Heartfelt thanks as well to all the tea lovers, tea shop owners, book clubs, tea clubs, bookshop folks, librarians, reviewers, magazine editors and writers, websites, social media sites, broadcasters, and bloggers who have enjoyed the Tea Shop Mysteries and helped spread the word. You are all so kind to help make this possible!

And I am filled with gratitude for all the special readers and tea lovers who've embraced Theodosia, Drayton, Haley, Earl Grey, and the rest of the tea shop gang as friends and family. Thank you so much and I promise many more Tea Shop Mysteries to come!

KEEP READING FOR AN EXCERPT
FROM LAURA CHILDS'S NEXT
TEA SHOP MYSTERY . . .

Murder in the Tea Leaves

"Quiet on the set! Quiet on the set!"

As if someone had suddenly spun a dial and cut the volume, there was complete and utter silence in the darkened living room of the dilapidated Brittlebank Manor.

"Roll film, and . . . *action!*" shouted Duncan Mills, the film's director.

Theodosia Browning watched, fascinated, as actors recited lines, cameras dollied in for close-ups, and producers, assistant directors, storyboard artists, set dressers, grips, writers, gaffers, production assistants, makeup artists, and costumers stood ready to jump at the director's every command.

It was the first day of filming for *Dark Fortunes,* a Peregrine Pictures feature film. And the first time tea shop owner Theodosia had ever seen a full-fledged movie in the making. Of course, she wasn't actually *in* the movie. But this week was still extra special for Theodosia and Drayton Conneley, her dapper, sixty-something tea sommelier. They'd been tapped to handle the craft services table, an all-day munch fest for the movie crew, instead of playing host at the Indigo Tea Shop on Charleston's famed Church Street where they'd normally juggle morning cream tea, lunch, tea parties, afternoon tea, special events, and catering.

Catering. Yes, that's exactly why Theodosia and Drayton had loaded their craft services table with a bounty of tea sandwiches, lemon scones, brownie bites, banana muffins, cranberry tea bread, and hand-made chocolates. And of course tea, which was Drayton's specialty.

"This is exciting, yes?" Theodosia whispered to Drayton. The director had called a sudden halt to filming and now the crew milled about the darkened set like shadows flitting through a graveyard.

"Exciting but strange," Drayton said, touching a hand to his bow tie. "I had no idea so much work went into filming one single scene." He peered through the darkness to where the director was whispering to a cameraman. "And that director seems to be constantly in an uproar."

Duncan Mills, the director, was most certainly upset. "Gimme some light, will you?" he barked. And lights immediately came up revealing the shabby interior. "We need something more dynamic here. A line or action that propels us into the heart of the storyline." He turned to Bryan Cole, the scriptwriter, and raised his eyebrows in a questioning look.

"It's already in the script, babe," Cole shouted back at him. Cole was Hollywood hyper, rail-thin with a pinched face and shock of bright red Woody Woodpecker hair.

"No, it's not. The script is dreck," Mills cried as he leaped from his chair, knocking it over backwards in the process. He was tall and angular, dressed in jeans and a faded Def Leppard T-shirt. Good-looking, handsome even, Duncan Mills had intense jade-green eyes and wore a now-popular-again gunslinger mustache.

Cole's face contorted in anger. "Watch it pal. I *wrote* that script." His lips barely touched his teeth as he spat out his words.

Mills shook his head tiredly. "C'mon man, 'fess up. You plagiarized a Japanese film that won a *Nippon Akademii-shou* back in ninety-five."

Cole's face turned bright red to match his hair. "That might have been the seminal inspiration," he shot back, "but the dialogue is completely mine!"

The director stared thoughtfully at the small round table where a woman wearing a purple-and-gold tunic and matching turban sat across from Andrea Blair, the film's leading actress.

"She should read the tea leaves," Mills said slowly. "That's what we need. The fortune teller has to *read* the tea leaves before she delivers her line."

"Brilliant," Lewin Usher trilled. He was the film's main investor and executive producer, a slick looking hedge fund manager in a three-piece Zegna suit with a Rolex the size of an alarm clock. He seemed positively giddy to be on set today.

Duncan Mills pointed a finger at the fortune teller. "Fortune teller lady. What I want you to do is pour out the tea, then peer into Andrea's cup and actually *read* the tea leaves. Tell her, um, that her life is in terrible danger."

"That's not in the script," Cole called out.

"Well, it should be," Mills said. He stared earnestly at the fortune teller. "You got that?"

"No problem," said the fortune teller.

"Lights down, quiet, and roll film," Mills instructed. He stood there, tense, arms crossed, watching his actors.

The fortune teller lifted the teapot and tilted it at a forty-five-degree angle. At which point the lid promptly fell off and clattered noisily to the floor while the teabag tumbled out and landed in the teacup with a wet plop.

"No, no!" Mills shouted. "That's not going to work, you're doing it all wrong. Everybody, take five while we figure this out." He sighed deeply and gazed in the direction of Theodosia's craft services table as if there were an answer to be found there.

Turns out there was.

"Loose leaf tea," Theodosia said. "You have to brew loose tea leaves in order to achieve the effect you want."

"Huh?" The director peered at Theodosia as if really seeing her for the first time. "You know something about tea?"

"She should," Drayton said, suddenly speaking up. "She owns a tea shop."

"Come over here, will you?" Mills said, waggling his fingers.

Theodosia slipped around the table and walked toward the director, aware that more than a few eyes were following her. She stepped over a tangle of wires and black cables that connected lights, cameras, and sound equipment to the main power source.

"So you're a tea expert?" Mills asked.

Theodosia lifted a shoulder. "Of sorts."

"Because you own a tea shop."

"The Indigo Tea Shop over on Church Street."

The director seemed to relax. "Truth be told, I've been known to imbibe a cup or two of tea myself. You might say Earl Grey was my gateway drug."

"Because of the bergamot," Theodosia said.

Duncan Mills reached out, gently grabbed Theodosia's arm, and pulled her toward him. "Right."

"Hard to resist that rich flavor."

Mills looked as if he was suddenly struck by a wonderful idea. "Since you seem to know what you're doing, we'll have *you* pour the tea and read the tea leaves!"

"What!" screeched the fortune teller, who suddenly saw her big scene going up in smoke.

"Oh no," Theodosia said, holding up her hands and slowly backing away.

Mills gazed at her. "Oh yes. I want *you* to read the tea leaves and be in the scene."

"I can't do that," Theodosia said.

Mills's brows puckered together. "Why not?"

"Because I'm not an actress," Theodosia said. She glanced around quickly, looking for confirmation. Wasn't it glaringly apparent that she was only here to oversee the craft services table? Wasn't it? Come on, somebody kindly pitch in and give her some backup.

But Duncan Mills had already made up his mind. He looked over to where Andrea Blair, the star of the movie, was now lounging in a folding chair as she scrolled through her phone messages. Her script lay on the floor next to her, unopened. "You're no actress?" Mills said. "Neither is she." Then he lifted a hand, snapped his fingers, and called out, "Beverly, we're going to need hair, makeup, and wardrobe for . . . what's your name?"

"Theodosia. Theodosia Browning. But I really can't . . ."

"Do it," Drayton urged from across the room. "It'll be fun."

"No, it won't," Theodosia said, shaking her head. "I'm not an actress, I don't even look like an actress."

"Actually, you do," Mills said. "You're young enough so you'll look great in a close-up, but you also possess a seriousness and quiet maturity that should come across on screen. A believability the audience can connect with." He appraised her from head to toe. "Good figure, ice chip blue eyes that go nicely with that English rose complexion only a few women are naturally gifted with, and . . . well, I do love your tangle of auburn hair." He hesitated. "Though we'll have to tone it down some to fit under the turban."

Theodosia shook her head. "No," she said again. But even as she continued her protest, two production assistants rushed to her side, grabbed her, and lead her down the hallway toward the makeshift makeup and dressing room.

"This isn't going to work," Theodosia protested as they guided her in, plunked her down in a pink plastic swivel chair, and bombarded her with bright lights.

"Of course it will, honey," Beverly, the head makeup artist said. "All we need to do is line your eyes, pat on some makeup, and tone down that hair of yours." She ran a brush through Theodosia's locks and said to her assistant, "Joanie, have you ever seen so much hair?"

Shaking her head, Joanie snapped her gum and said, "Only on wigs."

"Really," Theodosia said, gripping the arms of her chair. "I can't go through with this."

"Honey, you gotta trust us," Beverly said. She was a bleached blond with over-plucked brows and a spray tan. A fake bake as Theodosia and her friends would say. "We're gonna glam you up so good you'll look like a genuine Hollywood actress."

"Good enough to be on TMZ," Joanie echoed as she draped a plastic cape around Theodosia's shoulders.

"Oh dear," said Theodosia.

But ten minutes later, once Beverly had sponged on a light base coat, artfully powdered it down, then added some blusher to highlight her cheekbones, Theodosia started to feel a little better. And when Beverly gelled her brows and added eyeliner with a slight cat eye oomph at the outer corners, she peered in the mirror and liked what she saw.

"Not bad," Theodosia said.

"See? You're a natural," Beverly said.

Meanwhile, Joanie had sussed out a cute tangle of curls to peek out from under her turban.

"You live here, honey?" Beverly asked as she carefully lined Theodosia's lips.

Theodosia nodded. "Born and bred in Charleston, South Carolina."

"Quite the place," Beverly said. "I've never seen so much historic architecture in my life. Then again, I'm from LA where anything before nineteen eighty is considered ancient history."

"Some of our homes and churches date back to the Revolutionary War," Theodosia said. "There are churches that George Washington worshiped in, narrow alleys where duels were fought, and Fort Sumter where the Civil War began."

"This house must be plenty historic, too," Joanie said. "I mean, it sure is a spooky old place. Dark and drafty, practically falling down—it gives me the creeps being here. I can understand why the location scouts chose this place. It's the perfect set for a scary movie."

"It feels as if nobody's lived here in years," Beverly added.

"That's because nobody has," Theodosia said. "This place is known as Brittlebank Manor and it's reputed to be haunted."

"No!" Beverly cried. "Seriously?"

"Charleston is full of ghosts," Theodosia said playfully. "We've got haunted houses, haunted hotels, a haunted dungeon, and even a haunted cemetery. Actually, two haunted cemeteries."

Joanie gave an appreciative shiver. "This place, Brittlebank Manor, is there some kind of legend behind it?"

"I don't know all of it," Theodosia said. "But apparently a woman was kept locked in the attic and then was killed when an enormous bolt of lightning struck the building."

"Why on earth was she locked in the attic?" Beverly asked as she helped Theodosia into a long, purple velvet coat embroidered with silver stars.

"Not sure," Theodosia said as Joanie situated a turban on her head and gave a final touch to the swirl of hair that peeked out. "I never did hear the whole story."

Back on set, Drayton had brewed a proper pot of tea, lights and camera angles were being adjusted and Helene Deveroix, one of the members of the Charleston Film Board, rushed up to greet her.

"Sweet dogs, Theodosia, I hardly recognized you!" Helene said. "You're done up like a bona fide actress!"

"It wasn't my idea," Theodosia explained, patting nervously at her turban. "But the directors wanted a more authentic read."

"Can you do that?" Helene asked. She was a tad theatrical herself with her mop of curly blond hair, zaftig figure, and overly broad gestures.

"If I follow the director's lead, then sure," Theodosia said. "I mean, I guess so."

Helene grabbed Theodosia's arm and gave an encouraging tug. "Aren't you glad that Delaine set you up with this gig?" Delaine Dish was a friend of Theodosia's and also served on the Charleston Film Board.

"I'll let you know once we shoot this scene."

Helene grinned. "It'll have to be later, sweetie, right now I have to bounce. Got to deliver some signed papers to the City Film Office." And she was gone.

"Are you ready?" the director asked. He was suddenly in Theodosia's face.

"Hope so," she said.

Theodosia and Andrea did a couple of rehearsals, with Theodosia feeling more confident as they went along.

"This is working," Duncan Mills said. "Very believable. I think we're ready for a take. Now Andrea, when Theodosia tips your cup sideways and stares into it to read the tea leaves, I want you to look apprehensive. Do you know what that is? Can you give me apprehensive?"

Andrea pulled her mouth into a pout and widened her eyes.

"That looks more like a case of indigestion," Duncan said. "Try to work up some genuine emotion. Try to actually . . . act. And Rollie . . ." Duncan turned to his cameraman, "I want you to dolly in slowly for an extreme close-up on that teacup." He glanced up to his left. "Lighting guys, let's throw up a scrim and add a blue light to create a spooky vibe. Then, when Rollie goes in for his ECU, amp up the key light and give me a medium-sized flicker, okay?"

"Okay, boss," called the lighting director.

"And somebody get me a chair," Duncan said. There was a flurry behind him as somebody set down a metal folding chair. Duncan plopped down, crossed his legs, and said, "Quiet on set. Lights all the way down." There was sudden quiet as the lights dimmed and everyone held their breath. "And I want *aaaction.*"

At which point the lights came up slowly, revealing Theodosia and Andrea huddled at the tea table. Theodosia picked up the teapot, poured tea into a floral teacup, and waited as Ashely took a couple of sips. Then she reached over and took the teacup back. As Theodosia leaned forward to peer at the tea leaves, she was aware of the camera moving in close and of a strange, almost electrical, feeling in the air. There was a weird rumble, then a profoundly loud SIZZLE, CRACK, POP, as if someone had suddenly thrown the master switch in Dr. Frankenstein's laboratory. Electrical flashes lit up the room like a string of exploding Black Cat firecrackers and Theodosia smelled a hint of phosphorous. To add to the mayhem, a horrible, loud gagging sound rang out then slowly morphed into a strangled scream.

This isn't in the script, Theodosia told herself. At which point she jumped to her feet, glanced around, and spotted Duncan Mills, the director, thrashing wildly on the floor. He'd flipped over backwards in his metal folding chair and was writhing in agony. His eyes were popped open so wide the whites were enormous, like a couple of boiled eggs. And for some bizarre reason Duncan seemed almost welded to his chair as his arms flailed crazily, pounding out a drumbeat against the sagging wooden floor, caught in the throes of what had to be a terrible seizure. Seconds later, his back arched spasmodically and his legs kicked and jerked, as if dancing to some unholy tune.

"Somebody help him!" Andrea cried, setting off a cacophony of screams and shouts.

There was another terrible gurgling sound as white foam spewed from Duncan Mills's open mouth. Then, in one final convulsive act, Mills's head snapped back and banged against the floor with a deafening CRACK. Then his crumpled body seemed to run out of steam as he let out a slow expulsion of air that sounded like a vampire's dying hiss.